The Water Spider

J. SCHLENKER

ISBN: 978-0-9994278-8-0

To all sisters

"All dreams spin out from the same web."

HOPI TRIBE

Contents

One

"Will we be trading places like we did that night?" she asks, her cold, unblinking eyes fixated on mine. We had both grown weary of waiting for this day, losing faith that this would ever happen.

"It's time, don't you think?"

"Yes." She smiles.

The day has finally arrived. The Halloween bash, doubling as my birthday party, begins in two hours—more like two and a half since those selected to attend will compete to be fashionably late. My birthday is not until tomorrow, but Saturday is better for a party. My sister insists we call it a bash because she says the word denotes grandeur, better fitting my persona as Carter Hudson. Since she is the most practical and wisest of us two, I always defer to her judgment on these matters.

Other than my sister and I, Maria, my housekeeper, and the caterers remain. The decorators were here earlier, but they packed their gear and left. Not a minute too soon. Earlier this morning, they complained vehemently regarding my last-minute change of plan, but offering to pay whatever it took solved the problem as it does in most matters in this town. I assume any town. I'm just relieved the six-member team performed the miracle of transforming the entryway and main room according to my instructions and didn't recoil too badly when I handed them the handmade party streamers. Carl's face drooped like red melted butter if there was such a thing, and I thought he would surely hurl, but his wife and partner, Meg, tugged at his belt and said, "Let's do this and get out of here." As she turned, I heard her mutter, "Because of fame, she's gone off the deep end." Carl pinched her waist. Considering the time constraint and the fact I needed them, I pretended I didn't hear. I wanted to tell both of them I'd gone off the deep end long before fame.

There was no time to change the outside, which was decorated days ago to resemble Dracula's castle—Arthur's idea since he intended to come as Dracula. I'm sure the guests will wonder about the drastic change of theme from the outside to the inside.

I cautioned the decorating team to steer clear of the west wing, as I instruct every worker who enters this house to do. Of course, they were only decorating the house's central area, but one can't be too careful. My sister lives in the west wing and likes her privacy. She came to live with me a few months ago. Until then, she had been in and out of different care facilities. I insisted she move in with me despite Arthur's protests. He considers the arrangement strange, but since Arthur hasn't officially resided here for over a year, I saw no point in my sister not using the unoccupied part of the house.

I take one more trip through the party area to ensure everything looks perfect before heading to my bedroom. I hope to get some shut-eye before the guests arrive. Rest will help me focus.

After checking on the caterers, I leave the kitchen. Halfway down the hall to my bedroom, the noise from the kitchen fades into utter silence. The quiet is eerie. It was the same thirty-three years ago on Halloween on the rez. I remember my mother looking up at the sky and commenting she didn't have a good feeling. That same feeling creeps in now, filling every vein in my body like dry ice. I shake my body in an effort to relax and rid myself of the sensation.

In my bedroom, I stare at the pills on the nightstand, inching my hand toward the plastic bottle, but withdraw it, thinking tonight, of all nights, I don't want to be numb to the world. A brief nap will revive me. After tossing and turning for what seems like an eternity, I look at the clock and see I have an hour left before the party officially begins; the time on the invitations, the ones I had specially printed and signed individually, sometimes with personal notes. I expect they will be valuable one day, sold to the highest bidder on eBay.

I should dress, but flashes of lightning illuminate the room, and thunder rattles the windows, shattering the cunning lull of tranquility. I curl my body into the fetal position, put my hands over my ears, close my eyes, and try to think about happier times, attempting to ride out my fear of impending disaster. In the past, I downed whiskey and pharmaceuticals, whatever it took to sleep through storms.

I move my hands at a snail's pace from my ears and rise in bed. With a shaky voice, I sing a kachina song my mother taught me when I was young. She related the story to my sister and me about how Spider Grandmother thought outward into space and sang and spun the world into existence. Like Spider Grandmother, I'm also spinning. I'm creating a new direction for myself, one in which I can take back what I sacrificed. I hum softly but increase my volume to silence the loud booms and clench my eyes shut to block the quick blazes of light coming through the gap of the thick, gold-embroidered curtains. I struggle to direct my thoughts and prayers the way my mother taught me. She said our thoughts and feelings affect the balance of the world around us. Somewhere, I got off track.

In the dimly lit room, I hear my sister's voice, "You know what our mother always said. If you drive down the paved road of the white man, you lose your way."

I look over and see her sitting in the chair. With all the racket outside, I hadn't heard her come in.

"I'm glad you're here," I say. "It's a big night for both of us."

While still in my robe, I stare at my costume, perfectly pressed on its extra-large wooden hanger that accommodates the outfit's broad shoulders. I've decided on Frankenstein's monster. It could be nothing other. Plus, no one would ever expect me to dress in such unflattering, hideous garb, but it's perfect for setting the tone for the evening. My therapist urges me to face my fears. So, I must deal with the marauding monster Dr. Frankenstein created. My therapist doesn't know my *real* fears. She definitely doesn't know my guilt. No one does. Even after thirty-three years, I haven't been able to divulge them fully. Dressing as the creature in Shelly's Frankenstein will be a step in the right direction. My sister, the only one who knows the whole story, concurs.

When I first told her my idea, she tensed and looked at me as if I had lost my mind, but then, after a moment of reflection, she nodded and said, "Yes, it will be perfect."

I had expected her to scold me. Like me, she has adopted too many of the white men's ways. She attributes it to our mother not following the birthing ritual practiced in the Hopi tradition of placing an ear of corn beside us to represent the corn mother and keeping us in darkness for twenty days. The Hopi consider the corn plant to be a living entity. Even though a child is born into this world, it is still under the protection of the corn mother and sun father, who unite to ensure the glorious birth of a baby. Our births were hardly glorious.

"How could she? We were off the Hopi land, born in the cab of a beaten-up pickup truck, while our father drove us across the country into the mountains of North Carolina to live with his people, the Cherokee. She tried. She did the next best thing," I argue.

She frowns. "Placing candy corn on our tongues, purchased from a gas station, is hardly the tradition of our people."

Over the last thirty-three years, my sister has immersed herself in our traditions. Growing up, she never was interested. It was always me who leaned toward our teachings, even though I had the conflicting desire to be an actress in the white man's world.

"Yes, we got a poor start in life, especially you, but tonight will be a new beginning," I reply.

Nervous tension seizes me, and I wonder if we can pull it off, but I offer an encouraging smile and say, "Don't worry. It will be fine. It was meant to be."

"I know, but still..."

"You're worried something will go wrong."

"Of course I am. Everything went wrong on our sixteenth birthday," she says.

"This is different. We're older. Wiser," I insist.

Not buying the wisdom thing, she changes the subject. "We should make Halloween streamers. Could you bring me crepe paper in orange and black? Remember, you, Mom, and I were making those for the barn that night?"

"How could I forget?"

"Carter, do you remember how Mom sounded?" she asks in a quivering voice.

I realize she's crying, and a tear flows down my cheek, but I wipe it away. I summon my acting skills and, with detachment, say, "I don't know. She sounded like our mom. You know, always telling us Hopi stuff and sometimes Cherokee stuff."

"I know, but I mean the sound of her voice."

Why does she ask me such a question? I close my eyes and try to clear my mind. Traveling back in time, I hear the small waterfall in the stream behind our house, the chickens clucking, and that crazy old rooster crowing from dawn to dusk. I even remember the smells—the awful stink of the outhouse, the liquor on my father's breath when he kissed my cheek, and the hay in the barn. I never want to see or smell hay again, not after tonight.

"No," I say.

"I remember it like it was yesterday," she says.

I want to tell her she has the advantage of time over me, but I hold my tongue. Easy enough, but keeping my thoughts from her is a different matter, having the psychic connection with my sister that I do.

"What about Dad's voice?" she asks.

"I can still hear him bragging to Victor about you playing the part of Frankenstein's monster in the school play and asking him to stick around for the party." I feel ashamed recalling that and not my mother's voice.

A flash of lightning floods the room. A deafening crack of thunder that surely can be heard by our Hopi and Cherokee kin across the land follows. Even my sister, bathed in a serenity I don't possess, is startled.

I never dreamed the Great Spirit would provide all the atmospheric effects befitting the costume. I contemplate backing out of this. In a trembling voice, I say, "I don't know if I can go through with it."

"You must," my sister says. "This party will go down in the annals of Hollywood lore and make national news. It will be your best performance, better than your role as a mute."

"But I didn't win the Oscar."

"No, but that movie propelled you into stardom and out of a career in B movies. It made you a legend, along with Marilyn Monroe."

"Her life ended tragically," I counter.

"We will be different. Like the phoenix, we will rise from the ashes," my sister says confidently. She sometimes refers to us as one. I don't know if this is common with all identical twins, but it is with us.

I only wish Arthur were here. We had a bitter quarrel yesterday, and I haven't heard from him. No matter how often I call and leave messages, he doesn't answer. My second biggest fear after storms is that Arthur will abandon me.

Ever since he found me at age sixteen on that sleazy street corner almost thirty-three years ago, we've been together through three marriages and three divorces—all to each other, sometimes husband and wife, always best friends, after my sister, that is.

I should never have said what I did. Arthur's father is his Achilles heel. I was tense and anxious, worried about this party.

Two

CARTER

The infamous party was six months ago, on Halloween, during one of the fiercest storms in the history of Los Angeles. While surrounded by pretenders such as myself decked out in elaborate costumes borrowed from the wardrobe departments of the major movie studios, I vowed to face my fear head-on.

On the day of the party, there had been rumblings of a brewing storm all day—a teaser or precursor to a night of wicked parties enclosed in ghostly mansions decked out for the occasion all over the city, an utter disappointment for miniature goblins roaming affluent neighborhoods in hopes of full-sized bars of chocolate. I was determined, though. While enormous trepidation penetrated every cell of my body, those around me held their drinks high and cheered on the rare, growling Los Angeles storm, ready to fully unleash its demons on the one night that welcomed them with open arms.

As guests arrived, they were asked to deposit their cell phones into a box—no exceptions. If anyone refused, they would be asked to leave. I gave no prior warning lest someone try to sneak one in. I had little idea of what might unfold during the evening. No matter how much planning goes into something, one never knows the outcome. It's similar to a movie set. As an actor, I'm always shocked to see the final result on the big screen after numerous takes out of sequence.

I had no script. It would be almost totally ad-lib juxtaposed with guests' reactions. I only knew that whatever was to happen, the interpretations had to be left to people's mental and emotional impressions, with no video recordings to counter their imaginations. A one-woman act, vague, mysterious, fitting for the occasion of Halloween and my forty-ninth birthday party, something spectacular to make up for what happened thirty-three years ago—something to right the wrong for my sister.

The people attending the party knew nothing of my phobia or my past. In reality, even though they passed themselves off as some of my dearest and closest friends, they didn't know me. Not like Arthur, who discovered me homeless, crying, and ready to take my life while sitting on that street corner all those years ago.

I shouted into the empty street, "They're all gone, and it's my fault."

Call it fate that he passed by at just that time. He said that usually, he would have crossed over to the other side of the road to avoid someone deranged, a druggie, or a runaway, homeless on an LA street, but he wondered how anyone as beautiful as me could be so hopeless.

"Who's gone?" he asked. He casually reached into his coat pocket and pulled out a pack of cigarettes and a lighter, offering me a smoke. The tiny flame from the lighter startled me, sending me into my former panic mode. His expression was one of puzzlement. He returned the cigarettes and lighter to his pocket. "I need to quit these, anyway."

Perhaps it was the kindness in his eyes. I laughed, and he

did, too. For a moment, I forgot everything that had happened. I didn't deserve to laugh.

Dressed in a leather jacket, polo shirt, and jeans that I knew came out of one of the expensive Hollywood stores, he stood, looking down at me, listening to me tell my story while people walked around us. I omitted specific details. Still, the look on his face was one of horror.

"What's your name?"

I kept my head down, staring at the dirty street, and shook my head.

"Okay, if you don't want to tell me. It's all right. Can you tell me how old you are?"

I looked up at him but didn't answer.

"I see. Jailbait," he said as he reached for my grimy hand and pulled me to my feet. He took me to his apartment, showed me the bathroom, and told me to get cleaned up. He handed me a robe, which I assumed a girlfriend had left. I saw no signs of a wife. Nor was there a ring on his finger. He was twenty-five then and had just passed the bar exam.

"My name is Kachina," I blurted out. Why I said that, I don't know. Attempting to rectify what I had just said, my lips parted, but he reacted as if he had won the lottery, which simultaneously scared and exhilarated me. He smiled with pride the way I remembered my father doing after buying my mother, sister, and me ice cream cones on a trip into town. All the emotions of the moment merged into a calmness I hadn't known in months when he told me he would sleep on the couch and I would take his bedroom. I promised myself I would tell him the truth another day.

The next morning, after breakfast, which I gobbled down like the stray dog I remember my mom feeding one day on the reservation, he said he had to take care of some business, which would take at least a couple of hours. He instructed me to lock the door behind him and stay put. I thought his business might be going to the nearest police station or visiting Child Protection Services. Even so, I didn't run. Instead, while he was gone, I took a long hot bath and polished off the remainder of a box of donuts and the juice in his refrigerator, settling into Arthur's life like that same stray dog who never left after my mom fed him.

Within the week, he had moved us into a bigger, more expensive apartment, where I had my own bedroom and bathroom. I lived with Arthur, hidden away like a nun in a convent. I didn't question being tutored and groomed for something. I attributed it to my mother's spirit watching over me. From a distance, I watched girlfriends come and go out of Arthur's life until, on my twenty-first birthday, he dropped his code of chivalry concerning me. Significant events always seem to happen on my birthday.

The party didn't go as planned. Neither for me nor my sister. The monstrous storm that occurred on Halloween night half a year ago did end in tragedy. Any joy left for me in this life slipped away that night. Some might say I died. If Arthur had been there, he might have saved me, but he was absent, too angry to attend. He attributed it to something as minor as a lover's spat. For me, it was much more. I label it as abandonment in my time of need, the way I abandoned my sister thirty-three years ago, but it's okay. Kimi and I are together now, and she forgives me.

My second biggest fear after thunder and lightning is that Arthur might leave my life altogether one day.

Three

ARTHUR—THIRTY-THREE YEARS EARLIER

I left Kachina, whom I found only the night before, alone in my apartment, to drive to Malibu to see Connor, the man I work for. On my way out the door, I asked if I could trust her not to leave. She told me she wouldn't, and something in her dark brown eyes said I could trust her not to run. I asked her to keep the door locked and not to let anyone in other than me. I had no reason to think she might, nor did I expect anyone to knock on my door, but I couldn't lose her after searching so hard for her.

He'll be disappointed I only found one. From what little she told me, I'm assuming her twin died, along with her parents, in a fire, all having something to do with a man named Victor, who is the reason for her being alone and helpless on a questionable street in LA. Not being a psychiatrist or psychologist—what this girl needed—I let her do all the talking lest I should say the wrong thing, causing her to bolt.

"It's like looking for a needle in a haystack—two homeless girls, twins with dark hair, aged sixteen in LA. Maybe in LA," I complained to him.

"I know. It's a tall order," Connor said. "I can hire someone else if you're not up to it, but your father's firm has always handled any job I needed."

"No, no," I insisted. "Twins, of course, would make it easier. And you say they are of Hopi descent?"

"Yes."

"I'll get right on it," I say, not wanting to turn down the money, also hoping, if they are to be found, I need to make it happen before my father returns from abroad. Possibly, I can do something right in his eyes for a change—complete a job on my own.

Connor's expecting me because I left a message saying I would be by first thing the following day. I told him nothing else, keeping my voice calm, not wanting him to get his hopes up. I don't know how he will react. Will he be happy I found at least one of them, or will he be disappointed? I thought it best to deliver my news in person. Until now, we have conducted all our business over the phone.

I press the doorbell attached to the white brick beside the massive double doors of his Malibu mansion. His glum young secretary, Kyle, opens the door. If Kyle has a last name, I don't know it. I wonder if he has any life outside of his employer. I've heard he hardly ever leaves his side.

Kyle looks at his watch, a knock-off Rolex, which seems out of place in the plush surroundings in which he works. "Good, you're here and early," he says. "He's in his study waiting for you. Luckily, his wife is out of town."

We pass through the entrance, where a man and a woman

dressed in black are removing Christmas decorations, wrapping each thoroughly in tissue paper, and carefully placing them in boxes. I assume they are a maid and a butler. They go about the job, speaking with muffled voices, never looking in our direction.

Kyle doesn't mention Connor's son, but it's January, and I know he's away at boarding school. Since taking on this task, I've researched Connor and his family as much as possible. Why he considers this girl so important or why he wants to keep it a secret from his family is a mystery to me. From all reports, his marriage is sound, a rarity in Hollywood, and he dotes on his son. I can only speculate.

I knock on the door of his study.

A robust and business-like voice says, "Enter."

Even I, a twenty-five-year-old male, am struck by this man's appearance. At forty, with dark, slightly wavy hair, he's the colorized version of a film star from a golden era. Gregory Peck comes to mind. I honestly didn't think he would be as handsome in person as portrayed in films. I've met plenty of stars; the men are always shorter, and the women's features are harder than the soft focus lens of a camera portrays them.

He sits behind a massive mahogany desk in front of a wall-to-wall bookcase filled with leather-bound books. He looks up from what I presume to be a script.

A bark startles me.

"Down, Bear," he says, turning to the large black lump I failed to see on a pillow in the corner. He reaches into one of his desk drawers, and the dog immediately runs to his side. "You just wanted one of these, didn't you, girl?" He hands the dog a treat, and she retreats to her pillow with it, perfectly satisfied.

"Have a seat, Arthur. I hope this is good news. Perhaps you found them?" His eyes light up.

"Only one."

I relate everything she told me, the horrific story of the barn fire and that her sister died, although Kachina didn't explicitly say that. I think he is going to lose it. He grips both hands on the edge of his desk until his knuckles turn white. His eyes water. He turns toward the window and stares at a small palm tree, its leaves beating against the glass by the breeze coming off the ocean.

"Which one? Kachina or Kimi?" he asks in a shaky voice, still gazing out the window.

"Kachina."

"Aw, Kachina," he says softly.

I pull a Polaroid snapshot I took of her standing next to the Christmas tree and hand it to him. She's cleaned up and is in a robe. He studies her face. Not taking his eyes from the photograph, he says, "Yes, it's her. She looks just like her mother."

I'm curious why I was to locate her and how he even knew about a runaway girl from a Cherokee reservation in North Carolina, but like his private secretary, Kyle, I only do what he asks.

"You still have your Christmas tree up," he says.

It's small, a poor excuse for one. It came with lights and decorations already attached, the kind a pathetic bachelor like me would have. "Yes, I haven't had time to take it down."

"My wife and I wanted to wait until our son returned to school to take ours down. I told her I would take care of it while she was out of town."

"Yes, I passed your staff boxing up the decorations."

"I imagine you've been too busy scouring the streets looking for them," he acknowledges. "I gave you an almost impossible task, and you came through. As I recall, you said it would be like searching for a needle in a haystack. The sad part is that there was only one needle."

"Yes, but when I saw her on the street corner, I knew immediately it had to be one of the twins."

His gaze returns to the picture that hasn't left his hand since I gave it to him. "She's distinctive."

"She's certainly that," I concur.

"She's in a robe? You haven't touched her, have you, Arthur?" His eyes narrow.

"No."

"See that you don't." His warning echoes across the room in a voice that reminds me of a Shakespearian actor on stage. "This girl is to remain as pure as the driven snow."

It's hard for me to fathom her being a virgin after being alone on the streets for months. Possibly, her haggard appearance and deranged behavior might have rebuffed lustful predators. I keep these opinions to myself, considering Connor only hired me to find her, not to opine on her purity or lack thereof.

"She's young, sir. I don't do that sort of thing. Her clothes were disgusting, ready to be thrown into an incinerator. The robe was the only thing I had for her to wear."

"I figured as much." His face grows more relaxed.

He picks up the phone and asks his secretary to bring some things.

After he hangs up the phone, he asks, "She said her father was dead?"

"Yes."

Kyle returns carrying three enormous shopping bags, all with the logos of Los Angeles high-end shops. He sets them in the chair next to mine. Beautiful, professionally wrapped presents protrude from the bags.

"Mostly personal items, things a young girl needs, some clothes, nothing flashy. She was on the streets during Christmas and New Year's. I don't want to think about what may have happened to her. I had Kyle buy enough for two girls. So she should have plenty for now. The receipts are in one bag. I guessed at what size she might be. Whatever she returns, don't let her get anything indecent. Understood?"

"Yes, sir. But don't you want to come get her?"

"I would like nothing better, but that's not possible."

"What should I do with her?"

"You are to take care of her for now."

"Me?"

"Yes, Arthur. You will be paid well."

"But sir..."

"We must keep her a secret. Trust me. It's for the best. You, Kyle, and I are the only ones who know about her."

"Wouldn't she be better off staying with an older woman?"

"Probably, but I don't want to bring anyone else into this."

"This arrangement is for how long?"

"For however long it takes."

He puts the Polaroid snapshot inside his desk drawer, locks it, and rises from his chair. I also rise. He turns, facing his bookcase, and pulls a book from it. He walks over and hands the hardcover to me.

I examine what appears to be an original tightly woven green cloth binding, still in good condition. I carefully flip through the pages. They're clean. No notes, marks, or book-plates. The only wear I see is at the edges, and that's minimal.

"It's a first edition, first printing. Mark Twain's *The Prince and the Pauper*. My mother gave it to me before I went to college, right before she died. Have you read it, Arthur?"

"I've seen the movie," I say.

"Yes, I suppose you have little time for reading except for legal documents."

"No, sir."

Knowing its value, my hands grow sweaty. I hand it back toward him.

"No, Arthur. It's for her." He looks over at Kyle, who has faithfully stood in the corner all this time. "Would you get something to wrap the book in for him?"

After Kyle closes the door to the study, he says, "After my mother's death, I wanted to be the pauper. I had my fill of being the prince. I went off on my own."

I know the story. It was in all the magazines about the handsome leading man taking a break from acting—his whereabouts unknown—but I don't interrupt.

"I learned a lot from that trip. I saw what it was like to live the simplest of lives, something far removed from my own. I could have lived that life, but things didn't work out. Possibly, it was my fate to be the prince and not the pauper. This girl has lived the poorest of lives. With your help, Arthur, we will make her a princess, but we will do it right, take it slowly. She will be a star without all the grime and coarseness usually accompanying it. Besides, she's traumatized."

Kyle returns, takes the book from my hands, carefully wraps it in cloth, places it in a bag, and returns it to me.

"First, we see she gets an education—not school, of course. I want you to hire a private tutor for her, one who shows her the world through books. After that, we'll expose her to what's out there. Nice job, Arthur."

He reaches for my hand, and we shake.

"You should keep the Christmas tree up for her—for a while, at least. It might comfort her. Put all these things in the bags under your tree, and have her open them like it's Christmas morning. I need to make a phone call now. Kyle will show you out."

He sits back at his desk and picks up the receiver, waiting for us to leave before dialing.

I gather the bags and follow Kyle, wondering what I've

gotten myself into. Does he expect me to be a parent to a teenage girl? He can't be serious. However long it takes? She needs a woman's supervision, not mine. Surely, he knows this. I tell myself I shouldn't be responsible for her for too long. The phone call, I'm sure, is to make permanent arrangements.

On my way out, I hear, "Hello, it's me." There is a tightness in his voice. I look back to see I haven't fully closed the door to his study in maneuvering all the bags through the doorway. I think I hear him crying, but I can't be sure.

Why did he ask if her father was dead and not her mother?

Four

KIMI

Both my sister and I share a terror of storms. Our panic stems from the tragic one that happened on the eve of All Saint's Day thirty-three years ago. Even though I fear storms, I harbor mixed feelings concerning Halloween.

There is delight and dread. I delight in disguise and look forward to the adventure of roaming freely, melding myself into the character of my outer garment, and losing my true identity, whatever that is. Sadly, I've never been able to define who I am.

I can't help but associate storms with that night. They bring dread and foreboding, a reminder of what happened decades ago, drastically cutting short my parents' lives. They were in their mid-thirties. It changed the lives of my sister and me forever. We were only sixteen.

The storm that night also came close to taking my life. It did—that is, it crushed the life I thought lay ahead for me. A miraculous intervention, possibly from our mother looking down upon our horror while ascending to the afterlife, spared me from meeting my maker. Carter and I discussed it years later.

"I'll always have your back. That's what sisters do. Besides, we are all we have in this world," she declared.

"We have Arthur," I reminded her.

"Of course," she said. I sensed an air of uncertainty in her voice. Carter has never been able to hide anything from me, even giving it her best acting skills. Our bond formed in the womb, and her insistence on trading places with me that night overrides everything else.

Before the party, she exclaimed, "I want an angel guarding my grave. You'll see to it, won't you, K?" She often referred to me as K. It made things simpler—less of a guilt trip. Blame plagued my sister. She camouflaged her inner struggles with love affairs, alcohol, and drugs. "Kachina or Kimi. What does it matter? We're identical twins, after all."

I don't think my mother knew how fitting my name would become. Kimi, in Cherokee, means secret.

Whenever my sister spoke of death, which was often, I would smile—a half-crooked smile, all my distorted face would allow, and say, "And why would you think that you'll die before me?"

"It's just a feeling. Let's leave it at that."

I left it as always because not doing so only invited heartache and regret. My smile was fake, but I could pull it off because I was born to be an actress, not Kachina.

Our mom always told me I would be a great actress, like the ones on the covers of the magazines she brought home from the beauty shop where she worked. In retrospect, I don't think she meant it, but it was something my mother told me, a long-abandoned dream of her own, passed on to me.

I often wonder where our mother's stardom dream came from, considering she grew up on a Hopi reservation. Even if she could have afforded to go, the nearest movie theater was miles away, and there was no television on the rez. Nor did we have one in Cherokee. The beauty shop where she worked had one, though, and the lady who was the owner kept it running all day long, loud enough to counter the sound of the dryers the women sat under. To go to work at that beauty shop, my mom traveled fifteen miles one way to the nearest white town from the edge of the Cherokee reservation where we lived in the mountains of North Carolina in our beat-up old Ford Pickup, the same one we were born in, the one our father struggled to keep running all those many years.

Whenever my mom would hand me one of the outdated, tattered magazines from the beauty shop, I would smile radiantly or pout my lips sultrily, like the women on the cover. "You have the actress gene," she said, patting me on my head.

I never saw Indians on the cover, and I asked our mom why that was.

"Maybe you'll be the first."

Our mom didn't like my sister or me using the term Indian. She said it's what Christopher Columbus called us, and who wants to believe anything coming from a white man who got lost, not to mention the other things he was capable of?

"What other things?" I asked.

"We'll save that little talk for when you are older," she said.

She also said it was a way to group all the tribes into one, even though we each had our distinctive cultures. She was always clear about the differences between our Cherokee heritage and Hopi tradition. "Both are equally important," she said.

We had the same thick, dark hair as our parents, which didn't bode well for Kachina. Everyone had black hair on the reservation. Nothing good ever came for the lacquered black-haired people living in our segregated place on the mountain. The flea-market Barbie doll my sister and I shared had yellow hair. Barbie, or rather the idea of her, was what we aspired to become. As we grew older, our mother compared us to Elizabeth Taylor, Sophia Loren, Audrey Hepburn, and Hedy Lemarr. You would think she knew these stars intimately the way she talked. She would relate stories about them that didn't appear in any magazines. Our father said these stories came from her wild imagination. I sometimes think her obsession with celebrities caused our father to drink, but then there were a myriad of reasons Cherokee men living on a reservation drank.

If you looked beyond our mother's preoccupation with female movie stars, she was the only grounded member of our family, other than me. Back then, I considered myself seriously grounded and determined to make the best of both worlds the way she did. I could listen to her chattering about Hollywood stars or espousing Hopi wisdom for hours. According to her, all of it was dreams spinning from the same great web. I think I'm only now beginning to grasp the meaning of her words.

While I was content to be compared to any of these legends, Kachina was prone to idolizing Marilyn Monroe, even emulating her whispery, sultry voice. Unbeknownst to my parents or sister, I longed to be like Katharine Hepburn. By 1968, she had already won three Oscars for the best actress.

When we were only five, my sister asked, "What was *I* born to be, Mama?"

My father burst through the door, bottle in hand, declaring, "You are a born politician and a mighty pretty one, at that."

At five, neither of us knew what a politician was.

"Is that a good thing?" she asked.

"Oh, my little Kachina. You have both looks and personality and a charm that could convince anyone of anything," our mom answered. "You take that after your father."

Our dad winked at our mother and said while proceeding to hug her, "I won your mother, didn't I?" She pushed him away the way she usually did when he was drunk.

While I took after my mother, Kachina had the traits of our father. We all knew deep down she would end up married young, living either in a trailer or shack on the reservation or on the outskirts.

My father was a salesman and farmer. Our mother met him when he traveled the back roads from North Carolina to Arizona.

"Why would anyone here need a vacuum cleaner?" My grandmother said. "We have dirt floors."

Hiding in the corner, my mother, fifteen then, laughed. Their eyes locked, and the rest is history. That's how our mother related their brief courtship before our father hauled her away to the nearest Justice of the Peace, a white man, since our grandmother, whom we've only heard stories about from our mother, was against the marriage at first.

"How dumb can someone be trying to sell vacuum cleaners to women with dirt floors?" my grandmother scoffed.

According to the Hopi, it was customary for the son-in-law to move in with the wife's family, but Grandma gave our mom her blessing to leave their tribe to join his. Prospective sons-in-law were judged by their work ethic, and our dad's was less than stellar.

He changed his strategy to selling brushes and hair combs, something any woman needed, especially tribal women possessing long, thick hair. He was an excellent salesman when he wasn't drinking and a poor farmer, even at his soberest.

"Our chickens won't even eat this corn," I remember our mother complaining. But our father had this way about him, and Kachina did too. By fourteen, she could wrap boys around her little finger. The problem was they were all Cherokee boys living on the reservation with no aspirations of ever leaving. My sister saw no future with them, and she was right. We lived in a climate of poverty and alcoholism.

Two nights before our sixteenth birthday, a white man named Victor Wildman, a shady-looking man decked out in garb from one of the touristy shops along our mountainous road, appeared on our doorstep. He claimed to be traveling through the area, looking for baskets and other Indian goods he might resell. That was the original story he told. Kachina and I tell our mom we saw him hanging around the schoolyard earlier. Red flags automatically go up for our mother. There had been talk about him at the beauty shop where she works. Gladys, the owner, told our mother he was in earlier asking about her. "Why would such a man be asking about you?" Gladys asked.

"He's seen our girls, how beautiful they are," our mother says. Everyone in the area thought our mother was a raving beauty and that Kachina and I had already surpassed even *her* good looks.

She tells our father to get rid of him, but he is drunk. When our father drinks, he doesn't get mean—just the opposite. He and Victor are outside, standing among the chickens, talking like old friends. My mother is peeking out the window, cringing, and telling us to stay inside. "That man is nothing but trouble," she warns us. "Victor Wildman is some made-up name."

I ask her how she knows.

"There's been talk about him at the beauty shop." She wouldn't say anymore.

Before we knew it, our father invited him for dinner. He tells us he has Cherokee roots on his mother's side and suggests that we could be related. The man with his big white hat with a feather sticking out of it grins and winks at us while our mother pulls our father aside. "If he is Cherokee, which I seriously doubt, he is possessed by Uyaga."

We are sure Victor overhears, but he doesn't seem to know

what Uyaga means, nor does he seem to care, as he can't take his eyes off of us, particularly Kachina, who is smiling back. I nudge her, but she ignores me.

Uyaga is an evil earth spirit opposed to the forces of right. It's a Cherokee tradition, and although our mother is Hopi, she says if Victor is indeed Cherokee, he must follow his tribe's traditions. Our mom, even though she takes pleasure in the goings-on of the white world, refuses to leave behind the conventions of our people, whether they stem from the Cherokee or the Hopi. Like her mother before her, she is deeply entrenched in the old ways, which she says carries a lot of wisdom. She always cautioned us to keep the old ways in our hearts, even though the white world was swallowing us up daily, as it was determined to do.

At dinner, my mother looks like she may hurl her food at any moment. While Kachina and our dad are friendly, my mother has her guard up, seeing this man as some threat. It is as if she knows him or his true purpose in being here, but how could she?

My dad passed the cheap liquor, the only variety he ever had. Victor, in his white suit that won't button because of his protruding belly, decked in faux gold chains and turquoise, his hat now removed, revealing greasy hair gel coating several strands combed over the top to hide his baldness, eagerly gulps it down.

Victor brags he has traveled the globe. Whereas our dad becomes what Mom calls an exaggerated boaster when drunk, Victor leaks truth the way our old pickup leaks oil. It turns out, in reality, he had been as far north as New York and as far west as Oklahoma and never any further south than our mountainous region because he said the South still carried the scars of slavery. He proclaims to have business in California and announces he's headed there to join a cousin already working for a Hollywood movie studio. He winks in Kachina's and my direction and says, "Too bad your daughters can't go with me. They're so beautiful, they could be models. Or actresses."

Of course, my sister's and my eyes light up—Kachina's more than mine. Like my mother, I was initially cautious regarding Victor, but when the conversation went in this direction, I was ready to give him the benefit of the doubt. This could be our chance—my chance. I want to believe him, but I see the look in our mother's eyes. She's always been an excellent judge of people, except for men in matters of the heart.

Even though she married young, there was someone before our father. The only reason we know about it is because our father has brought it up on several of his drunk binges. He's never hit our mom, but when they fight, it's usually about this man, and I think he might. Our mom would only say in her defense she was young, a child who didn't know any better, too pretty for her own good, well-endowed, and easy prey when it came to flattery. She admitted she had no sense regarding men when she was young. Kachina takes after her in that respect. My mom knows this and worries. So does our father when he is not drunk.

"They can't go with you. They're not even sixteen yet and have another year of school."

I don't think I had ever seen my mom so tense or frightened. Our mom was determined that we would finish school. Still, I detected something else, possibly something coming from that Hopi wisdom she believed so firmly in, although I don't think the sageness of it fully sunk in until she had children of her own.

"They can make their own decisions when they graduate, but not until then." She pushes her chair back from the table and starts clearing the dishes. "We don't want to hold you up from your trip, Victor," our mom says, standing as rigid as an oak, her back to us, holding a plate so tightly in her hand that I think even if she restrains from throwing it, it will break because of the sheer force of her grip.

Victor might have taken the strong hint if our dad had stayed quiet, but the liquor wouldn't let him. "You can't leave before our Halloween party. The girls and their mother have been decorating the barn all week. And the girls are in the school play on Friday. Our Kachina is the lead as Frankenstein's monster," our dad announces, to which Mom storms from the room with a plate still in her hand and demands we go with her. We retreat to the living room, only a few feet away, since our house is nothing more than a small shack. We can still hear everything, especially since their voices become progressively louder with each gulp of liquor.

"Oh, the lead? Impressive," Victor says, taking the last drink of liquor, winking at Kachina, who stands just beyond the doorway.

After Victor left, Kachina's only goal was to leave the reservation when she turned sixteen. "We'll leave together. We'll find rich men who will take care of us. We'll hitchhike to Gatlinburg and hook up with rich tourists," she declared.

I hadn't even thought about leaving until Kachina and Victor put the idea into my head, but I wanted to be an actress, and talent agents didn't visit reservations.

Our good looks were legendary in the area. We were identical twins, not so much as an errant eyebrow hair to set us apart, yet we were radically different in our manner and behavior. My sister had all the charm and personality. I was studious and shy, an introvert except when acting. I could become anyone I wanted to be then, even Kachina.

While my sister experimented with makeup and collected

boyfriends, I studied a box of old scripts with half of the pages gone, which our mom picked up at the flea market where she acquired our Barbie doll. My favorite was *Frankenstein* by Alexander Utz, based on Mary Shelley's *Frankenstein, Or The Modern Prometheus.* I was thrilled when Mr. Harrison, our teacher at the reservation on an educational grant, said we should do the play for Halloween. I don't know that it would have been my first choice, except for the fact it was the only fully intact script. Or perhaps this particular play prophesied what was yet to come.

I practiced relentlessly, playing all the parts and even fashioned costumes with the help of my mom and her archaic Singer sewing machine, another flea market bargain. I don't know what I was thinking. There were only so many parts, and our class lacked boys. Some parts would need to be taken by girls, sort of the reverse of Shakespeare's plays.

I had made the costume specifically to fit me, thinking I was a shoo-in. However, any outfit designed explicitly for me meant it would also fit Kachina, so Mr. Harrison gave her the part of the monster.

Seeing my disappointment, he took me aside and lectured, "Listen, Kimi, I have faith that you will graduate and do great things. Let's let Kachina do this. There are virtually no lines for her to memorize. What does it matter? No one will even know who is beneath the costume."

"I'll know," I muttered under my breath.

"You're the director. Do you know how important that is? Not to mention your artistic abilities and organizational skills. The set you've created is marvelous. This play would fall apart without you."

"Will worked on it too."

"Yes, of course. Credit goes to Will as well."

I gave in. I knew what Mr. Harrison said was true. While I was a straight-A student, Kachina did well to bring home a C.

Mr. Harrison was under the false impression that giving Kachina the lead might propel her into caring about school. I never let on that it hurt me not to get the part. Nor did I let on to Mr. Harrison Kachina could have cared less. All she could talk about was the party we were throwing in our barn the next night after the play.

Despite our differences, my sister and I were best friends.

I don't blame her for what happened to either of us. Neither do I blame my mom, whom I found out after the play convinced Mr. Harrison to give the part to Kachina. "Kimi, you'll do fine in life, but Kachina needs an extra boost. She did great, didn't she?"

I try not to blame either of them. I'm sure if my mom were still alive, she would blame Victor. He could have saved both of us, but he didn't.

It turns out my sister was right. She did die before me. Not once, but twice.

Five

KIMI

It's been six months since my sister's death—a death that still makes headlines and invites speculation and conspiracy theories, and two months since Arthur found me in the house, standing amid broken glass shards, bleeding, unaware of who or where I was.

Only I know the actual truth of it. The only problem is that legally, I don't exist. I'm Kimi. I'm a secret.

I look down at myself. I'm not alarmed by the blood on my clothes, but this strange man standing behind me is. I do not know who he is nor question him being here. He is holding a bag and a cup. I smell the brew I recognize as coffee. I see a picture of a green mermaid on the cup. I know these minute details, although I don't associate them with anything. I seem to know mundane things. The bigger picture is lost on me, and I feel serenely calm as if an entire life of baggage has been lifted from me, whoever "me" is. I also know I've been waiting for this inner peace all my life, even though I have no knowledge of this life.

I'm standing amid shards of glass in front of a splintered full-length wall mirror with only a tiny fraction of glass still intact, stunned at the image staring back at me—stunned but not alarmed.

I'm not even startled that suddenly, through what's left of the mirror standing behind me, I see the reflection of a gray-haired man dressed in a dark blue suit with a blue-striped tie. He drops the bag he is holding to the floor. It lands on the shattered glass strewn about the floor. He puts his hands on my shoulders and asks, "Carter?"

I stare blankly at him. I know nothing. I reach up, placing my sticky, bloody hand on his warm one. There is something about his watch, perhaps some flicker of a memory trying to come through. It quickly fades.

His face changes as if he is addressing a different person. "Kimi, what have you done?"

I don't recognize this name either, but I turn toward him. He examines both my wrists. He pulls out his phone and taps a number on his speed dial. I stand motionless.

"No, it doesn't appear she has cut her wrists. Pieces of glass are embedded in her hands from where she has probably banged her fists against a mirror, and she doesn't seem to know who she is." There is a pause. "Yes, possibly she could have suffered a stroke."

The rest of the conversation is Arthur saying either yes or no as he walks to the far corner of the room, occasionally looking my way before responding.

Another pause. "Yes, we will be here. I'll leave the door unlocked. Be careful. The entrance is covered in glass and blood." He puts his phone back into his jacket pocket.

He looks in my direction. "Dr. Ferguson will be here within the hour."

I don't respond.

"Kimi, come with me."

Even though neither the name Carter nor this new one he calls me is familiar, I comply as he leads me into the nearest bathroom. It's immaculate, with a marble-topped vanity and a black-and-white tiled floor. Plush white towels hang from brass fixtures. Upon closer inspection, I see a layer of dust over the neatly draped towels, which tells me no one has used this bathroom in a while. I look around while this man holds my hands under lukewarm water streaming from a gold-plated faucet. He picks tiny shards of glass from my hands and places a clean towel over them. I realize this man, who appears to be in his late fifties or early sixties, is familiar with this house and knows me. I wonder if he might be my husband, but I'm wearing no wedding band, and neither is he.

I sense we are close, and I can trust him, although not trusting anyone at this point seems foreign, as foreign as my surroundings and identity. I'm perfectly calm, free, and at peace, lifted above my baggage, although I don't know what that could have been.

He is talking to me, trying to get me to respond, asking me benign questions. He wants me to say something, but I don't know what to say. I stare at him dumbly until the word Carter spills out of his mouth in what I perceive as audible slow motion.

I jerk back upon hearing the name. Memories rush back with the force of Niagara Falls.

"Arthur?" I question.

"Yes, yes, I'm Arthur. Can you tell me what happened?"

Arthur, a semi-retired lawyer, looks after me. He is also the power of attorney for my sister, whom the world knew as Carter Hudson. I knew her as Kachina, my twin sister, although I rarely called her that. Kachina died long before Carter did.

I suddenly realize that Arthur might think that I tried to commit suicide. What if he had come in and found me dead? How would he explain me? Perhaps some dazed, deformed, obsessed fan who somehow gained entrance to Carter Hudson's mansion. Or he might hire a clean-up crew. Arthur probably has access to such people. I wonder if he might mourn my death.

Or would the police suspect Arthur? Considering his history with Carter, it is a likely scenario. They always blame the husband, in this case, the ex.

After my sister died, I inherited everything, and Arthur inherited *me.* It's only logical that Arthur would want to get rid of me—logical, but not probable. Arthur doesn't have it in him. Even though memories are seeping back slowly, I know this about him.

I remember that he always comes in the wee hours of the morning before heading to the office. He comes through the door using his key, bringing my favorite poppyseed bagels. Of course, he would mourn me. Arthur once told me our morning visits were the highlight of his day. He misses Carter, I'm sure, and I remind him of her.

I recollect wandering around the massive limestone stone mansion in a daze, curious about my whereabouts, leaving a bloody trail in my wake, before returning to the broken mirror to stare into what is left of it.

I look down at my hands in shock and fall slightly backward. Arthur holds me. I'm limp in his grasp. From my five-foot-four frame, I look up at Arthur's over six-foot-tall one, only slightly stooped with age. I've always thought him handsome, but more importantly—kind.

He opens a drawer in the vanity, pulls out a first aid kit, and puts hydrogen peroxide on my wounds.

"Now, tell me what happened," Arthur asks while blood diluted by water runs down the sink. I don't think it's hard to figure out, but I know Arthur is testing me, trying to gather as much information as possible before Dr. Ferguson arrives. It will be a while, considering he has to come across town, and rush hour has started by now. I'm glad. Arthur is the only person I want to be around at the moment. Dr. Ferguson has this clinical coldness about him.

"He doesn't like me," I say.

"Who doesn't like you?" Arthur asks while examining my hands.

"Dr. Ferguson."

"Everyone loves Carter Hudson," he says, forgetting.

"But not Kimi," I remind him.

He admonishes, "Now, now. It's all in your mind, Kimi." He hesitates before saying Kimi.

"Everything is in our minds," I remind Arthur.

"You've read too many of those new-age books," he says and smiles.

Carter was the one who read those, but I don't correct him.

I'll never be able to step out of Carter's shadow. As children, even though we were identical, she always took the lead. Every baby is the most beautiful child to grace this planet, according to the mother or grandmother of that child, but in Carter's case, this was true. Throughout her life, she never lost her beauty—a beautiful baby, child, and teenager—and as she entered womanhood, every alluring physical feature became more enhanced. Plastered on the covers of magazines, people described her as the most enticing woman on the planet, with Marilyn Monroe coming in as a close second. Carter was the nearest thing to royalty in the United States.

Carter never aged. People accused her of having plastic surgery, but I can attest to the fact she hadn't. A magazine article once compared her to Dorian Gray, claiming she must have an aging portrait hidden in her mansion. The piece alluded the picture was kept on a covered easel hidden away in the west wing that always stays shut up for redecorating or repairs. Little do they know how close to the truth they are. I'm the portrait, a scarred face that has gone through a trial by fire.

I suddenly remember my rampage through the house, the part of the house I only dared enter when no one was about. I had stopped in front of the hallway mirror, seeing my reflection. A hideous and horrible monster stared back at me.

I look down at my hands, which don't look all that bad after Arthur has cleaned away the sticky, crusty blood from them. He releases a heavy breath before reaching into the medicine cabinet to pull out a bandage. His touch is gentle as he presses the adhesive next to my skin.

I turn away from the medicine cabinet's mirror, focusing on my hands or, rather, Arthur's.

He looks into my eyes. "It's going to be all right."

"No more scars," I say. I feel tears forming, and I desperately want to return to my previous state of serenity. I, too, like Arthur, realize I must have suffered a stroke, or maybe I willed myself to forget everything, if only temporarily. I've read enough medical and psychology books because of my condition during my decades as a hermit to know the signs of both. I remember Arthur suggesting both possibilities while on the phone with Dr. Ferguson. I realize who I am or who I'm not and that I can't go to the hospital like an average person. If an ambulance were to pull up to the vacant house of Carter Hudson and leave with an unknown person and Carter's attorney and former husband close in pursuit, the paparazzi would be thicker than molasses.

The man he called—Dr. Ferguson—is my physician, one of the few who know about my existence. He's on a hefty retainer provided by Carter, now Carter's estate, to make house calls and keep my life secret. Doctors who make house calls and keep secrets aren't uncommon in Los Angeles. Money speaks.

Arthur cleans himself up, wiping away the blood from his hands. I stare at the bloodstains on his jacket and say, "I'm sorry."

He smiles and says, "It's only a jacket."

I smile my weird grin, realizing he will throw it out with the shirt and tie. It's easier than coming up with an explanation to the dry cleaners why there is blood on his clothes. He can hardly say he cut himself shaving. Who shaves after fully dressing? I'm sure LA dry cleaners see all sorts of suspicious things, but Arthur has always been so careful regarding my sister and me that I can't imagine a slip-up.

I hold my arms forward as Arthur leads me out of the bathroom. We walk into the sitting room together, passing through the trail of blood with pieces of glass mingled with it. We pass another mirror with a French-style frame devoid of most of the glass it once encased. It leans against a burgundy velvet chair. I realize I put it there. Carter loved opulence and, after a trip to France, hired an interior designer to emulate the richness of the Versailles Palace.

We pass another large room. It smells of smoke. I peer inside to see a room vacated of furniture with soot-blackened walls. This alarms me, but my memory is still fuzzy. I ask, "What happened in here?"

"You don't remember?"

I shake my head.

"It's why you moved into the west wing. It's when things changed."

We continue through a dining area into the kitchen. Arthur pulls a chair from beneath the table and motions for me to sit.

"Are you hungry?"

I shake my head.

"Come on, Kimi. I know you haven't had breakfast and must have worked up an appetite..." He stalls.

"You mean, after breaking mirrors?" I sometimes think my sister's obsession with mirrors was not only to admire herself but also to keep me secluded in my part of the house, where mirrors are non-existent except for the small handheld one I bring out when necessary. Carter used mirrors to keep me in my place the way someone uses garlic to ward off vampires. Kachina would have never done that.

"Well, I've only seen two thus far."

I laugh, and Arthur does, too. He turns and opens the refrigerator door. He sighs, staring into the empty shelves. "I forgot," he says.

"Remember, when you let Maria go, you told her to take home all the food when she cautioned it would draw mice in what she assumes is an unoccupied house."

"We couldn't let her know the house was in use." Smacking his head with the palm of his hand, he exclaimed, "I also forgot amid this morning's happenings that I brought bagels."

"We could go to the west wing, where we usually have breakfast," I say.

"No, stay where you are. I'll be back in a jiffy."

Jiffy. What an unusual word for prim and proper Arthur to use.

In Arthur's absence, I look down at my bandaged hands.

Regret grips me, realizing Arthur will be the one who will clean up the mess I made. He let go of most of the staff shortly after Carter's death. Keeping them on would have been hard to explain in a supposedly empty house, and hiring anyone to clean up broken glass and blood would have been more difficult to account for.

"How do you feel?" he asks upon returning with his

coffee, now cold, no doubt. He also has my poppyseed bagel and his blueberry one. He turns on the teapot.

"Oh, Arthur, you know me. I go through a plethora of emotions. I'm calmer now, but earlier, I was angry."

"You know, we have to do something about this, don't you?" he says.

"Yes, I know, but I don't know what."

True to his word, Dr. Ferguson arrives within forty-five minutes. We hear him cussing as he maneuvers through the wake of my mental breakdown. The full extent of what had happened before the stroke or nervous breakdown suddenly registers. After some reflection, I'm prone to thinking it was the latter. I'm sure Dr. Ferguson will concur.

"We're in here," Arthur calls out.

Dr. Ferguson follows Arthur's voice into the kitchen.

He places his bag on the table and exchanges a look with Arthur—a look that tells me that together, they will decide my fate. Things are no longer in my control if they ever were.

After taking my temperature, checking my pulse, taking my blood pressure, and listening to my heart, he says, "Yes, more than likely a stroke—a mild one, I would guess."

"Or possibly a nervous breakdown," I interject.

"We would need an MRI to be sure," he says.

I feel the panic creeping through my body. "That would mean a hospital."

"Yes," Dr. Ferguson says.

"But I feel perfectly fine now," I say.

"You're not fine," Arthur scolds.

My heart races thinking one of them has already called an ambulance, that Arthur wants an end to this charade once and for all, and that Dr. Ferguson does as well, wanting to return to the "do-no-harm" code of ethics he vowed to uphold before leaving medical school strapped with insurmountable student loans prompting him into a behind-the-scenes, cover-up doctor to the stars.

The doctor, probably two inches shorter than me, pauses again and rubs his chin while looking up at Arthur. "Maybe the question I should ask is, did she know who she was after she regained her memory?"

I'm thinking, what an odd question. However, Arthur doesn't seem to think it odd at all. He merely answers, "No."

The doctor replies, "Perhaps there is a solution."

At this moment, I know I will not be going to a hospital. If the good doctor breaks his vows of silence concerning me, all the others who seek his discreetness will get it elsewhere. A multitude of so-called professionals are ready to rush in and take his place—physicians who are not listed in the Yellow Pages but ones who people like Arthur know and can connect anyone with for a fee.

I also know I will no longer be living without supervision. Until this moment, I had been perfectly content to live out the rest of my days in the limestone house, almost hidden from view by the massive shrubbery. But my destructive temper tantrums—yes, there have been more than one—and compromised health brought on by this last one force their hands on the matter.

I have never feared death. There have been times I've welcomed it, but I do fear life coupled with the terror of dying alone in this twenty-two-room house. So, I agree with their proposal of moving somewhere where I can still retain anonymity but have the care I need.

Dr. Ferguson takes Arthur aside. "You know she could have died."

"But she didn't," he says sternly.

"Well, the next time..."

Arthur interrupts him, "There won't be a next time."

"No, there can't be. I don't want to be involved in a scandal so close to retirement. And neither should you. Aren't you thinking of retiring soon?"

"This place you recommend...?"

In much the same manner Dr. Ferguson pulls individual pills from his coat pocket, he hands Arthur a yellow Post-it note, a ubiquitous, untraceable item with something scribbled on it. Arthur takes it, looks at it, and merely nods.

Dr. Ferguson retrieves his bag from the kitchen table and says, "I'll show myself out."

Six

KIMI

For the past week, the time it took Arthur to make arrangements, a task only someone with his expertise and influence could pull off in such a short amount of time, I've gone over everything I can think of—what to take, what I can do without, and what should go to charity—not only the things I've accumulated since living here but those items belonging to my sister. I thought I would have more time, but I find time moves more rapidly at forty-nine. I have to choose wisely regarding what I take. I can hardly fit the contents of a twenty-two-room mansion into a small studio apartment. Arthur assured me it was nearly the size of the west wing, the part of the house I've occupied since coming to live with my sister. There's not much I want that belonged to Kachina or Carter, as our styles are radically different. These days, I desire little in the way of material possessions—possibly my books and paints.

I've often asked Carter what drew her to this house. She told me she always had me in mind when picking it. "I knew you would come back to me one day," she said, following it with her distinctive wink and smile. "Plus, I loved the house's unusual layout. Arthur and I had quite an argument when I told him I wanted to connect the guest house to the main structure, but I knew it would make it easier for us."

"But you didn't tell him I would be living here."

"No, not then. He didn't like the idea because of the cost, and he also wanted to keep the guest area, which we never used, separate."

"But you won out."

"I always do." She winked again and, after a pause, said, "People say it's haunted."

"The guest house?"

"Yes."

"Haunted by whom? Me?"

"No, not you. This was before we moved here, and no one knows. This house is old, you know. But I have a theory."

It's not like Carter to have theories. This immediately intrigues me.

"Do you think future ghosts could haunt a place, Kimi?"

After some reflection, which isn't necessary since I know Carter's mind as well as I do my own, maybe better, I said, "I suppose."

"I think the ghost is what sold me. I wanted someone to keep me company when I'm between films or Arthur is working. Too much rattles around in my brain when I'm alone."

"I rattle in your brain."

She frowns briefly, then pretends to ignore my last statement.

"I instructed Arthur to purchase it. For us. But there was no ghost."

"Until me."

"Until you," she agrees.

While Arthur thought she meant for her and him, I knew she meant for her and me.

"I had more than enough money to do so after making

The Muted Girl, and new offers were pouring in by the dozens. I'll have to admit, Kimi, it frightened me. Not the idea of the haunted house. God knows, our lives have been haunted enough. I feared I couldn't pull this acting thing off. I needed you. You were the one born to be an actress."

"Yes, it's what Mom always said. Do you think about her, Carter?"

"Every day. Don't you, Kimi?"

"Of course I do. I feel she is guiding me, as well as you."

"It was her spirit telling me to buy the house. I immediately hired an architect to draw up plans to join the guest house to the main structure. Deep down, I knew you would join me here someday. It took long enough, don't you think? Well, I didn't want us separated by an outside walkway. Don't you think making a secret entrance into my bedroom was marvelous? A secret that only you and I knew about?"

Secrets—one of the many, I think.

"I don't know, Carter. That idea was rather creepy, like something one might see on *Dark Shadows,* not to mention bypassing your stinky shoes to get here."

Carter didn't like me bringing up that show or her stinky feet. Before becoming famous, she had auditioned for one of the child leads. She didn't get it—not even a callback.

"Such a low-budget show," she snapped.

"Maybe so, but it's a classic. Besides, although you looked younger than your age, you were too old for a child's part."

"Yes, you're right. I don't know why I ever tried out for it. Anyway, I'm sure you or Mom channeled the idea of the secret passageway to me."

"Yes, one of us," I assure her.

"Not our father."

I laugh. "I'm sure he's sitting on a cloud drinking the good liquor."

"Anyway, *The Chronicles of Narnia* was my inspiration. You know, a secret passage through the wardrobe."

Carter loved to remind me of all the books she read when she was still going by Kachina. Arthur brought books home almost daily shortly after retrieving her from the LA street corner.

I miss these conversations with Carter. Since the Halloween party, there has only been me. Without Carter's presence, the house is drained of all spirit. I don't expect her to appear at The Woodlands, but I feel she is happy I'm going there, thinking it is best for me. I believe our mother thinks so, too.

I look around. Carter's silk robe is still strewn across the bed as if she will walk from the bath any moment and drape it over her body. Private pictures of her and Arthur adorn the dresser: them on a skiing trip, another of them on a boat on the Mediterranean, and Carter by herself posing in front of the Versailles Palace. In Cherokee, Kachina had a picture of the Versailles Palace torn from a magazine on her bedroom wall. I wonder if I should take them with me, but how can I? Why would I have never-before-seen pictures of Carter Hudson? They rightfully belong to Arthur. Besides, they're only memories—Arthur and Carter's—not mine.

Writing a memoir about my sister briefly crosses my mind, but the whole point of this, or at least part of the point, is a new life. The goal is to leave Carter behind and take up my true identity. I don't need the reminder of Carter's possessions, nor mine, since most are intrinsically related to Carter. Everything I have is what she has given to me. I left everything behind thirty-three years ago except for the clothes on my back, and I can do it again.

Even though Arthur initially suggested moving back in one day, I can't see myself ever returning to this house.

"Arthur, sell it, along with the contents."

As soon as I uttered those words, a multitude of stresses evaporated from Arthur's face. I think the same must have been true for me as well, although looking in a mirror for proof could only bring them back.

Carter Hudson's possessions alone will bring a small fortune. After I move out, Arthur will hand over the house to a real estate agent and auction off Carter Hudson's furniture and personal items. We couldn't have potential buyers exploring while I'm still in residence. There would be questions.

The main living area will have to be renovated before selling the house. People probably wonder why Arthur, whom everyone knows to be my sister's power of attorney and who everyone believes to be the sole beneficiary, even though the last divorce was nearly a year before her death, has not begun reconstructing the burned-out shell. It's because of me, who, in actuality, is the sole beneficiary. Arthur has cared for my needs, the hidden-away sister, as much as he ever did for Carter.

Except for the personal items I will need in the morning, my luggage, or rather the luggage belonging to my sister, the red leather ones engraved with C.H. in the fancy script, is packed. I've never needed luggage since I've never traveled. I wonder if anyone will question the initials. I'll say I bought them in a plush vintage shop. For my life, I can't remember the name of the shop. I simply fell in love with them.

There is too much to think about. My brain is overloaded, and my body feels heavy. Even my facial scars, deadened over time, tingle like they are returning to life. I know I need rest, but my mind won't quit. After midnight, I finally lay my head on the goose-feather pillow, but I only lie on top of the comforter as if making the bed is one last thing I can avoid in the morning. I don't want to leave that for Arthur. An unmade bed in a supposedly unused part of the house would look suspicious.

I've often noticed the sounds in the dead of night, but more so now since it's my last night here. I stare at shadows on the ceiling made by the faint light of the streetlight. I try to read the dark splotches that move as the blades of the ceiling fan whisk past as if I'm reading tea leaves. I'm far from psychic. Thinking about the psychic Carter smuggled into the house one day for a private reading, I laugh. Arthur, the pragmatist that he is, had felt it complete nonsense. She thought she could talk to our mother and ask for some Hopi wisdom. The woman, recommended by certain celebrities, was a complete fraud. When she spoke of her love life and recent breakup, she said, "I didn't see it coming at all," I quickly held both hands to my mouth to stifle a laugh. Our mother could probably gain insight from the shadows moving across the ceiling.

My mind moves from the shadows to the sounds. Even though the mansion hides behind enormous shrubbery, there are noises. It's two a.m. Early Sunday morning. I hear people's cars returning from Saturday night parties. This town has lots of partygoers. Parties are another thing I've missed out on. I wonder if they have parties at The Woodlands.

I don't know when I finally drift off, but it is still dark when I awake. I squint and look at the clock's numbers blinking—5:03 a.m. I'm exhausted from little sleep and anticipation. Arthur will not be here until eight to pick me up. We agreed on the earliest time possible on a Sunday morning to avoid people. Still, it's LA. I'm afraid to doze off now. So, I lie here, imagining every scenario I can imagine how the trip across town to The Woodlands Retirement and Convalescent Home will go. I'm neither retired nor convalescing. I haven't worked a day since I was a teenager, and I've long ago recuperated from my injuries. Still, I scratch at a hallucinatory itch on my face. Recognizing it's nerves, I pull my hand away. There have been times when I've thought I could magically pull away the outer layer of skin like a facial mask, revealing a fresh, unflawed complexion. Unfortunately, the scars remain.

Arthur and I agreed The Woodlands would be the best choice since I could no longer live alone in this giant, empty house. The staff, who didn't even know of my existence, have not been here for months, except for the gardener, who comes once a week. I think he spied me peeking from the window two days ago. He knows no one is supposed to be here. He looked scared, and I knew he revitalized the rumor of this place being haunted. Perhaps they're right. I sometimes think I feel Carter's presence. At other times, Kachina's.

When the sun finally teases me through the curtains, I rise, make myself a cup of tea, and warm up a croissant. The house has been shut up for six months, except for the west wing where I live. I miss Maria, but how could we explain me, the mansion's one lone occupant without an identity, needing sustenance, to her? All of Arthur's expensive blends of coffee were gone. Maria was a Java junkie. Luckily, she left the boxes of tea bags behind.

I have a small kitchen area in the section where I live, although I rarely cook. Arthur brings small bags of groceries twice a week and checks on me. He either calls or comes by both morning and night. He would have moved me out of the house sooner, but I fought him every step of the way until he found me in the state I was in last week.

I hear Arthur's car pull up outside. My heart pounds. I had begun to relish the idea of different surroundings—people in my life, but now that the moment is here, I want to retreat into the life that I have known, hidden in the shadows—Carter's shadow, but she is no longer here to cast one. I take a deep breath, attempting to relax, but it does little good. I look over to see I've left the dirty plate and teacup on the table. I grab them to rinse off and put them in the sink, but they slip from my shaking hands I didn't realize were shaking until now. I step back to avoid the shards. So much broken glass lately. What does it mean? I bend down and begin picking up the pieces but quickly rise back up. It doesn't matter. The real estate agent Arthur hires to sell the house will ensure everything is spotless. And I'm sure Arthur will do a police-like scrub down of my living quarters, hiding any trace of evidence of my existence.

I smile, trying to think of my leaving this place as a continuance of the life stolen from me at sixteen. I will experience being outside in the daytime for the first time in over thirty-three years. Both Arthur and Carter have kept me hidden away for the longest time.

Seven

KIMI

There is no knock on the door. There is no need. Even though Carter and Arthur have been through three divorces, Carter never changed the locks. Nor has Ernie, the openly gay security guard who has a thing for Arthur, never refused to open the gate at the security guard house and wave him through. When Carter teased him about it, Arthur would say, "Ernie has been a trusted servant for decades." Sometimes, she referred to Arthur in the same manner—when they were on the outs, which was a good deal of the time. Sadly, they were arguing right before the Halloween party. I warned her that one day, she would push Arthur too far. That's one of the many differences between me and Kachina. Even as a toddler, she could manipulate people, something she began honing to perfection when she hit puberty. She wielded power over men like no other woman. I lack those skills entirely unless I'm acting. Unlike Carter, I don't act around Arthur. He is my best and only friend.

"You look good. I like that dress," he declares. "I've always loved that dress on you."

I don't understand why he is saying this since I've never

worn this dress, but then I have my head slightly turned, hiding my scars. I'm sure he mistakes me for Carter. He's not over her death.

The one good side of my face blushes at the compliment. I don't think he's ever seen me in anything but yoga attire. Other than pajamas or swimsuits for a midnight swim, which are rare, I've only worn what is comfortable. At first, it was only loose-fitting clothes. It took a decade for me to feel confident enough to put fabric so close to my skin.

"I stole it from Carter's closet," I confess. Of course, anything that once belonged to Carter is now technically mine. It was one of the few things she owned with long sleeves. Longer sleeves are necessary, as the burns cover the top part of my right arm.

He sighs slightly as if I've said something distasteful—something fatiguing to deal with, but quickly changes his mood with a compliment. "Well, that shade of blue looks good on you. What do you call it?"

"Thank you. Periwinkle."

"Interesting name for a color."

"I think so too. It comes from a flower."

"I'm afraid, as for choosing names, I haven't been so creative. I've listed you under the name of Kimi Stone."

Arthur's voice is stoic. He doesn't want me to use Kimi but knows I would insist. Our mother felt names were significant, given to us for a reason.

I failed to consider my surname. Surely, people wouldn't associate the name Kimi Ahoka with my twin sister. Only a few know the name Carter was born with, and none would tell. She used a stage name from her first role, an ad for a soft drink. The only one who might tell is long dead. It didn't surprise Kachina when Arthur told her Victor had died of a drug overdose a couple of years after Arthur discovered her on that street corner. Arthur had kept as close a tab as possible on him since his disappearance shortly after taking my sixteen-year-old sister, Kachina Ahoka, across several state lines, only to abandon her on the outskirts of LA in California.

"Is it necessary? I mean, Carter is dead. What does it matter now?" I don't know why I ask. My sister, after being dead for six months, still makes headlines. Most of them are about her still being alive, hanging on by a thread alone in her mansion. She had gone crazy, totally off her rocker. Covertly, I read what people say on social media. I sometimes laugh at the absurdities fans come up with regarding her. It's almost always about a man or men—Carter had plenty of them. Arthur was a constant throughout her affairs—her rock, although sometimes she forgot. As Kachina, she never could stick with someone truly good.

"It's you I worry about, Kimi."

His words warm my heart. "I'm glad you let me keep my first name. I'm glad you remembered it." I smile. I can't imagine hearing another name on Arthur's lips now. Not even Carter's. I want to remember her as Kachina.

Since the first day Carter introduced us, he has been my advocate and protector. I could easily fall in love with Arthur —only now that Kachina is gone, of course. Why do I say I could? I *have* been in love with Arthur, five years my senior, since probably the first day I met him, despite his relationship with my sister.

It was shortly after I saw Kachina in a movie, one she made right before she made *The Muted Girl*. The world knew her as Carter Hudson. I knew her as my sister.

Ads with Kachina's face flashed across the tiny television screen mounted on the wall of my room. All the nurses here were talking about the newcomer, Carter Hudson, a virtual unknown given the starring role alongside one of the biggest male leads in Hollywood. I immediately thought of my mother and how proud she would be if she were still alive.

Then I saw Kachina's picture and an article about her in a magazine. It was about her upcoming marriage to Arthur Burke, the lawyer who handled her affairs. I knew I could never reach Carter Hudson, but surely Arthur Burke's law firm had to be listed in the Yellow Pages.

I called his office, leaving a cryptic message for Arthur Burke to get to Carter Hudson. I asked the secretary to tell Mr. Burke to get a message to my sister. I merely said, "This is your sister, Kimi Ahoka. I'm alive at the burn unit in Louisville, Kentucky, where you left me. Please come for me."

I can only imagine Kachina's fright. Possibly, she thought it was some prank. But how could it be? People on the reservation where we grew up and went to school would know that Kachina had an identical twin who supposedly died in a fire with the rest of her family. However, they couldn't have known that I had survived after being dropped off in a couple of states over from North Carolina to a hospital.

My phone call got their attention enough for Kachina to hop on the first plane to see if it was indeed me, the charred bundle Victor and she covered in horse blankets, drifting in and out of consciousness in the back seat of a car for the six-hour trip. I can only imagine their shock when Carter told Arthur's family's law firm about the circumstances of an identical twin sister who was in a Kentucky burn unit. Not once did Victor nor Carter ever make a phone call to check on me, not even an anonymous one.

Kachina, meeker than I expected, came into my room wearing a black scarf, an old coat, and beat-up tennis shoes, with oversized dark sunglasses hiding a good deal of her face. Red hair stuck out from beneath the scarf. As soon as the nurse left, she removed her sunglasses. "I have to go incognito these days."

I lifted a piece of gauze that covered the damaged part of my face. Kachina gasped and turned away but slowly got the courage to turn back toward me. "I've missed you so much, Kimi."

"And I you. Why did you leave me here? No calls or anything."

"I thought you had died. It's what Victor told me." Tears streamed down her face, taking heavy makeup and blush with it. She held me awkwardly. "Does it hurt?"

"Like crazy," I said.

"Is it just your face?"

"It goes down the right side of my neck and arm, almost to my elbow."

"Oh," she said, pulling her grip from that side.

"Kimi…"

"I know. You can't let anyone know you abandoned your sister in a burn unit. It could destroy your career."

"Kimi, I didn't…"

"No, not intentionally. I'm sorry."

"So, Victor came good on his promise. He made you a star."

"Victor! No, on the contrary. He dropped me off just outside of Los Angeles. Said he no longer wanted a part of this —that I was too much trouble."

"I don't understand."

"Neither do I. I only know he was tired of me crying during the entire trip and constantly told me to shut up. I half expected to find his car had vanished from the parking lot when I returned from the restroom every time we stopped for gas. From outside of LA, I hitchhiked the rest of the way. I was homeless for two months. Then Arthur found me."

"The man you're marrying?"

"Yes, how did you know?"

I point to the magazine beside my bed.

"Yes, I guess it's all over the news. I don't read stuff about myself. It's mostly gossip." A big smile erupted across her mouth, and she squeezed my left hand. "Kimi, I know you will fall in love with Arthur, just like me."

"Well, not just like you."

"No, of course not, but you'll have a brother."

"You mean, I'll meet him."

"Of course you will."

We hear a rapid knock on the door, and my nurse, Kimberly, says, "Miss Ahoka, sorry to interrupt, but it's time for your medication."

Kachina donned her sunglasses and walked over to the window, keeping her back to us.

Kimberly poured water from the metal pitcher into a paper cup and handed it to Kimi. "Who is your visitor?"

"A friend from the reservation."

"That's nice," she said, pushing the tray out of the way. She looked at my sister's backside and started to say something but suddenly changed her mind. "Oh, well, I'll let you get back to your visit. It's nice Kimi has company. I'm afraid I didn't get your name."

"Carla... Carla Smith," Kachina said, never turning around.

"Well, I'm sure you have much to catch up on."

We both snickered as soon as her footsteps faded far enough down the hallway.

"Carla Smith? Who has a name like that on a Cherokee reservation?"

"I was never good at ad-lib. I'm getting you out of here."

"What?"

"I have a big house. A giant house. It has so many rooms that I haven't seen them all yet. You can have your own wing. I've prepared it for you."

"Prepared it for me?"

"Yes, you'll have all the care you need. A private doctor.

One who makes house calls. I'll call Arthur when I leave here and have him arrange a private plane to pick us up."

"A private plane?"

"Well, we can hardly fly commercial. I came on a commercial flight and signed autographs the whole time. And well, what would they say about my traveling companion? There would be questions."

I stare, marveling at how much she has changed—how differently she acts from how she was growing up. The only thing I can think to say is, "Kachina, why did you dye your beautiful dark hair red?"

"I didn't, silly. It's a wig, but I'm looking at a script now, and if I decide to take the roll, I'll be a blonde."

"Like Marilyn Monroe."

"Yes." She smiled. "Oh, and Kimi, call me Carter now. I've left Kachina behind."

True to her word, Kachina—Carter—brought me straight to this house, where I've been ever since.

When Arthur first saw me, pity and kindness permeated his eyes. The pity has vanished. The kindness remains. I want to think that mutual respect and caring have developed between us.

I've lent a listening ear and a shoulder to cry on, metaphorically speaking, because I've never actually seen Arthur cry through his three divorces. I've watched him rise in the ranks at his father's law firm, encouraging him until he finally took it over. I was there when he had doubts about continuing in law. For selfish reasons, I dissuaded him from giving it up. What would I do without him? I had grown to depend more on him than on my sister. He has always been the voice of reason between us.

"Of course you do." I smile. "You have always been the one to worry about me."

"You have friends. They worry about you."

"Carter had friends. Insincere friends. Not real ones." I think back to the party.

Arthur sighs, and I think he will be glad to have a vacation from me for two weeks. Two weeks is the time recommended to settle in. No visitors.

In a loud voice, I exclaim, "The truth shall set you free."

He tilts his head to the right with a pitiful glance. "Not in your case, Kimi. I fear the stress of the truth being made public would send you..." He casts his eyes upward and points to the chandelier above them. "...before your time," he finishes.

I look up to see the light seeping through the slit beside the doorway, reflecting off the crystals. I wonder if Arthur envisions this as a symbol of heaven. Arthur avoids mentioning Carter. If he were a betting man, he would lay odds on her going in the other direction, even though a large stone angel guards her grave. Kachina Ahoka is not the name on the tombstone.

I've only seen pictures of my sister's grave online, and before that, when I picked it out. I decided on how her funeral should be handled, and Arthur carried out my wishes. Since Carter had no plans of dying so soon, she had no wishes other than an angel over her grave.

I couldn't attend for obvious reasons. Even so, I pleaded with Arthur.

"I will only be at the graveside service, covered in black from head to toe. A black lace veil will cover my face. I can stand off in the distance like the weird stranger one sees at funerals in movies," I had argued.

"Exactly. For just that reason, the paparazzi will tackle you."

"I'll run."

He laughed. "I doubt it, but if you escaped them, there would be even more reason to hunt you down. Besides, cameras will be all over the place. News crews will be there. Do you want to see yourself on the nightly news?"

"No, I suppose it's a bad idea."

"Do you have everything packed you will need for the next couple of weeks?" he asks.

I nod and point to the three matching pieces of red leather luggage in the hallway. There is one large suitcase, one medium-sized, and a carry-on. His expression says he recognizes them as belonging to Carter. He knows I have no reason to have luggage.

"And the rest of what you want is in boxes?"

"Yes, they're in my private library."

"So, what you've mostly packed is books." He smiles. "And I suppose that is what is in the largest suitcase?" He grimaces and places his hand on his lower back.

"Arthur, you know, reading, delving into the fantasy world, has kept me going for these past six months."

"How well I know. I'm glad your luggage is on wheels. I'll bring the boxes by in two weeks. That will give you time to get settled in."

"Good. The boxes have my paints and canvases in them," I say.

I don't know how I can live without seeing Arthur for two weeks, but it's what The Woodlands recommends, and Arthur is a rule follower.

Arthur takes a deep breath and exhales slowly. He and I

take a last look through the hallway leading into the west wing. Neither of us is sorry to leave this house behind. Well, I'm leaving it behind. Arthur will still have to deal with it for a while.

"What are we waiting for?" I ask.

Arthur bends and kisses me on the forehead, half of his lips touching my scars. "Shall we, Kimi Ahoka?"

"I'm no longer Kimi Ahoka, Arthur."

"I thought I would use it one last time."

I smile. "As soon as we go through the door, I'll be Kimi Stone."

"I should have asked you what name you preferred, but I hadn't thought of it until the last minute, and I needed to sign the papers."

"I'm glad you chose Stone. Perhaps it's fate. Stone symbolizes the passage from one life to the next. I see it as a new beginning. My mother taught me there is no death, only transition. I hope something better. Something peaceful."

"I hope so, too, Kimi."

I remember Kachina's story about changing her name to Carter Hudson. She was with her agent, the one Arthur arranged for her, after Victor, in a drunken rage, fled the scene, telling her she was too stupid to become an actress. The agent told her Kachina Ahoka would not do. "People won't go for it," he said.

Of course, they wouldn't. Something foreign or exotic but not Indian. This was before the polite term became Native American.

"People can see I'm Indian," she complained.

"Makeup does wonders these days. Just stay out of the sun."

"If I can't use my real name, I want something bold."

"Let me think on it," he said and told her to have a seat. He lit a cigarette and picked up the newspaper lying on his desk, ruffling the pages as he searched for the sports section. The cover had something about Jimmy Carter and the Hudson River in the headlines, two different stories.

"Carter Hudson," she said meekly.

"What did you say?" He looked up from his paper.

"Carter Hudson," she forcefully expelled from her larynx.

Initially, his expression was uncertain but slowly changed to a smile. "I like it. A bit masculine, but a name with the balls of Kathryn Hepburn written all over it."

The minute he equated the name she chose with the grit of Kathryn Hepburn, she clutched onto it with all of her heart, taking it in like the kernel of corn that was due to us but never received after our births.

I lower the veil over my face and grab hold of the carry-on. Arthur picks up the medium-sized suitcase and grasps the handle of the larger one.

"Okay, no looking back."

"Yes, no looking back," I agree.

We turn into the main hallway and head out the double doorway, down the three steps to the circular drive where Arthur's Lincoln Town Car is parked. I look up at the sun, feel its warmth through my dress, and almost feel faint. Slightly giddy. Arthur sees me staggering and lets go of both suitcases, leaving them on the steps, and grabs my arm. He leads me out to the passenger side of the car. After shutting the door, he places the luggage in the trunk.

Before turning onto the main drive, he asks, "Are you okay?"

"It's all overwhelming, but I'll be fine."

He smiles. "I know you will." Then he says, "Kimi, if you don't mind ducking down until we get through the gate?"

I immediately think, yes, we must keep up my non-existence. There will be paparazzi hanging around, if not for Carter, for some other star. There are plenty in the neighborhood. Arthur drove in alone, and everyone knows his only client in this gated community is Carter Hudson and that he has a power of attorney for her. Speculation that they were still lovers, even after and through the divorces, was all over social media. About this, they were right.

I do as he wishes, my head against his thigh.

Eight

KIMI

"It's okay. You can sit back up now."

A part of me wants to stay where I am, but I've waited so long to see the outside world in the daytime—what lies beyond the shrubbery outside my west-wing view and what lies beyond the darkness of the eve of All Saint's Day. I rise slowly, adjust my veil, and peer through the tinted window. I wonder if Arthur purposely requested tinted windows in this car because he knew this day of my leaving would eventually come.

Again, he asks if I'm okay.

"Yes, fine," I assure him. "I forgot to ask. There has been so much to think about. You got my email where I sent you the route I want to take, right?"

"Yes, and it's loaded into my GPS."

I smile back with my crooked mouth. I'm happy the good side is the one Arthur sees.

I knew Arthur would not let me down on this. Via Google Earth, I turned what might typically be twenty minutes through LA traffic into an hour's drive. Since 2005, when Google Earth first came out, I've been pushing the little man along roads all over the planet, traveling vicariously through the application. Although I've never had a license, I pretend I'm driving through busy thoroughfares and country boulevards. And ever since Arthur insisted I could no longer live out the rest of my days in solitude in my sister's mansion, I've mapped out different roads exploring buildings and landmarks I've only seen as 2-D on screens or heard Carter talk about, winding a long scenic route to The Woodlands.

I gaze out the window so hard I think I might get a kink in my neck. I silently pray for the slow-moving gridlock I see on the Los Angeles local news reports. Perhaps because it's only a little after eight on a Sunday morning, everyone is either in church or sleeping off Saturday night's drugs and parties. More than likely, the latter.

"Slow down," I beg Arthur.

He laughs. "If I were going any slower, I'd be going backward."

I've always thought Arthur was witty and funny, but I'm too busy taking everything in to laugh.

Arthur comes to a complete stop in the middle of the road as we travel through the Venice Beach area. "If you peek between those two buildings," he points, "you can see the jacked-up men at the outdoor gym." Stuff like this was a pastime for him and Carter.

Even though I have perfect eyesight, something the fire spared me, I see nothing through the buildings, but to the right, I see young girls clad, or rather unclad, in string bikinis playing volleyball. I glance at Arthur to see they are in his direct line of vision.

A car comes up from behind. Arthur opens his window and waves it around. He presses the button that closes the window and proceeds onward. "I didn't want him honking at us to speed up," he explains.

That's the least of my concerns. "Arthur, if only we could

roll down the window just a couple of inches?" I briefly turn my head from the outside view to plead with him.

He hesitates but says, "Okay, but only crack it."

He is probably relieved to suck in the warm California air. The air conditioner is turned to the max. Whenever he came to the west wing to visit me, he would ask for a cup of hot tea, which he never finished. Carter, when present, winked at him while he gripped the mug with both hands. Winking was a trademark of Carter's. While Marilyn Monroe's infamous picture is of her standing over a grate with the air blowing up her skirt, Carter's famous pose is just as legendary—her winking as if she has a tremendous secret, which she did. Me.

I've gotten used to cold air and cold baths and showers. While sitting in my frigid section of the house, Carter complained it was something I had gotten used to over the years. "You have a fear of anything hot," she said. She was right. The burns have conditioned me to live in what most would consider ice-age temperatures. Whenever Carter visited my section of the house to tell me about something remarkable that had happened on set or to practice lines, she wore socks, a wool beanie, and a heavy sweater. On those rare impromptu visits, she would curl up in an armchair in a blanket. Usually, I visited Carter's room to practice lines with her, almost always in the wee hours of the morning when no one was about or at other times through our private entrance.

Arthur never complained about the thermometer setting. He remained professional concerning me, at least until Carter's death. I don't think it's my imagination that, inwardly, he's more relaxed in many ways. Still, ever since the stroke, he has been feeling stressed about me. I sometimes wonder if he promised Carter he would take care of me should something happen to her first. Maybe the rumors of them being lovers even through the divorces are true. No, no, I would have seen it. I could read my sister like a book.

Sometimes, I feel as if I'm his obligation, while at other times, I think it's more than that—he cares. If only I had her charms. But my appearance negates the slightest possibility of allure.

We travel down a side street, passing a coffee shop in Venice Beach. We come to an assortment of people: young women in jogging tights and sports bras, men and women out for a Sunday run or walking their dogs, and lean, fit older men in bicycle pants, all grabbing a quick cup of coffee. I look over briefly at Arthur, imagining him like the elderly cyclers on days when he is not on the clock, although I've rarely seen Arthur in anything other than a suit and tie. For lack of a better designation, these yuppies artfully and skillfully maneuver around the homeless who shadow the main entrance looking for a handout.

I knew homelessness was a problem in Los Angeles, but I didn't know how widespread it was. Our plights are similar— misfits shunned by society. I ponder if I would trade places with them if given the chance. If I were that sixteen-year-old girl before the fire, I would have, but now, I wouldn't. I traded my sense of adventure for security and comfort. I could never brave the outside world at this stage in life, particularly with my appearance.

Arthur's slow pace comes to a stop. A man staggers down the street. He approaches a middle-aged couple walking hand in hand. The man pushes the woman out of the scraggly man's way while a police officer runs up from behind, yelling, and motions him onto the sidewalk after the couple has passed. The officer laughs. "LA isn't what you see in the movies."

Everyone ignores us, even though we are only a few feet away. Arthur speeds up, and we leave that scene.

The officer didn't know how right he was. The actual

world appears much different from the 2D version I'm accustomed to seeing on screens.

The officer, probably through training and experience, knew the couple were tourists. Probably their first time in Los Angeles. Even I picked up on that. There was compassion on the face of the female. I imagine them from a rural town where homelessness doesn't exist. I see all this because it's the truth written on their facial expressions, even in their clothing, which says they've picked the best from their wardrobe to visit the big city. The police officer immediately concluded this, as did the homeless man, who saw them as an easy pick. I've always grilled Carter on how vital every element is when coaching her with her acting.

"Body movements and facial expressions are as important as learning your lines, Carter."

"Yes, yes, I know. Don't you think the director tells me the same thing?"

One thing about my sister—as big of a star as she was, she never had a reputation for being difficult, but she did have a reputation for the actor having to go through more takes than any other.

I remember the first time she asked for my help. It was a month after I had moved in with her. "Kimi, you're a natural at this. Or you were when we were kids." She throws down the script on the table where I'm having my lunch of a tuna sandwich. "It's the role of a lifetime, even bigger than *The Muted Girl*. I can't flub this up. I'm playing the battered wife of an alcoholic."

"Hmm, even bigger than *The Muted Girl*," I say. I look up, push my sandwich aside, and reach for the script. I flip through the pages. "Think of our father," I say.

"But our father didn't beat our mother."

"No, but he was an alcoholic. There were women on our reservation who their alcoholic husbands abused. Draw on what you remember of that—their pain."

She looks at me in wonderment. "I knew you could help me, Kimi."

I look back at the couple before we are totally out of view and see the man pull out a bill to give to a bearded, slumped man pushing a grocery cart before he and his wife enter the coffee shop.

I think it might be nice to have a coffee from one of the many coffee shops and utter, "Arthur, do you think…" But his attention is on entering a more heavily traveled thoroughfare, and he doesn't hear me amid the engine's acceleration and the air conditioner's roar.

We turn onto a different road and come to a different scene. We go through several blocks of office buildings, practically deserted on a Sunday morning, except for a red convertible parked in front of a law office. I'm assuming the vehicle belongs to a middle-aged man with the work ethic of Arthur. Or, perhaps, he is having a rendezvous with a woman, or even a man, in his office while his wife still lies in bed.

Arthur takes a right turn. The long street is a mixture of businesses and residences, small, crumbling ones needing a paint job. These houses don't fit the persona of Los Angeles, and for that reason, developers will tear them down in the not-too-distant future for the sake of commerce.

Arthur puts on his signal to turn left and makes a rolling stop through the stop sign before entering a nicer neighborhood. "We're almost there." His voice startles me out of my coma-like observation of my surroundings. "You sure you have everything?"

"Yes, yes." I suddenly consider the alternative. "No, no. I forgot my toothbrush and toothpaste. I remember I left them out to pack at the last minute, but I'm sure I didn't." I'm lying, but I see a strip mall up ahead. It looks new, the kind that caters to middle-and-upper-income families where mothers drive SUVs with two kids in the back seat or maybe a dog. I'm stalling like a kid afraid of being dropped off to fend for herself on the first day of school. I'm not ready for The Woodlands. I want to experience more of the outside world before being pushed into a different plush jail cell.

"Kimi, they'll have that there, I'm sure."

"But Arthur, I use a special brand." That much is true. I give him the name of an herbal blend. Hopefully, it's something one of the stores up ahead might have. "I could wait in the car while you went into the store to get it. You can roll up the window."

He looks at me with doubt. "I can trust you to stay in the car?" He pulls his wire-rimmed glasses down while asking. Arthur has worn glasses ever since I've known him. Carter said he only started wearing them right before they married. Too many legal documents to read. Another thing I missed—their wedding. The first one was an enormous affair—the next two elopements.

"Yes, I swear. I'll be good."

He exits the car, leaving it running with the air conditioner still going full blast.

"Oh, and a purple toothbrush if they have it," I shout from the still partially rolled-down window. I don't care about the color, but looking for a hard-to-find color, I reason, will give me more time to view the life I missed out on or one possibility of life.

He quickly reopens the driver's door and hits the button to roll up the windows. "Someone could walk right past the car."

I know he's right, even though the parking lot is practically vacant. The sight of me, even a brief glimpse, would scare children and repulse adults. Someone might even pull out a gun or call the police. The world I'm locked away from, condemned only to observe in a fishbowl sort of way, has grown increasingly crazy. I watch enough news. The types of neighborhoods no longer matter.

Carter had argued the world was no more off track than it had always been. Perhaps, when you're a part of it, you don't notice.

Arthur comes back, pulling a purple toothbrush from the bag for me to see before getting into the car. "Only a couple more miles," he says.

I know we are close when we pass the cemetery.

"Please take me by her grave," I beg. "We won't get out. I promise." He swiftly swings the car around in a U-turn. I grab my veil as if a sudden turn might dislodge it. "Couldn't you get a ticket for that?"

"Do you care?" he barks.

"No, I don't suppose I do."

We travel up the hill, which is actually a small knoll, meandering through the well-kept lawn with old and new graves, the newer ones larger and more ornate. "I see it," I say.

Arthur pulls the car over to the side. My window faces the grave. This early morning, the cemetery is vacant—not even a runner. I suppose they have better places to run.

"Could we…"

Before I finish, he pushes the button down, and the window descends. Once again, I take in the slight breeze and smell nature's fragrance in the shrubs and flowering plants juxtaposed with bouquet arrangements bordering on artificiality, emitting conflicting scents, their competing blooms resembling a cheap perfume. Carter sure received enough of them while alive.

I work my way down from the angel's face. The white marble face looks downward, one arm resting on Carter's tomb, the other holding a bouquet of roses. White roses were her favorite. The wings are relaxed. They don't point upward toward heaven. Nor does the figure bend down as in grief over an untimely death, even though my sister was only forty-nine. The likeness to Carter is apparent. What people don't realize is that it is also my likeness. I both mourn my sister's passing, yet know it came at the appropriate time.

I come to Carter's name in bold script. Below it, her autograph is sketched into the marble. And below that, the date of her birth, October 31, 1961, also mine. There is no date of death.

I turn. "Arthur, there's no…"

"Date."

"Carter, you know…"

"You just called me Carter. It's because we are here at her grave. You miss her terribly, don't you?"

He stares into my eyes for the longest time. "Yes, I do. If only she would come back to me."

I place my hand on his arm, and he grasps it.

"You know that's not possible."

"All things are possible, Kimi."

"But what should we do about the missing date?"

He huffs as if he is losing patience. "I'll call tomorrow. I'm sure there was some slip-up."

"Slip up," I repeat. "On their part. I can't imagine you slipping up. I also can't imagine the stonecutter forgetting. You must be one of the most influential and powerful people in town."

"I would hardly say that, Kimi." He rolls the window up just as a couple of walkers pass. "We should be going," he says.

Nine

KIMI

Arthur slows. The road he turns into is bordered on both sides with palm trees. We stop at a booth like the one Ernie sits in, standard issue in Los Angeles. The man in uniform opens the glass he sits behind. I turn my head toward the window so as not to elicit stares. It would be foolish for Arthur to ask me to duck at this point.

Arthur gives the man his name. He picks up a clipboard and checks something off. He turns, looks down, and pushes a button I imagine being on some control panel I can't see, and the black ornate gates open. He turns back toward us and nods us ahead. Flowering shrubs and palm trees line both sides of the entrance. Arthur stops in front of a three-story white brick building with white alabaster columns gracing the double-door entry.

Although more massive, it reminds me of the house I just left. Perhaps the reason Arthur picked The Woodlands, my new home away from my old home. I've always trusted Arthur on these matters. Carter might have rebelled. Although she never caused trouble on the movie set, other than her failure to remember her lines correctly, she took any inner anger she may have been experiencing out on either Arthur or me, whoever was the handiest. It never lasted long, and besides, Carter, using the diplomatic nature our parents dubbed Kachina blessed with at age five, was always easy to forgive.

My eyes travel to the third and top story. I see someone staring, partially hiding behind a curtain, a thin, elderly man with long white hair and a beard. Of course, he would be old. He seems familiar, but I shrug it off. At the moment, I have much more to consider than trying to remember a face, someone I would have to have seen on television. Arthur cautioned there would be a few retired actors here, some who might have even known Carter, but assured me their memories were more in the past if they recalled anything.

"What they remember is the black-and-white era of movies and television. Most are stuck in the beginning scenes of *The Wizard of Oz* in Kansas. A few are even stuck in the era of silent movies," he says.

I laugh. I suddenly realize how calm I've been. I had imagined I would have been a basket case, curled up in the car's backseat within a mile of this place. It occurs to me that Arthur may have slipped something in the orange juice he handed me when we got in the car this morning. He was insistent I drink it. "You need the vitamin C," he practically demanded, holding it to my lips.

I replied, "Yes, I've read when we age, our minds go back to when we were young."

"Why did you laugh a minute ago?"

"Because I can't imagine anyone still alive from the silent movie era."

"Oh, I don't know. But, at any rate, you'll be the youngest resident here."

"I don't consider forty-nine to be young."

"Ca... Kimi, you're ageless." People said that about Carter. While almost everyone was getting facelifts, she refrained. She was still getting roles that would have gone to women in their twenties.

The expression on Arthur's face reminds me of a young Jimmy Stewart, Cary Grant, or Gregory Peck running in a bucolic scene toward his lover. The reference to old movies makes me think of my mother, who adored these actors, and then my thoughts turn back to Arthur. I realize he is seeing Carter instead of me. He almost called me her name again but caught himself.

A young man dressed casually in khakis and a dark green polo shirt taps on Arthur's window, bringing us both out of the moment. Arthur steps out of the car, has a few words with him, and pops the car's trunk lid before handing him the keys. I breathe a sigh of relief, thinking this means the attendant will whisk, or rather meander carefully, into a visitor parking lot since anyone can see Arthur takes great pride in his vehicles. I take comfort in the fact that Arthur will be here for a while.

I watch Arthur raise his hand and rub it through his gray-streaked hair. I'm surprised he's kept such a thick mop of it at his age. His father was practically bald. I only ever saw Arthur's father once. He wore a dark blue suit, a starched white shirt, a blue-patterned tie, and a matching pocket square. He was lying stiff in a bronze casket that looked extremely expensive, surrounded by more flowers than I had ever seen in my life. After the funeral, I questioned Arthur as to how expensive the casket was, thinking my own family's charred bones would have been in wooden boxes.

"Kachina, it's not polite to ask those questions."

I remember holding my head in shame. He lifted it and said, "The tie and pocket square alone were nearly one thousand dollars." I could feel my eyes bulging from my skull.

During the brief time, I peered into the casket as we walked in a stream past it, I tried to see if there was a resemblance to Arthur but found none. Perhaps it was the grayness of his skin.

Arthur told me his father was prematurely bald when I questioned him about it several days after the funeral. My face must have registered shock. "Don't worry; I take my physical characteristics after my mother." He smiled. It was the first time I had seen him smile since the funeral. I think it was then I realized I was in love with Arthur. Or maybe it was a crush. At sixteen, how could one know for sure?

I never got to meet either of Arthur's parents officially. His mother had died a year earlier from cancer. I had never even attended a funeral before. Arthur insisted I stay home, but after all he had done for me, I thought I might be a comfort and begged to attend. "We're both orphans. My family didn't get to have a funeral," I told him, although I didn't know that. There could have been one in Cherokee for my whole family, including me.

Per Arthur's instructions, I sat in the back pew, careful not to draw any attention to myself. I knew I was a secret. The First Presbyterian Church was packed. I had never seen so many well-dressed people in one place—most wore black. Some looked in my direction, possibly wondering who I was. I merely put my head down, sometimes with tears which were not only for Arthur but for myself and my own family. I noticed one man in particular, a handsome man who stared in my direction more than once. I asked Arthur later who he was.

"Connor Scott."

"The actor, Connor Scott?" I asked. Of course, I should have recognized him right off, but I was out of my element and trying to both fit in and do as Arthur instructed me.

"Yes. He is one of my father's law firm's clients."

"You mean your law firm, now," I said.

Arthur's expression indicated that he didn't want to deal

with that so close to his father's demise. He changed the subject, saying, "Maybe you will meet him one day."

"Perhaps he could help me with my acting career."

"Perhaps," he said.

As Arthur continues to rub his fingers through his hair, he squints at the blaring sun, and the rays catch his watch. I remember seeing it on the day of the episode. Something about it sparked my return to harsh reality, jolting me from my journey into nothingness, a state I was content to stay in.

I gaze back up at the top window and see the man is no longer there. I imagine him, along with most of the residents here, flitter back and forth between this existence and a state of nothingness. Or maybe he was called to a game of Bingo. I cringe at the thought that one of the activities here might be Bingo, along with Bridge, Gin Rummy, or jigsaw puzzles that, after residents complete them, get lacquered, framed, and hung on the hallway walls.

Arthur opens the car door for me. I straighten my veil before taking Arthur's hand, helping me out of the car. Another attendant, wearing the same khaki pants and dark green polo shirt, is going up the ramp with my luggage. A forty-something woman on the verge of obesity comes out to greet us. She's wearing a flowered-print dress, which only draws focus to the extra pounds.

"Miss Stone," she says as she reaches her hand toward me. After a light nudge to my elbow by Arthur, I awkwardly stretch my hand to hers. She smiles. I smell her perfume, or maybe it's soap. I can't imagine the employees wearing fragrance on the job. It seems unprofessional, a distraction, and perhaps even something the patients here might be hypersensitive to, although I've read smell and taste fade as people age. I catch my thoughts of referring to the building's occupants as patients. Arthur says residents, not patients. In old folks' homes, the term I was brought up with means one and the same.

She grips my hand and smiles. "I'm Mrs. Bell, the director." The smile is meant to reassure me, while the firm clasp ensures I won't bolt. I gaze at the building rising from the neatly groomed grounds behind her, thinking it has all the airs of the finest hotel, and wonder why anyone would run.

She lets go of my hand. I lower my own in slow motion. I wish Arthur had instructed me on the ubiquitous gestures and small interactions in the world of humans—a world I'm not accustomed to. Her hand was warm and fleshy, the opposite of Carter's. My sister's hands were as slender as her body. Carter ate like a hummingbird. However, she drank like a sailor. Salads and rare steaks comprised twenty-five percent of her daily calorie allotment, while alcohol comprised the remaining seventy-five percent. She always said the camera added twenty pounds.

Our mother would turn over in her grave if she even has one. I must take this up with Arthur. The plot where we buried Carter is big enough for my parents and me. Why had I not thought of this before? There would be no bodies, but it would be symbolic. I can see their spirits smiling down at me. While my mother believed, as the Hopi, that her spirit would leave through her mouth and go to another world, my father's Cherokee tradition taught he would live on as a spirit or perhaps return as an animal. He said he preferred a wolf.

"Miss Stone, we are so happy to have you here."

It takes me a moment to realize she is talking to me. Responding to my new name is another thing Arthur and I should have practiced.

She escorts us into the main room. Ornately carved white tiles grace the ceiling. White columns like those out front lead down to a black and white tiled floor. I imagine this type of floor is the softest, other than a soft wood such as pine, considering older people tend to fall. Meditation music is playing faintly in the background, coming from no particular direction but surrounding us. I imagine it's to calm the residents, along with a daily routine of pills. I'm glad no one can see my expression behind my veil as my mind wanders to Nurse Ratched. The smell, though... It's vibrant and clean, like the mountain air I remember in North Carolina. Piped in like the music, no doubt.

The memory of our mother taking us to visit an old white lady who had been one of her beauty shop customers surfaces. She was in an old folks' home. The smell was worse than that of our chicken coop. Kachina and I practically gagged and held our noses the whole time. When we walked out into the fresh air, our mother held our wrists so tightly that we both had red marks for most of the day. "I was never so embarrassed," she scolded. "That lady was the kindest customer I had. She always gave me a dollar tip. Who do you think paid for your Barbie doll?"

"I'm sure you want to get settled in." The elevated voice of Mrs. Bell disrupts my thoughts. I imagine she has to be loud in the land of hard of hearing.

I hear something classical, perhaps Mozart or Chopin. Classical artists are not my forte. I look toward the piano and see a petite, silver-haired woman sitting at a baby grand, her eyes shut, her head tilted to the side, her lips turned upward, and her body swaying to the sound. Her fingers move fluidly and hard on the black and white keys. I imagine to drown out the competing music coming from the hidden speakers.

"Oh, that's Gloria Morton. She plays the piano this time every day. She was famous in her youth. Perhaps you've heard of her?"

Both Arthur and I shake our heads.

"Well, I'm sure you'll get to know her and appreciate her music as much as I and the residents here do. I'll accompany you and Mr. Burke to your suite and let you settle in. Since it's Sunday, we serve brunch, and it will begin..." She pauses to look at her watch. "In one hour and fifteen minutes. I'll return to your suite and escort you both to our dining area. I hope you'll dine with us on Miss Stone's first day here, Mr. Burke?"

Arthur stumbles.

I blurt out, "I thought we could have meals brought to our rooms."

"Of course, if that is what you want. I'll have someone bring you down a menu."

We walk down a hallway toward an oversized elevator, which I assume is to accommodate wheelchairs and walkers. My apartment is on the second floor. I say, "I'd rather take the steps if you don't mind."

She looks at me as if confronted by a first but says, "Of course. If you wish."

I want her to know that despite the burns on one side of my body, I'm perfectly fit. Also, it's partly to convince myself I am not old or frail like some residents using walkers or being pushed in wheelchairs we've already passed by.

We enter the stairwell and climb the vacant steps, me at a hurried pace. Arthur is trailing behind Mrs. Bell, who loses momentum with each step, her breath clearly audible. I look back at Arthur, who has disapproval plastered all over his face. Mrs. Bell forges ahead, too labored to notice, as I knew she would be.

Upon arriving at the second floor, I'm holding the door open for both her and Arthur, who still expresses disappointment in his facial expression at my need to prove my fitness. I also detect he worries that I will tell him I've changed my mind about being here.

After the heavy stairwell door closes behind us, Mrs. Bell stops momentarily to tug at her dress, pulling it downward from where it has risen above her knees in the brief climb up the stairwell. Her breathing calms as we tread down the level floor of the hallway toward my new habitat. She stops at the door marked 201. I think easy enough to remember and then recall my mini-stroke and not remembering anything, hoping there is no reoccurrence.

She announces the number on the door as if programming me where I belong and says in a cheery voice, "Well, we're here." She retrieves a key card from her pocket and waves it over the lock. I assume this key card is a master gaining her admittance into each apartment or room. After two swipes, a green light appears. We follow her in. My luggage has already arrived and is sitting near a flower-print couch, a pattern that is not too different from Mrs. Bell's dress.

She travels over to the balcony window and pulls back the curtains. "Let's let in some light, shall we?"

Arthur and I walk into the center of the room where Mrs. Bell now stands. She hands me the brown oversized envelope packet she has had lodged under one armpit the entire time and explains, "This is our manual, along with your key card. Don't worry; if you ever get locked out, any of the staff can let you in. The manual includes a map of the property. It also lists times for meals and activities. You know, all the usual stuff. The dos and don'ts." She laughed. "There are rules for every place you know."

"Yes," I agree, trying to make small talk with another human, something I'm rusty at, although I never had a knack for it before the accident. Carter would have no problem.

"I think that is everything. You've already sent in the questionnaire regarding your interests, likes, and dislikes, and we have your medical file."

"But I didn't..."

"I did," Arthur piped in.

Mrs. Bell doesn't seem to think it inappropriate that Arthur might have answered the most personal questions regarding me. I surmise it's usually a relative, or, in my case, a power-of-attorney, who takes on this task, not the patient.

"Let me show you around," she says.

I think, what is there to show? From the sitting area, I can see the kitchen, the doorway to the bedroom, and one into the bathroom. "I'm sure we can find everything," I say.

"I'm sure you can, but the designers of this complex installed helpful measures into all these studio apartments. Please follow me into the bathroom." Chrome handles seem to be the theme. White towels. Okay, I'm used to those. It's what Carter preferred, except they bore the CH monogram in a fancy handwritten-style script. These are plain. There is no monogram, not even one bearing the name of The Woodlands. They are plush. Carter always told me you could tell a good hotel by their towels and robes. I see no robe, but then I brought my own.

Mrs. Bell directs our attention to a chord hanging from the ceiling within reach of the toilet after she sees me staring at it. "This is what you pull in case of an emergency." Similarly, I see a button with a red light right outside the walk-in shower and beside the handicapped-accessible bathtub. "We have either buttons to push or strings to pull in every room," she says.

I want to say I think you've gone a bit overboard, but instead, say, "I'm not handicapped."

"No, of course not, but many of our residents have some form of disability or can no longer maneuver with the agility they had in their younger days." She pauses as if regaining her composure over the recent climb up one flight of stairs. "They're here for your convenience. They are in all the rooms." The defiance in her tone is only something I sense, even though she expertly tries to hide it. I feel Mrs. Bell sees me as a problem. Perhaps I'm overreacting, seeing things not there. I'm not used to people.

She seems oblivious to my mood, directing her attention mainly to Arthur as she walks us through the bedroom and kitchen, showing us all the little extras built into the residence for protection the way one might protect a toddler.

I sigh. Arthur's facial expression is one of concern, seeing there is so much here we didn't anticipate. Mrs. Bell doesn't notice, but then she doesn't know Arthur the way I do, and only Arthur is privy to my change of emotions and my skillful way of hiding them, all the things I tried to teach Carter when we were reading her lines together.

When we return to the living room area, I see the remote for the flat-screen television affixed to the wall. The numbers on it are enormous.

"Do you have any questions or thoughts you wish to convey?" she asks.

I look blankly at Arthur.

"I guess not," he says to Mrs. Bell.

The door closes, leaving Arthur and me alone to peruse my new surroundings. I feel more relaxed now that, once again, there are just the two of us.

Ten

KIMI

"This was not what I expected," I say while removing my veil. I'm used to taking it off when I'm with Arthur. My scars have grown invisible to him.

"I should have prepared you more."

"How could you? This is all new to you, too."

I realize Arthur must have inspected the apartment before signing any papers. He's thorough in that regard. I'm sure Arthur will guide me the way he always guided Carter—almost as if he had her whole life planned, from hiring an agent, advising her to take it slow—to work her way up, that she was young and had plenty of time. Even though he wasn't in the business, he was always sure of everything. She wouldn't have landed the part in *The Muted Girl* if it weren't for him. He would only ever tell her, "I knew a guy who knew a guy, who knew a guy. That's how it's done in this town."

Carter once told her, "Kimi, I think I fell in love with Arthur from the first moment I saw him cross that street toward me. It's as if he had a purpose, and that purpose was me."

I reminded her she was always flying off the handle,

doubting Arthur, thinking him dishonest about things, and divorcing him three times. "Who keeps divorcing someone and remarrying him? What would our parents say?"

"Oh, Kimi," she would say, "that's how things are done in this town."

I wanted to say that we always fall in love with our rescuer, but I held my tongue.

Arthur's voice broke back through. "To accommodate most people who live here, and also for insurance, they've standardized all the rooms. While you don't need these precautions, most here do, and it wouldn't be economically feasible not to include them in all the rooms."

Arthur. Always so practical. It was his practicality that made Carter a star. His common sense made up for Carter's lack of it. I saw why they made such a good pair even though others didn't.

I can see in his eyes he feels bad about evicting me from my fortress of solitude and depositing me in this glorified receptacle of the aged and societal misfits, myself being the latter. He feels terrible, perhaps not only for me but for the aging process of humans in general and our need for such safety measures.

Arthur is thinking that, eventually, this will be *his* fate. He's fifty-eight and plans on retiring next year, hoping to spend his retirement on the golf course. But there is me. He assured me he would still handle my affairs after retiring and that we would see each other daily. I worry, though. Since Carter's death, I've watched new creases and wrinkles appear on him. Her death hit him hard. I tried to warn him it would happen, but he refused to see it. He should have listened. He should have known that identical twins know what's going on with each other.

"I suppose I will get used to them," I say, putting my hand

on his arm. We are sitting on the floral sofa. I kick off my shoes, or rather, Carter's. "These heels are killing me."

He laughs. "Those look comfortable in comparison—"

"To what she usually wore?" I finish.

"Yes."

"Do you want me to help you unpack?" he asks.

I don't want to move. I only want to sit with him undisturbed in this unfamiliar environment. I rub my hand across the texture of the bright orange flowers, no particular variety, something the artist created from their imagination. I laugh.

"A bit brash," he says, following the movement of my hand across the fabric.

"I guess I can get used to it, although I would have preferred a solid color such as blue." I look into his eyes.

"The only thing I might need help with is the heavy suitcase," I say, moving my eyes to the unpacked luggage.

"You mean your books?"

"Yes," I say, smiling, but my smile fades as I look around the room and see the absence of bookcases.

Arthur, who knows what I'm thinking, says, "We can get a bookcase."

I nod, thinking we can hardly bring one from home, considering they're built into the wall. Home. "Will this be my permanent address?"

"This is only temporary," he says.

"Oh, people leave this place by foot locomotion and not in a body bag?"

He frowns. "Don't be so glum."

I rise and move over to the window, which overlooks a garden area to one side and a pool to the other. Older women, some in not-so-modest bathing suits, are swinging their arms at the shallow end in a water aerobics class. I see the instructor, a young girl, standing in the water, only a couple of feet from the other end. I then realize the entire pool is shallow—another one of those precautions.

Arthur now stands behind me, pulling the curtains to the side for a clearer view.

"See anything that turns you on?" I tease. I can't resist.

He laughs. "You." Or did he say, "You!"

He doesn't elaborate. I don't know if he is referring to me or asking me if I'm turned on by the old, primarily bald men in their Bermuda shorts playing cards at the table below.

"Perhaps you can take those midnight swims you like."

"Carter liked them too," I say.

"Yes, she did."

"I remember that sometimes you joined her."

He lets the curtain drop. I turn toward him. He looks into my eyes like he is searching for something.

Like in one of Carter's movie plots, a knock on the door interrupts the moment. Arthur walks over and answers, letting in an orderly who wheels in a cart carrying food protected by stainless steel covers. A matching stainless-steel teapot is also on the cart. "Where can I sit this up for you?" he asks.

Arthur points to the kitchen table.

After removing everything from the cart, the orderly, whose name tag bears the name Luke Jones, R.N., opens cabinets and drawers, pulls out plates, utensils, and cups, and places them on the table. It's like he has done it a million times before, although it is strange why a registered nurse would perform this mundane task.

After setting the table, Luke bids us a good evening, pushing the tray through the door and into the hall.

Arthur removes the lids. "It looks like Thai."

"I guess you checked that as one of my favorites."

He smiles, pulls out a chair for me, and sits across from me.

We eat in silence. The situation is strange for both of us.

We are used to eating in the privacy of the west wing inside a sprawling house with no one but us. We are both cautious of this new arrangement, wondering if it will truly help.

Outside the apartment's thin walls, we hear the openings and closings of elevator doors and the comings and goings in the hallway. At the opposite end of the room, sounds drift up from the pool area through the open doors leading to the balcony. I imagine it will become routine in time, and I'll get used to it.

Eleven

KIMI—SUNDAY MORNING

It's Sunday, my two-week anniversary here, although I find nothing to celebrate. I didn't think the day would ever come.

Two weeks ago, I paced about my lonely wing of the house, making last-minute checks, worrying if I had packed what I needed, not having much of a clue of what that would be, lying on top of a duvet, so as not to get clean-crisp sheets wet with anxious perspiration, getting hardly any sleep worrying over the big step of coming here. Last night was much the same, tossing and turning in anticipation of Arthur's arrival today. To refrain from rolling about, I stared at the bare walls because Mrs. Bell thought I would want to bring my own to hang since I dabbled in art. I tried to imagine which ones would go best and how they should be arranged in the dim light of the bedroom.

Bringing some of my paintings had crossed my mind. Although my work mainly involved simple landscapes and still lifes, it was the drawings of life on the reservation that got left behind that truly mattered. I wonder what happened to them, who moved into our old house. I should have brought paint, canvases, or a drawing pad to pass the time. A lot of good the books did me, not even a bookcase. I brought too many. I should have brought at least one box of my art supplies. But Arthur will be bringing them today.

Two weeks have passed, and not so much as a phone call or text from Arthur. I haven't left my apartment. Arthur, true to his word and The Woodlands' recommendations to help me transition to my new surroundings, has stayed away. And true to mine, I haven't left my apartment. I told Arthur I wouldn't. It hasn't been difficult, considering self-imposed confinement was my existence before.

I'm confident that Arthur has checked in with Mrs. Bell. She comes by at unannounced times every day to see how I'm doing and if I'm adjusting. I tell her I'm fine when I'm in limbo, awaiting the next big thing, not knowing what it will be. Yet, I know it's coming, the way my mother knew things were coming. Sadly, all the things she foresaw seemed to concern doom.

I wonder if Mrs. Bell reports back to Arthur. She's always cheery and wearing bold colors. I see through her. It's all an act —lousy acting, at that. I sometimes think she knows my true identity. If she does, the fact that I'm Carter Hudson's sister elicits no special treatment from her. I suppose many important residents here are more demanding of her time and favors.

The only other time I see anyone is at mealtimes. Luke has brought my meals a few times, usually the noon one, but mostly, it's been other staff. I feel comfortable around Luke, even though he occasionally drops subtle hints that I should leave the apartment. None of the others do. They merely do their jobs like robots, avoiding conversation, but they stare. Luke doesn't ogle like the others. Nor is he condescending.

I sit out on my balcony, my chair pushed back from the railing, wearing my veil, and watch the residents come and go into the garden and pool area. The same group of women always show up for water aerobics. They do their flutter kicks and arm curls, exposing the neglected parts of their bodies worn down by age, smiling with Botox lips at the young, ripped male instructor whose job is to give them hope. In the early morning hours, there are yoga and tai chi classes for both men and women. The instructor looks Japanese. She is young, and although she teaches modified poses for her students whose flexibility has all but atrophied, I watch her in the wee morning hours before the classes begin doing her practice with the agility of a Cirque du Soleil performer. I've seen her look curiously in my direction.

Watching the world as it carries on outside my balcony and practicing small talk with Mrs. Bell and the orderlies who come and go helps me pass my probation period until Arthur's return. I imagine him bursting through the door, holding a bouquet of blue roses, my favorite. But I forget. Blue roses were Carter's favorite. I suppose they are mine, too. No one has ever given me roses. Blue ones don't actually exist in nature, but, in a way, I don't either. Perhaps a freak of nature. Blue roses are merely white roses dyed blue. The mystery of blue replaces the innocence of white. Other than mystery, the blue rose symbolizes rebellion. Carter was both mysterious and rebellious. Blue is also the color denoting an unrealized dream and unattainable love. I'm reminded of that when the time for Arthur's arrival finally comes, and there is no Arthur or flowers—instead, my cell rings.

"Kimi?" he asks hesitantly, expecting someone else to answer. Perhaps it's because my number will light up with Carter's name and her picture on his end. I could hardly have a cell phone in my name, being a secret.

"Yes, Arthur," I respond, already disappointed, sensing something is wrong.

"Kimi, something important has come up. I need to make a trip out east for a... matter. I can't put it off."

"On a Sunday?"

"It's urgent," he says.

"New York," I ask. That is usually where Arthur goes on business. I've never known the details of Arthur's business. He's always been guarded about it. Perhaps it's why Carter found it so hard to trust him.

"No, not New York. The thing is, I'm not sure how long I'll be gone. Probably only a couple of days. But it could take longer. I'll call you as soon as I return."

My heart drops, but what can I do? I know Arthur has been trying to settle many things before he retires. With no heirs to inherit the business, he must have everything up to snuff to sell it.

Unlike Carter, I resolve to be understanding. It's how Kimi would be. "Of course, Arthur. You have other things to take care of besides me. It's not like you are abandoning me for a game of golf. I understand."

I'm on the verge of tears, but draw on all my acting skills, the ones I forsook so long ago, trying to remain cheerful. He should have known how important this day would be for me and how I eagerly anticipated it.

"You've always been understanding."

I think, good ole Kimi, but I can't resist. "Unlike Carter?" In my mind, I hear Carter blow up at him, as she often did. During one rough patch of their marriage, I forget which one, she threw things. I hid in the closet because she didn't want Arthur to know I was there.

There is a brief pause on the other end.

"I have to go, Kimi. I'm pulling into long-term parking now."

"But, Arthur..."

The phone goes dead.

Long term? I tell myself that's just what they call it. It doesn't actually mean long-term. I want to ask him where in the east, but he seems rushed. My mind analyzes every word uttered over the phone conversation. He referred to it as a matter. He never said it was business. I'm the one who said that. Could it be something else?

I'm no longer hungry but could use a drink. I call the dining room, canceling our lunch for two, and ask if they could bring me a dry martini with an olive.

Arthur, never on time. That's why I gave him the watch.

Twelve

ARTHUR—SUNDAY MORNING

I had no choice but to cut her off mid-sentence. She has a way of extracting the truth from you, much like *he* does. Sometimes, I feel I'm being pulled in two different directions. Over the years, I've become confused about who has the most power over me—him or her. Perhaps by acting on this alone, I can somehow come out ahead. Before leaving for The Woodlands, she said, "The truth shall set you free." There have been so many lies over the years, and I long to be free.

Kimi—she's just like Carter, although she says while on the outside they were identical, they couldn't be further apart on the inside. "Still, we're bonded like no other."

"What about *our* bond?" I ask.

"Yes, Arthur. Our connection is deep." She says it more through her sensual brown eyes than her voice. "But our connection is not as deep as my one with my sister. How can you understand, Arthur? How can anyone understand? You didn't share a womb with me. You weren't the one sharing the universe's secrets as we clung to each other in the soft, syrupy void. Maybe the secrets that only the same sex can share. You see, Arthur, you and I share different kinds of secrets, the type a man can share with a woman and vice versa. And on the more practical side, the side you will undoubtedly always take, you didn't grow up with me. Even though I tell you what it was like on that reservation, you'll never truly understand. You came from affluence and wealth."

"Affluence and wealth," I mutter sarcastically, banging my carry-on, almost losing the wheel while stepping onto the curb of the airport entrance. Yes, we were born into different worlds. Each carries its own burdens. The little boy, hurriedly dragged along by his mother coming from the opposite direction, looks up at me as if I'm mad. *I don't mean to scowl at you*, I say mentally, as if the young have some unique skills of understanding we lost when becoming adults. *I never got to have a child, and I'm jealous.* Luckily, his mother is too busy to notice.

Children were something Carter neither had the time nor the heart for. "We could lose them or one of them," she said, of course, constantly referring to her tragedy.

Still, I brought it up to her repeatedly, only at the most opportune moments after a sufficient amount of time had passed since my last plea.

"Arthur, why do we need children when we have each other?"

At one point, she told me she couldn't have children. I insisted on rigorous checkups. We both were diagnosed to be above average on the fertility scale, according to the doctor handpicked by him, one on his payroll. No amount of money could get him to lie for her. He has that kind of power.

To me, she is Carter. Sometimes, she was Kachina, but after she became Carter, the name the world knew her as, she begged me never to use her birth name again. The fear in her voice scared me. I didn't understand, and sometimes, the name would slip from my lips in the bedroom. I first knew her as Kachina, that desperate and frightened little girl whose charms I somehow resisted until her eighteenth birthday. I was under his orders not to touch her.

His was the only money I had coming in. I couldn't flub this up, especially after my dad said everything I did, I screwed up. If only he had lived long enough to see me take the firm to new heights, even if I mainly subsist off of one client, one who is of a somewhat seedier caliber than what the public sees him as, and to know that I had married the most sought-after woman in the world, not once, but three times.

The third and last time I accidentally called her Kachina, the room grew cold. Her posture stiffened, and her voice tightened as she turned away and told me to leave. I could never get her to reveal what troubled her about the name her parents gave her. When I asked, she tensed, changed the subject, or walked away. I knew it was something other than what she had confided in me. I slept in one of the guest bedrooms that night—the ones that never got used other than by me. The next morning, even though she seemed to have forgotten the incident over a breakfast of poached eggs and toast, I recommended a therapist.

She initially scoffed at the idea but started naming out loud all the actresses she knew who were seeing therapists. "I guess it couldn't hurt," she conceded. "It's what *she* would do."

She? I take it by she, Carter was referring to Kachina, although she couldn't bring herself to say her name. Carter would often refer to whoever as she or her. I knew, or at least I thought she meant Kachina. But then, Kimi came into our lives, the elusive Kimi who stayed in the west wing most of the time, the sister who turned up out of the blue and who Carter insisted we keep a secret.

I suddenly learn the real story, and I think Carter either carries so much survivor guilt that she can't cope, or she would have been a shoo-in for the part of Rhoda Penmark in *The Bad Seed*. That's when *I* started seeing a therapist.

I came to think of Kimi as another version of Carter. I know she knows this. Carter—Kimi. Kimi—Carter. After all this time, it no longer matters.

I stopped seeing the therapist. It defies logic to me to go around in circles with no progress. Plus, the therapist was delving into my past with my father even though I kept reminding her I was there because of my relationship with Carter. She told me everything was interrelated. Besides, I've learned to accept. Acceptance, in my book, is progress.

After that night, when Kimi called me on the phone, crying hysterically, proclaiming, "Carter is dead," she talked incessantly about Kachina. Whether or not that is progress, I'll never know.

Unlike Carter, Kimi is needy. It's as if Kimi draws what little strength she has from Carter, and Carter absorbs Kimi's vulnerability as well as a subtle, unrelenting ambition.

She said, amid sobs, "I can finally let Kachina rest in peace. We can now be who we were both meant to be."

She speaks in such riddles. After all that's happened to her, she can't help but be disturbed. But sometimes, I want to shake her and tell her to quit acting. Even though I've known her since she was sixteen, I can't tell if she's genuinely mental or if it's all an act.

From day one, she has had this alluring manner. She could take your breath away even with filthy hair that looked like it hadn't seen a comb in days. Like a siren, she beckons sailors onto the rocks. It's the same with all men, but especially me. I have to admit, even though most of my time with her has been splendid, a good portion of it is as if I've been scraped against the jagged edge of stones and washed up along the beach with the sea salt burning into my wounds. Women, on the other hand, view her with jealousy. They either avoid her or use her

—gossip columnists trying to get a scoop and look into her life and mine. Women want to be her, and men want her. Most never understood what she saw in me. Most don't know it was me who saved her long ago on that dark street corner. They know nothing about her past, making her even more mysterious. And I know very little.

When I told the florist her favorite color was blue, he said, "Then you must take her blue roses."

"Blue? I never knew there was such a thing as blue roses."

He whispered as if it were some trade secret, "There isn't. They're dyed. But blue means mystery."

That's when I started calling her my mystery girl.

She's always refused talk shows and insisted I write it into her movie contracts. "You know how I get carried away, Arthur. I'm afraid I'll give away my mystery. Then what am I, if not a mystery?"

"You have no idea what you are, Carter," I said.

"Or rather, who I am, you mean."

If I had remained on the line with her any longer, she would have asked where I was off to. I've always told her my whereabouts, giving her my flight information and the name, even the room number when I have it, of the hotel I'll be at. But, in this instance, I'm going into the unknown, the place where she grew up. I have no clue what this information might do to her. The root of what's wrong with her stems from the place I'm traveling to. Maybe this man can tell me the absolute truth once and for all.

I had every intention of going to The Woodlands to see her today. A part of me was looking forward to it, counting down the days, but another part dreaded it. However, checking my messages from the office last night, I discovered a strange, unexpected one. The opening was, "I'm not sure if I'm calling the right person."

He said his name was Will and that he knew both Kachina and Kimi, that in a sort of way, he was dating Kimi. "Well, I think I was. We were young—teenagers. You know how that goes. They had this habit of trading places, trying to fool people. I honestly never knew who I was with. That is when I actually was with Kimi. She could pull off Kachina much better than Kachina could pretend to be Kimi. As far as I know, only their mother could tell them apart. Well, there is one way. I don't know. Maybe you know it. Their mother is why I'm calling."

He knew their whole family and was on his way to the big Halloween party they were throwing in their barn before the tragedy. He had even been there earlier, helping with the decorations. He said he had seen all the Carter Hudson movies and thought she was one of the twins, although everyone said they had died that night. The message became garbled, obscuring the rest. People shouting—no, cheering—drowned out his voice. It was apparent he was in a public place. "How could Carter not go see..." The message cut off. There was no second call from him.

This guy had a way of rambling on, and I'm used to succinctness in messages. There was no need to elaborate on the teenage dating stuff. It's irrelevant at this point. If he had not thought it pertinent to recompense about bygone memories on a limited phone message, he might have gotten to the main point of the call, giving me more to go on.

I look again at the message's time stamp: 11 p.m., Saturday night. Six hours earlier. I immediately called the number the message came from to find it was a landline from a casino in the Cherokee Nation in Cherokee, North Carolina. A woman answered, saying an older man named William worked there along with William Jr., but she said she was pretty sure everyone called them Bill. I told her, "The man sounded older, maybe fifty-ish."

"Doesn't matter. Neither of them are working at the moment."

"One of them, I don't know which, left a message at my office last night, but it got cut off. The number he called from came from this casino. If I could get the number for the older one..."

"I'm sorry, sir, but that's against our rules."

I expected as much, but I thought I would ask.

"Sorry, another call is coming in." That was the end of the conversation. Not even a last name.

It sounded as if Carter's mother had survived the fire. In all these years, why would she not have contacted Carter to let her know she was alright? Possibly, she's not.

I immediately Googled Cherokee, North Carolina. I also Googled the last name Ahoka. I rattled my brain. I don't think Carter ever mentioned her mother's or father's first name. I'm sure I would have remembered if she did. Sure, Carter talked about them, but I only remember her referring to them as Mother and Father. I should have asked her that day in the cemetery when she brought up graves for them, but there was too much happening at once—too much stress with the trip already. I looked in the White Pages to find a slew of Ahokas in the area, but none of them fit the age of what her mother would be. I'm guessing she would be in her mid or late sixties since Carter said she married as a teenager and birthed them eight months later. "Twins always come early," her mother had told her. And as for Will,... It's too common and not an easy name to trace.

I considered sending Harry, our firm's private investigator, to Cherokee but reconsidered, thinking I needed to handle this. Of course, Harry would be discreet. I pay him to be. But this is something I have a personal stake in, and even though

Harry is always thorough in his reports, I want to experience where Carter grew up. I'm sure a lot has changed, though. It's been thirty-three years since I found Carter in a suicidal state on that street corner. I think Carter has more secrets than I know, but I do, too. I never told her why I was in that part of town. Years later, after getting to know me, I thought she might have asked, but she never did. She always said I saved her life that night. What she doesn't know is that it was *she* who saved me.

I have to have personal knowledge of what happened. Possibly, others besides Will will remember her. Considering her state and the fact I, along with her physician, moved her into The Woodlands, not because of a minor stroke, probably brought on by a medication she was taking, but because of her mental condition, she wouldn't be able to handle it. According to my daily conversations with Mrs. Bell, she is adjusting, although she hasn't left her apartment. I expected that. I had hoped my visit this morning, the one I intended to make, that I might coax her at least to sit out by the pool, even if she insisted on covering herself from head to toe in a ridiculous garb that reminds me of a Middle Eastern burka. If that is what she chooses, I'll go along with it. She has been fragile ever since I've known her. The thing is, I honestly do love her. If I didn't, I wouldn't be putting myself through this.

So, I booked the earliest flight to the nearest airport to the Harrah's Casino, which is Asheville. I added a car rental and an SUV, considering I would be driving through the mountains, possibly in the snow. It's late April, and there might be snow in the higher elevations. I also reserved a room at the resort. Everything is open-ended since I don't know how long this could take. My flight is one-way, and since the hotel seems to have plenty of rooms available this time of year, I put in one night. I'll figure it out when I get there.

What if what this man said was true? What if her mother

is still alive? In the past, I've never been able to find an actual story in any newspaper regarding what happened that night. Newspapers covered little of what went on in Indian reservations. It's as if what went on there was a world of its own. I had found something about the school play announcement, probably only because a white teacher named Harrison had traveled there on a grant to teach a drama class. It could be a wild goose chase, but I have to do it for my sanity and maybe hers.

I pull out my travel bag and haphazardly throw in casual clothes, something one might wear into the mountains at this time of year. I have no clue. I need Carter's advice on this. I smile, thinking about the skiing trip she and I took in Colorado before Kimi came into our lives. This was after our first divorce. We were always best friends, even through three divorces. Carter calls and says, "We need to take a vacation."

Like it was the most perfectly normal thing in the world to take a vacation with your ex-wife, I asked, "Where do you suggest?"

"Skiing," I remember her exclaiming.

Carter was like that. Impulsive. Kimi is a different matter. Practical, Inquisitive, Intellectual.

Neither of us had ever skied in our lives, but it was what all celebrities did, so Carter said we had to. We spent a fortune on skiing gear after we arrived there but only had it on once. We were both too used to the California sunshine. We spent most of the time in the lodge by the fire, drinking hot chocolate or making love in our room. It thrilled me that we returned with no broken bones. We were so happy then.

I zip up my bag and head out the door, prepared to take on the role of some 1950s sleuth, investigating the old-fashioned way, tracking down information using cold calls and face-to-face questioning, not having the computer skills to do it the way one might today or going through a professional like Harry. It will be an organic experience, a new adventure for me. One Carter would cheer on if it involved anyone other than her. Kimi, on the other hand...

I can't think about it now. My flight leaves at 12:30. I have less than two hours to maneuver through LA traffic to LAX and get through the TSA line. From there, it will be a long day. Because of the time difference, I won't arrive in Asheville until close to 11 p.m. I'll have to pick up the rental vehicle and then drive for an hour and a half through mountainous roads. With luck, maybe I'll make it to the resort before two in the morning.

Will could be working at that time, but I'll be too exhausted. I'm already tired. I've been tired ever since Kimi called me to tell me her version of what happened six months ago and of having to deal with the repercussions of it ever since.

Thirteen

KIMI—SUNDAY AFTERNOON

I pace back and forth in my tiny space. I don't know how often I've done this, smoothing out a path from the kitchen bar to the couch on the Berber carpet with my bare feet. I can't imagine how something so important came up over the weekend that Arthur can't tell me even the meagerest of details about. This whole thing is so unlike him. I'm tempted to order another martini, as this one did little to quell my disappointment. But it might prompt a visit from Mrs. Bell to see if I'm alright. I'm sure she has reported my progress back to Arthur in the last two weeks. I flip on the television, hoping for something I can absorb myself into. I push the enormous forward buttons on the remote, finding nothing. I see at 6:00 that *The Muted Girl* is playing on the movie channel. I'm tempted, but I need something other than my sister or myself.

I realize tomorrow, my therapist's visit is scheduled. What is the thing about two weeks? Is something miraculous supposed to happen during this period? Is The Woodlands some magical place that cures all ills and sets one on the right path to a fulfilled life?

Maybe it's the martini, although I feel no effects. They skimp on the alcohol here. They discourage liquor stocks in the rooms. I'd be willing to bet the man inhabiting the entire upper story has a full bar. His familiar face keeps nagging at my mind. I've gleaned a little information about him from the workers who deliver my meals and come to check on me, taking my pulse, blood pressure, and heart rate regularly. Oddly, they never comment on my burn scars. If one looks closely enough, being right across from me, with a stethoscope against my chest or holding the blood pressure cuff to my arm, they could see right through the veil. I'm sure of it. I'm also sure they have been sworn to secrecy regarding the residents here and have been conditioned to oddities such as myself.

I've thrown subtle hints regarding the man upstairs to the staff who come to my apartment. Not Mrs. Bell, though. Whoever this man is, she protects his privacy. I think the staff are as curious as me. According to Luke, he's someone important and has lots of money. I think that goes without saying. The mysterious man inhabits the entire floor except for a personal assistant, who conveniently lives in an apartment like my own next door to him. He has no direct contact with the staff himself. His assistant attends to everything for him, and like me, he hasn't set foot outside his apartment since arriving, which, according to Luke, was shortly before I came here.

A part of me wonders if I could beat his record, but Arthur, standing me up today, has thrown everything off. I pace around some more, wearing a wider path in the carpet, before getting the nerve to go out my door. Before I lose my resolve, I grab my veil from the coffee table, adjust it over my face, and open the door. I only open it a crack at first and peek down the hallway. It's vacant. I bravely step outside. The door closes behind me, and I realize I've forgotten to grab my key card. My heart speeds up, and I fear the loudness of it will set off some alarm in the otherwise silent hallway. I remember the master key Mrs. Bell carries with her and telling me that most staff members could let me back in. I immediately think of Luke and hope he is working today. I check my pocket and realize I've also forgotten my cell phone.

I stand outside my door for the longest time, taking deep breaths to calm my heart. I'm also contemplating whether to take the stairs or the elevator. Dare I brave the elevator where there might be other people? I play it safe and take the stairs. I tremble with each step, but before I know it, I'm standing on the first floor of the stairwell behind the heavy door, debating whether to label this as a dry run and retreat upstairs to my apartment, but I don't have my key. While deciding, the door opens, startling me and almost knocking me down. Thank God, it's Luke. "Oh, sorry, Miss Stone."

I'm still not used to the name, even though people who come in and out of my room use it constantly, but I'm in an unfamiliar environment, and I'm more than a bit shaken.

"Miss Stone, are you okay?" he questions.

I say yes with a meek voice. I want to tell him to drop the Miss Stone and call me Kimi, but I think it better to wait. I've been through enough therapy to know subconsciously that I might be replacing Arthur with Luke.

"Where are you headed? To the dining room?"

"I don't know." I had thought nothing further than stepping beyond the confines of my apartment.

"Lamb is one of the selections today. I had some earlier. It's perfection. Unless you're vegetarian."

"No." I smile.

"I think Gloria Morton is the only vegetarian on the premises, which is strange for California."

"The lady who plays the piano?"

"Yes."

I guess if Arthur had shown up, that's what we would have had. Lamb with horseradish is a favorite of his, although the horseradish always upset his ulcer. Thinking of Arthur in this manner has calmed me somewhat. I ask, "The lamb?"

"Yes?"

"Does it come with horseradish?"

"Why, yes, I'm sure they have horseradish," he says.

"I guess I could have it brought up to my room."

"Yes, of course, if you like, but it's late, and most residents have already eaten lunch. There is a table in the far corner where you might be happy. It's away from the hustle and bustle of the dining room, although, since most everyone has already eaten, it will be quiet now."

We both stand there, him looking at me with pleading blue eyes in his matching blue scrubs. Luke could have easily been an actor. I'm thinking of possibly a leading man in a soap opera. Perhaps, other than checking heart rates and blood pressure all day, acting is required with this job.

"I'm afraid I've locked myself out of my room. I foolishly left the key card on the coffee table." This is a lie. I've never removed it from the original packet it came in.

"Well, I could let you back in if that's what you truly want, but I think if you wanted that, you wouldn't be standing out here."

I stand frozen.

"You might enjoy eating in the dining room today. I'd happily sit with you or at the next table, whatever makes you comfortable."

"Haven't you already eaten, Luke? You said—"

"Yes, but I didn't have time for dessert. You know, always on duty. They have blueberry cobbler today."

"Am I your duty, Luke?"

"No, Miss Stone, you're my pleasure." His eyes light up, and his dimple grows deeper with his smile.

"Blueberry," I repeat. I remember my mother's blueberry

plant on our small farm and Kachina and me picking them for the blueberry cobblers she made.

"Okay," I say. "You'll sit with me?"

"Of course."

"But weren't you headed upstairs to do something?"

"It can wait. But blueberry cobbler can't."

Fourteen

ARTHUR—SUNDAY MORNING

Perspiration fills my armpits from the anxiety of getting here in time, and I worry if I thought to pack deodorant. The TSA agent makes me go through the metal detector three times. This stuff is usually old hat for me. I typically go through the line in a well-thought-out sprint, but my anxiety trips me up. I keep removing things from my pocket that my hastiness caused me to forget to remove. The woman glares at me as if she could be at home spending a Sunday with her family, or more than likely wishing she had a family to go home to, taking her angst out on the customers. These types of jobs collect societal misfits who need a sense of power. I finally make it through and sit on the bench, tying my shoelaces. Then, I practically run down the concourse toward my plane.

Thankfully, my terminal is right around the corner. All the sections have been called by the time I get there. I'm three people back toward the end of the line. If I had gotten here earlier, I would already have boarded, being in first class. The woman flinches as she scans my ticket, making me think I need that deodorant. I'll head to the restroom and try to rectify the situation with soap as soon as we are in the air and can unbuckle our seatbelts.

There is an hour-and-a-half layover in Dallas. I've only been to that airport once. I missed a connecting flight because of its weird configuration. I'm hoping this won't be a repeat since I have more time between flights this go around. My tension eases a little, realizing the redundancy of that thought. Hopefully, this time, the terminal I'm supposed to get at won't be right next door but in the wrong direction. Hopefully, I'll be able to grab things I didn't pack in my hastiness, possibly, in addition to deodorant, a jacket for the mountain air. And if I don't have time, it's a resort. I'm sure it will have everything I need, no higher than airport prices.

I place my carry-on overhead and settle into my seat. The man behind me in line takes the aisle seat beside me and nods. The flight is packed.

We haven't taken off yet, but the air flight attendant bends down and asks me if I want anything. She calls me Mr. Burke. Of course, I'm on the list of first-class passengers, but I detect a hint of recognition. I've certainly been in the news enough, along with Carter. If so, she refrains from saying anything.

This first leg of the journey lasts almost five hours. I would love to sleep, but I know I won't be able to. Also, I didn't think to bring anything to relax me. "Something strong," I tell her.

She smiles. "Will a scotch and soda do?"

Ah, the typical drink for a nervous flyer. Maybe that's it. She mistakes me for a nervous flyer.

Within minutes, she mixed my drink and handed it to me over the man, who had already settled into a movie with his earbuds on.

I thank her and take a sip.

After all this time, why suddenly does someone from the Cherokee Nation call out of the blue? Possibly because all the papers and magazines carried the story about Carter's Halloween fiasco. But that was six months ago. I don't know what else to call it other than a fiasco. If only I had been there. I could have dragged Carter off into her room before it turned into an utter disaster. The signs of one coming are always clear. Maybe only to me, but then, I've been with her since she was practically a child, and yet, I know little of her life before that street corner. She hid most of her past, although sometimes she sprinkled bits and pieces of it in conversations. The paparazzi would have had a field day with it. For all I know, it could have been one of them calling to lure me in. Some bizarre ploy by a reporter willing to go to any length to get the story of the century. Or the call could be genuine. Or perhaps someone wanting money. Someone who knows something she wouldn't want to be revealed. I don't see how a tragic fire that supposedly killed everyone in her family except for her or her mother could put her in a bad light in the public eye. If anything, it would draw sympathy, possibly explaining her recent breakdowns. But if her mother is truly alive and Carter abandoned her, public opinion would be the opposite, destroying future movie deals. Hollywood is a fickle place. But then, it appears her career is probably already over unless a miracle in her condition occurs.

"Could you bring me a double martini with an olive," I ask the flight attendant as she collects my empty glass. I tell myself this is my limit. Carter always had one waiting for me in the evening when she wasn't on location. The flight attendant makes no judgment. I don't know why I'm so nervous. Flying is routine for me, as are business trips, but this one is different. It's personal.

The man beside me, who has removed his earbuds, tired of the movie, looks over my way. "Good idea." He turns to the air flight attendant and says, "The same for me."

While the attendant prepares our drinks on her cart, he

says, "I guess I'm starting early. Off to a convention. I hate these things. How about you?"

"No convention. A resort," I say.

"Lucky you," he says.

"Yes, lucky me."

Fifteen

ARTHUR—SUNDAY NIGHT TO MONDAY MORNING

Fortunately, the Asheville airport is small and easily maneuverable, unlike LA's airport or the other cities I'm used to traveling to. I head straight to the Avis rental desk. It's late. A headache is coming on. Only one person is in front of me, not a person, but a family of four. The parents take turns bouncing and trying to soothe two tired, cranky children—twin girls. I can't help but wonder if it's a sign, although they have sandy-colored hair, not black. Carter would say it's a sign. I tell myself it's just a coincidence—apophenia, the false belief that unrelated things are connected. The color of the girls' hair negates serendipity.

Once, trying to offer support, I unloaded a slew of self-help books recommended by the owner of the small new-age bookstore on Carter's nightstand. After reading them, she said coincidences are the universe's way of speaking to us. I suppose if you look at anything long enough, patterns will emerge.

The lady, holding one toddler per arm, her husband having handed one off to her to take care of the luggage and car seats—I'm guessing them to be around two years, although

I've never been around children much—turns to me, apologizing. "They'll go to sleep in their car seats as soon as we hit the road." The woman looks exasperated. I smile. I know how they feel. I'm tempted to cry with them, but I'm a grown man. At least they have the comfort of their parents' arms. The man finally gathers the rental company's paperwork, and the kids' screams grow distant as they walk through the glass doors out to the parking lot. I move up to the desk and give the lady my name. I want it to be quick, but these things never are. I'm impatient as she tries to sell me extras. She keeps smiling, rattling off each option robotically throughout my persistent nos.

Like the man before me, I sign on the dotted line, too tired to know what I'm endorsing as my legal obligation even though I'm a lawyer. I've often thought that if people took the time to read what they signed or initialed online, all this legal jargon would end, and I would be out of a job, or it would be pared down.

"Thank you, Mr. Burke. Just go through those doors, and the attendant will have your SUV ready."

I might consider this an adventure if things weren't so strange—if our relationship was ordinary. However, the relationships of Hollywood icons are never normal. If only I could travel back in time to these mountains with Carter, asking her to show me all the wonders and misfortunes of growing up in this area. Possibly, our road would not have been so rocky.

After departing Asheville, I find myself on a lonely, curvy stretch of road with a myriad of tunnels. The plus is that traffic is almost nonexistent after reaching the outskirts of the town. The farther I drive down the highway, the more the lights dim, making way for what is natural. An endless sea of trees covering the surrounding mountains. It's after midnight, and unlike LA, there is little nightlife here. It is a quiet place I would have loved to have visited with Carter.

Under more serene circumstances, I might find the roadway bordered by nature, primarily evergreens mixed with barren trees giving birth to minute buds, relaxing. In retrospect, I probably should have gotten a hotel near the airport and left early the next day. I don't know why I thought a man my age was cut out for this middle-of-the-night road trip.

Occasionally, I'm greeted by patches of light. Sometimes, it is the moonlight peeking between the tree branches. At other times, it's inhabited areas with lone porch lights or security lights shining into the darkness. I see beautiful homes securely affixed to the mountainous landscape, some mansions juxtaposed against smaller, more modest dwellings. Then, a few miles down the road, I come across mobile units with rusted-out cars parked on front lawns. So this is what Appalachian poverty looks like. Impoverishment comes in a different form in LA. The stretches I pass with houses and trailers are mere shadows out of place among vast areas of foliage. I'm sure it's beautiful in the daytime.

As I get out of inhabited areas, I find myself mesmerized by my headlights that are set on bright, illuminating the yellow line zig-zagging through the curls of the road. The only other lights are those above me. I do my best to take in every aspect to keep myself from dozing off. I gaze upward to see a cascade of stars, more numerous than I've ever seen, except possibly in the Rockies. In contrast to the Rockies' sharp peaks, the Appalachian Mountains, older, are worn down by billions of years of geological upheavals. The stars' brilliance dot the firmament with hope. It's the way nature is meant to be—miraculous—this majesty erased by man's artificial rendition of lights in the cities. I can only imagine what a pristine life the Native Americans had before the arrival of the white man.

When the attendant handed me the keys and directed me to the vehicle, he cautioned, "Watch out for bears." I had casually mentioned I was headed to Cherokee.

I'm exhausted and shouldn't be driving, but my racing mind propels me forward. I watch for the forewarned bears and deer, which I've seen a few of, or any other creature making their home in these parts that might dart across my path. I sometimes see the glare of red eyes poking out of the trees on the sides of the road. This is their rightful abode. They only answer to the rules nature doles out to them, unlike modern man, who does everything in his power to corrupt nature while harnessing it for monetary purposes.

I crack my window and take in the mountain air. I hear the gurgle of a stream and the sound of an owl's hooting. A thick line of trees camouflages its inhabitants. I imagine a cabin hidden deep in the woods—a lone author reflecting on the meaning of life, a Thoreau writing his equivalent of *Walden*. His shotgun rests in the corner, ready for aggressive bears. He kills for his food, contrary to his original purpose of the adventure. In the end, he discovers life is meaningless. We are all animals. The bear has just as much of a right to eat him as he does the bear. I think about how twice in my life, I might have set out on a similar path of self-reflection. One was after my first divorce from Carter. The first was the night I was packing the rest of my stuff at my father's house to take to my new apartment after a blow-out fight with him—the last time I saw him alive and also the night I met Carter, then Kachina, or was it actually Kimi? No wonder I have a headache.

While driving, I think about my life and the direction it has taken. All of this started with him—that one phone call from him I took while picking up my stuff that night. That call and meeting her changed the course of my life. Why was it so imperative that I find her, or rather *them*—sixteen-year-old twin girls transported across state lines by a Victor Wildman? She said through tears he promised to make her a star but dropped her off after declaring her not worth the trouble. I don't know how often I've thought the same thing, but unlike Victor, I kept coming back, a glutton for punishment.

I sigh, analyzing whether the good times were worth the bad. I have to say they were. The simplest experiences with her dart through my mind. Initially, she reminded me of a timid kitten, always afraid she would do something wrong and ruin the career she wanted so badly. Little did she know, he had her path to success carefully planned—laid out in steps spread across years.

It was after the success of *The Muted Girl* she became a household name—her picture spread across the covers of magazines, plastered across billboards, and on the sides of buses. And because it was written into her contract that she was released from doing interviews to promote the movie, people hadn't heard her voice, except for the guttural grunts her part called for. This made her even more of a mystery and the subject of gossip rags. Before that, we could go out to nice restaurants without the fear of our meal being interrupted. Business associates might come up to me occasionally. They regarded her as my latest love interest, of course, drawing plenty of stares because of her extraordinary beauty, but we could eat dinner in relative peace. But after that one movie, to go out in public meant donning disguises or paying maître d's for private, out-of-the-way tables.

After all the hoopla of *The Muted Girl*, her timidness crawled into the background, revealing a wild streak, an impulsiveness I sometimes couldn't control. I'll admit it could be fun; at other times, her antics got me called into his office.

Shortly after *The Muted Girl* came out, she insisted we take a drive. We found ourselves on the outskirts of Los Angeles. "Oh, look, Arthur. That looks like a good place to eat."

"You have to be kidding," I said as she grabbed the side of the steering wheel, forcing me into a U-turn. Although it was ten o'clock at night, the OPEN sign flashed, at least part of it. The O failed to light up.

"It looks like one of those cozy roadside diners you see in movies," she said.

The thing is, those diners are romanticized, always better than the real thing. But I know there is no use in arguing with her. Besides, we are already in the parking lot, a few spaces from one lone car, a dented Ford Falcon. I didn't even know they were still making them.

She put on her red wig, the one we kept in the backseat for times such as these, and donned her oversized sunglasses, which only drew attention in the poorly lit parking lot. The thing about Carter is almost every aspect of her life is an act, a scene out of a movie. This was no different. We pass a table of what appears to be migrant workers having pizza and beers while heading to the darkest corner of the restaurant. They glance up at us as we walk past. The bright side is that no one would ever expect Carter Hudson to be eating here.

The server, the same guy who told us to sit wherever we wanted, who looks Mexican, hands us a laminated, sticky menu with pictures of Venice, Italy, faded into the background of the entrees.

"So, what will it be, Carter?"

"Oh, no, Arthur. You must call me Alice."

I comply with her wishes, even though I'm confident no one here knows who she is or has even seen the movie.

We order a large pepperoni pizza and beers because Carter, or rather Alice, says we must fit in. I'm tempted to remind her this isn't a movie set, but I play along. The beers arrive, and Carter removes her glasses. She seems almost annoyed that the server doesn't gawk at her like a love-sick puppy but starts laughing so hard that I think her wig might fall off.

"What's so funny?" I ask.

"Don't you know, Arthur?"

I shake my head.

"Well, we're sitting in an Italian restaurant with a Mexican server and French music playing in the background."

She noticed these kinds of things.

The server, oblivious to her outburst, brings out the greasiest pizza I've ever seen. The pepperonis are floating on the fatty oil, but Carter doesn't complain. She accepts it as perfectly usual, while I'm wondering if the ulcer I've developed since knowing her will burst into flames.

"Growing up on the reservation, we didn't have pizza, only a dairy bar that served milkshakes, hamburgers, and hotdogs. One day, our father took us all out for ice cream cones. It's the simple things, Arthur."

She would occasionally add little tidbits about her life before stardom. I wish I had encouraged her to elaborate more.

And where was her twin sister? They had to leave her, was all she would say. They, meaning she and Victor. I told her Victor had died. I didn't know for sure. It was only a rumor, but news of his demise settled her the same way it soothed him. Both feared he might reappear one day. I suddenly wonder if the call might have been from Victor. I was never certain if he had died because Harry said he had more aliases than an internet stalker, but Carter had such a fear of him turning up again after she became famous, so I told her that.

Why was this girl and her sister so crucial to my boss? Did he have some sort of relationship with Victor Wildman? In all of these years, I've never asked, not directly. It wasn't my place. I'm paid well to follow his orders, not to ask questions. But I *do* question. This is the first time I'm taking matters into my own hands.

A little over an hour after leaving the airport and driving on winding roads in the middle of nowhere, I see faint lights up ahead. The road widens, revealing houses plucked sparsely along the fringes. I pass the sign that says CHEROKEE, NORTH CAROLINA, Population 27,435. Further along, as I climb the roadway, a mingling of modern and rustic log structures, the latter, I guess, dating back to when Kachina and Kimi grew up here, line both sides of the road, along with small mom-and-pop eateries. Everywhere, I see advertisements for local handmade crafts. Totems and Native American art decorate the buildings' entrances. I see my first bear, the wooden statuesque variety. Nothing is open, but a few stragglers who appear to be drunk stand by an old Chevy parked in front of one of the tourist traps. Or are they doing drugs?

I travel a couple more miles. Up ahead, one couldn't miss it; I see the casino, lit up like a small chunk of Las Vegas that broke off and somehow made its way across state lines to this remote area. It's massive, dwarfing everything else around it. I wind around to the hotel entrance, ready for a nightcap and a peaceful sleep, before starting my inquiries in the morning.

Sixteen

ARTHUR—MONDAY MORNING

I open my eyes and glance over at the clock, which registers 10:17 a.m. I don't remember the last time I slept this late. Then I do. I had woken up beside Carter after a late dinner we fixed ourselves. I use the word, we, loosely. Carter was the head chef, and I was her sous-chef. It was the day after Thanksgiving, and although we had plenty of leftovers in the refrigerator, all neatly labeled, complete with reheating instructions in Tupperware containers by our cook, who considered both Carter and me inept in the kitchen, Carter said it would be fun to cook a meal. "Why do we have this big luxurious kitchen if we don't use it?"

I had almost forgotten the meals prepared by the sixteen-year-old Kachina when we were first together. Never anything complicated, but home-style meals, something I wasn't used to. There were always corn or potato dishes. At other times, I would bring something home. I remember when she requested a Big Mac and fries early on.

"I've never had a MacDonald's meal," she said.

She lit up like a toddler when I not only brought a Big Mac with a large order of fries but also a Happy Meal. As far as

I know, she still has the prize, a MacDoodler stenciler. Shortly after that, MacDonald's put *Star Trek* paraphernalia in as prizes, and she had me stopping at least once a week for Happy Meals.

"So, at eighteen, she's collecting MacDonald's' toys?" He smiled like a pleased parent but quickly reprimanded me, "The toys are okay, but we can't have her consisting on a diet of burgers, soft drinks, and fries. See to it she eats healthy."

In some respects, Connor controlled her like movie executives of the past controlled stars like Judy Garland and Mickey Rooney.

"So, she likes Star Trek, does she?"

"I don't know. She likes the toys. She has them displayed on top of the chest in her room."

"I wish I could see that," he said with a faraway look in his eyes. His expression changed, turning to business. "That would be a perfect part for her. They are already making a sequel to the first Star Trek movie. Some minor part of an alien would be perfect to see if she has what it takes."

He consistently secured roles like this for her before casting her in *The Muted Girl.*

Our cook was right about me. I could barely boil water. However, Carter had her fooled. She could be quite the cook when she wanted to be.

"I don't know about you, Artie," that's what she called me when she was in a playful mood, "but I'm tired of the traditional white man's feast."

I distinctly remember saying, "I'm game."

"No game," she said. Hopi corn stew. It's simple and cheap. It's something my mother used to make."

It was one of the most delicious meals I have ever eaten, possibly because Carter made it.

I sit up in bed. My stomach growls. I realize my last bite of food was at the Denver airport—a Cinnabon and coffee, not much of a meal.

I push the sheets back, rise from bed, shower, and slip on my jeans and a light sweater, grabbing my wallet and room key card. I look over at my phone on the dresser. It will only be a distraction. How many times has she called? I put it in the room safe and lock it using our first wedding date for the code. I hop on the elevator to find a restaurant serving omelets. Carter could make a mean omelet. I remember her telling me they kept hens. I got pieces of Carter's or Kachina's life in crumbs, never the whole story, only small chunks that came up at the oddest moments.

After breakfast, I will inquire about Will, the man with no last name.

By three p.m., I must have spoken with every casino employee, an exaggeration since the whole town must be employed here. Everyone, it seems, except for Will. Thinking I've come on a wild goose chase, that the call was some prank, or it truly is Victor who called and is watching my every move from the shadows like the red-eyed creatures on the road last night, I walk outside for fresh air. A crew of gardeners are busy preparing the grounds for spring plants. One of the younger workers shouts, "Hey, Will, where do these lilac plants go?"

A middle-aged man who looks Cherokee walks over to the younger man and points to a particular spot near the front of the building. My heart races, hoping the universe is stepping in. It's what Carter would say.

I walk over. "Will?"

"Yes, can I help you?"

I reach out my hand to shake his. He pushes his shovel into the soil, leaving it standing upright. He rubs his dirt-covered hand on the side of his jeans before shaking mine.

"I certainly hope so. My name is Arthur Burke."

"You came!" He seems surprised.

"Then you are the Will I'm looking for?" I'm relieved that he doesn't fit Carter's description of Victor.

"I think so. I'm Will Catawnee." I see the name Catawnee Landscaping on the side of the white pickup truck. I see three trucks and count nine men who all look to be Cherokee, removing plants and laying them out in their new homes. I think he must be doing well for himself.

"You want to know about Kimi," he says.

"It's Carter I want to know about," I say.

"I knew her as Kimi."

"No, not Kimi, Carter or Kachina."

He looks puzzled.

I watch him grip the top part of his shovel with both hands while looking up at the clouds for direction. I wonder if this is some manner of Cherokee reflection, but I realize this type of pause is typical of anyone trying to sum up someone as complicated as her. I doubt if anyone could be more complex than Carter or Kimi.

"Okay then, Carter...," he concedes. "She was intricate. Smart. Extremely intelligent. If she would have finished school, she would have been the valedictorian. She would have done great things, but then, I guess she did."

He shovels more dirt from the hole he had previously

started digging and places the sapling inside the hole. I study how he turns the dirt with each twist of the shovel like he knows what he is doing. We had gardeners who came by once a week to tend the lawn, although I never paid them much heed.

It's like he is one with the earth. People walk by us, paying no attention. They're here to gamble, eat, drink, and take in the view from behind the safety glass of their hotel room, and the next day, more of the same. Possibly, when they gamble most of their money away out of desperation, they'll take a side excursion on one of the trails to reconnect with the bark of the tree and its newly forming buds or dip their toes into the frigid water of one of the babbling brooks because some ancient Native American spirit beckons them to do so. Or that's what they pretend is happening. Nature will go along steadily, true to its purpose, keeping its secrets, shrugging off the human nuisance because Mother Earth knows they're not sincere.

Will's dark hair with flecks of gray falls against rugged cheeks, a papery film of soil with streaks of sweat as he bends and delicately adjusts the small tree into its new home. He's careful to place an earthworm out of the path of the back of his shovel as he clamps down the dirt. The white truck beside him is equipped with an assortment of shovels neatly arranged on one inside one wall. I assume each one serves a different purpose.

He looks up at me and smiles. "Only nineteen more to go."

"Can I help?" I ask although I wouldn't even know what to do with a shovel. I've never gardened a day in my life. I don't even know why I offer. Perhaps because I'm avoiding asking questions and getting answers I might not want to hear.

He knows this. Letting me off the hook, he says, "I could get fired if someone sees me letting a customer do my work."

"You're right," I say.

"Are you staying at the casino's hotel?" he asks.

"Yes, I came in last night. I didn't expect to find a place this huge."

"On the top of a mountain?" he finishes. I have to admit, the guy is handsome. He's aged as well as Carter. It must be something inherent in having lived so close to nature.

"I have so many questions," I say.

"I don't know if I can answer them, but I'll try. I knew Kimi such a long time ago."

"You mean Kachina, right?"

"No, Kimi."

This adds to my confusion.

"I need to get back to work. He points to the plants still on the back of the truck. We need to get these planted today."

"Of course. When do you get off, Will? Could I take you to dinner?"

"Oh, no. My wife expects me home, but you can eat at our house. Six o'clock?"

This is unexpected. I hesitate.

"Sandy loves to entertain."

"If you don't think she would mind."

"No, not at all. She'll have a million questions for you. Not about Kimi, but about what it's like in Los Angeles. We've never had a chance to travel much."

"What can I bring?"

"Just yourself," he says. "It won't be anything fancy, just a good home-cooked meal."

"That sounds great. I haven't had one of those in a long time."

He grabs a pack of business cards from the cab of his truck and hands one to me.

I look at the colorful card decorated with plants. There is a dirty thumbprint on the edge. I rub my finger over it to remove the dirt and realize it's part of the card. Will laughs.

"Everyone does that. My wife designed them."

"They're great," I say.

"It's easy to find, about five miles from here. My cell number is on there if you have any problems."

Seventeen

KIMI—MONDAY AFTERNOON

It's been only one day since Arthur failed to show up and one day since I braved eating with Luke in the dining room. I consider it a dry run. By the time we reached the table, most residents had already eaten. Staff were clearing plates and removing tablecloths to wash.

I picked at the lamb while Luke gobbled down the blueberry cobbler and told me about his family. Then he walked me back up to my room, this time via the elevator.

I haven't ventured back to the dining hall since. Luke has brought most of my meals to me. He's careful not to push me out of my comfort zone. I wonder if Mrs. Bell has assigned him to me.

Unlike Arthur, Luke takes what I say seriously. Arthur dismisses so many things as figments of my imagination. Today, I think he might be one of those figments. No word from him. I've called his office. His secretary reports the same.

I've always considered Arthur my Orpheus, although I've never told him that. I've thought he would travel to the land of the dead if need be for me. Now, like Carter, I have my doubts. I lack the beauty and allure of Eurydice and Carter.

I need a distraction, and I need to build confidence and independence. It's 1 p.m. I passed on having lunch brought to my room. I watch as the time clicks by on my phone, mustering up my courage. The dining room shouldn't be crowded. Defiance over Arthur's desertion of me is rearing its head. So much so that I'm tempted to walk in without covering my scars, but insecurity seeps in, and I wrap one of my many scarves around my head, tying it in such a way as to hide half my face. I've become an expert at knots and various ways of draping veils and scarves.

I remember my key card. I walk down the hall, this time toward the elevator. I see no one until I get off on the first floor. Mrs. Bell looks surprised to see me. Her initial shock changes into a pleased smile. "Miss Stone, you are looking well."

I hold the edge of my scarf close to the side of my mouth and say, "Thank you."

"Can I help you with anything today?"

"I thought... I thought..."

She looks at me like I might have dementia.

"I thought I might have lunch in the dining room today."

"I'm so happy to hear it," she says, pleased that I'm not having another stroke and that I'm venturing out of my suite.

"I'll happily walk down with you if you like."

"No, I think I can do it on my own."

She smiles and presses the up button for the elevator. The door reopens, and she, in her pink dress with lipstick to match, disappears inside, telling me to have a pleasant lunch as the doors shut.

I walk down the black and white tiled hallway leading directly into the dining area. There are perhaps twenty-five people, most huddled together at three of the center tables. A few look my way but resume their eating and conversations. I might be the new person here, but I am a nonplus for them.

They probably think the scarf is hiding recent plastic surgery. I've noticed a few here who have overdone it.

Whenever Carter walked into a room, heads turned in her direction, the way plants reached toward the sun. She was always the main draw in a room. Even without the scars, I don't think I could be the moon.

I sit in the back, at the same table where I sat with Luke. The giant fern partially hides me. One of the wait staff walks over to me and tells me today's selections. "Would you have a hamburger and fries?" I ask. This is something I rarely indulge in, but rebellion wells up inside me, as well as nostalgia. It's what Will and I were having following the play rehearsal. I wonder if he ever thinks of me. We were kids. He's probably married with children, possibly even grandchildren.

The woman smiles. "I will ask the cook to rustle it up for you. "It may take a little longer not being on today's menu."

I seriously doubt it's ever on the menu, but say, "That's fine. Could you maybe bring me a Coke while I wait?"

"No problem," she says, but I don't think she means it. I know a bad actor when I see one but play along.

"No, no, Althea," I say as she turns to walk away. I'm pleased with myself for remembering the name on her badge.

She turns. "Yes, sweetheart?"

I hesitate at the word sweetheart. I remember my mom sometimes referring to the older customers in the beauty shop as sweethearts, as if growing wrinkled and having bluish-tinted hair, as many women back then did, opens a magical portal back into childhood. I squelch a laugh, thinking I could use one of those portals right now. Wouldn't it be great if I could go back and change everything that happened that night? How many people wish they could go back in time and change something that threw them down some trajectory in life they hadn't planned on? Probably most people my age. Certainly, most of the people in this room. I would rewind my life like a film, redoing all the scenes that fell short, even if it took hundreds of retakes.

"Would you possibly have an Orange Crush?"

Her eyebrows raise momentarily. I take it this is a first for her.

"I don't know if we have that, but I'll check."

I remember Will always had Orange Crushes. I hadn't thought of him in years. I don't know why suddenly I am now. I have so many regrets. I wonder what my life might have been like if I had stayed in Cherokee. We would have eventually ended up together with children and grandchildren. While forty-nine is young here for grandchildren, it wasn't then back in Cherokee.

I sit silently, taking in the conversations coming from the center of the room. I surmise the man doing most of the talking is Frank. One woman looks his way using this name. He is talking about his grandson, who is in rehab. One lady places her hand across his arm, the one connected to the hand still grasping a knife ready to cut into a steak. Her emerald ring, the stone so big that it might have come out of a pirate's treasure ship or from the Emerald City in *The Wizard of Oz*, clashes with the blood running from Frank's prime rib. Everything about this woman, her perfectly groomed ruby-red fingernails, also setting off her ring, says money. After an appropriate time, she removes her blue-veined hand from the sleeve of Frank's argyle sweater, and he resumes cutting, placing a bite into his mouth with the unsteady hand of a man on the last leg of his life after dipping it in a pool of Worcestershire sauce mixed with the blood of his steak. If anyone has a special diet here, I'm not seeing it. Everyone seems to eat whatever they want as if it's their last meal before execution. It might be for most of them.

Althea approaches my table carrying a Coke and a straw from which she has removed part of the wrapper. I guess most here are too feeble for such intricate tasks. "I'm sorry, we didn't have an Orange Crush."

I tell her no problem. Carter would have demanded, while Kimi accepts and shrinks into the background.

"I'm sorry. I didn't ask how you wanted your burger done. The cook just placed it on the grill."

I look back over at Frank and the diluted blood that his steak sets in. "Well done, please," I answer.

I remember Will always liked his dripping with blood, similar to Frank. Again, I am thinking about Will. I've read that if you think of someone, they are also thinking of you. No, he can't be. I'm sure he has forgotten me by now.

Althea brings my burger and fries. Catsup and mayonnaise are in small silver containers on the side. This is not McDonald's, after all. Gosh, I was a teenager the last time I had something from MacDonald's. I'm sure it would no longer taste the way I remember.

I can see they prepared this burger using the finest ground chuck. I relish each bite, swirling each fry into the catsup, similar to the way I dip my brushes into the paint on my pallet while listening as best I can to the conversations going on. I watch over the pink roses, three placed in the center of my table. The same arrangement is on every table. Will would sometimes bring me azaleas. He had a special knack for growing things, unlike my father, who failed miserably at gardening.

Frank is the only man at this center table. Three women sit with him, hanging onto his every word. My father used to tell the joke that whenever a man's wife died, the woman who brought him the first casserole had dibs on him. Kachina asked what that meant. He replied with a wink, "Ask your mother."

I suddenly realize this is where Carter got her infamous wink. Why I had never realized this.

The harder questions always got deferred to our mother,

as if Hopi wisdom outweighed Cherokee answers. At least, that was the case in our house. I could use that wisdom now.

Althea comes back to check on me several times. She does the same with the other tables. I watch them finish up and leave in groups. The consensus is they will return to their rooms to rest and meet up later for a game of cards before dinner. None of them pay attention to me, even though they all walk within five feet of my table to leave, two using walkers and one in a motorized wheelchair.

I pass on dessert and am about to return to my room. Rest seems like a good idea to me, too. However, Luke walks in carrying a can. "I hear someone ordered an Orange Crush."

Eighteen

ARTHUR—MONDAY NIGHT

I watch the numbers on the houses as I drive by, knowing I'm getting close.

All along the drive, I've seen sights I don't see back in LA: people outside in their front yards, sometimes talking with their neighbors, sometimes just standing or fiddling with a car in their driveway. But the most incredible thing is the children darting all around, some playing basketball on the pavement, only stopping for approaching vehicles.

My GPS says I will arrive at the destination within less than a minute. An ornate black mailbox with the street number on the side and a matching placard at the top with the name Catawnee leads me into a driveway paved with earth-toned stones winding up a slight hill to what I would term a storybook cottage. The front yard looks like something out of a *Home and Garden* magazine. I wonder if this might have been Carter's life had she never come to Los Angeles. Will mentioned they had dated in high school. Or would she have come to LA alone, like so many, hoping to make it big in the movies?

I pull up in the driveway, turn off the engine, and pick up

the flowers from the seat beside me, thinking it is a bad choice considering his profession. I immediately regret not going for the chocolates.

I ring the doorbell. A slightly plump woman answers. She's wearing black leggings and a v-necked sweater, almost reaching her knees. She smiles broadly. "You must be Mr. Burke."

"Arthur, please."

"Welcome, Arthur." She motions me in.

I hand her the flowers, a bouquet of several varieties. She takes in the fragrance and names each one, saying the lily stargazer is her favorite, pointing to that one.

"I wouldn't know one from the other, but I'm drawn to that one myself," I say.

"Will is out back watering the garden."

"Oh, there's more of your front yard beauty out back?"

"The front is for show and pollination. A bland lawn for Catawnee Landscaping wouldn't be a very good advertisement."

"If your front yard is any indication, you must be turning customers away."

She smiles. "I wish, but no. The commercial accounts, mainly the casino, are what keep us going. It's what keeps the whole town going. If Harrah's were ever to go, the rest of Cherokee would go with it."

The aroma of fish, lemon, and herbs penetrates the house. If I were to guess, rosemary and... maybe paprika. Carter knew a lot about herbs. She said she learned it from her mother.

I follow her through a living area and into a kitchen, where she opens a pantry door and pauses as if choosing between a particular glass vase and a brightly colored pottery one. She chooses the latter. I look over to see several pots over low flames on the stovetop.

"The hues on the vase and those of the flowers match,

don't you think?" She holds the vase forward for me to inspect.

"I think you're right. I've never given this stuff too much thought, I guess. That was Carter's department."

Carter slips from my mouth. It's habit. If my words were to come out in bubbles above my head, the name Carter would turn up at least once in every paragraph. I did not mean to bring up her name so soon. I had planned to ease into it—not look so needy, angry, rejected, suspicious, a love-sick puppy at my age, or all of the above. I want to cuss, but refrain. I've already made two faux pas—this and the flowers.

The mention of Carter's name doesn't seem to phase her. While most women are jealous of Carter, the fact her husband and Carter were high school sweethearts doesn't seem to bother this woman. She radiates a security I don't see in Hollywood among women. But then the men there are more insecure, always afraid that they can't cut the deal, provide for their current young wife and the string of exes, or the Viagra they so depend on to hold on to that young wife, other than the main draw, the money, will no longer work.

She places the flowers on their kitchen table. Off to the side, I see a dining area with a somewhat odd-looking floral arrangement that looks like it came straight from their front lawn. Three plates with napkins and silverware are already set. She sees me looking in the direction of the table. "Our grandchild, Allison, made that arrangement. She's eight," she says.

"It's striking. Tell her I said so."

"I will. Coming from a man from Hollywood will mean a lot to her. She considers it the land where all the stars and celebrities live, even the characters from *Toy Story*."

"Close. Same state. San Francisco, but don't tell her."

"I won't." She laughs. "There is enough to explain to an eight-year-old without adding to it. Fortunately, her mother, our daughter, is great with her."

I follow her outside and see Will holding a small head of cabbage. He holds it up, beaming proudly. "Our first this year."

I know little about produce, but I think this one looks relatively small for a head of cabbage.

I gather Sandy feels the same. She laughs. "Big enough for coleslaw for the two of us."

"My wife likes to make fun of me, Mr. Burke."

"Arthur, remember."

"Okay, Arthur."

He looks different from when I saw him earlier. He's wearing a Polo shirt and khakis, and I notice a long braid going down his back. Either he had it tucked under his hat earlier, or all the questions flitting through my mind about Carter distracted me.

"Let me just go in and wash my hands, and we'll have cocktails in the living room," he says and grins at his wife.

Sandy whacks him on the head playfully.

"I've embarrassed her. When I told her you were coming to dinner, she started searching the internet on how to make cocktails because she said it was what people in Hollywood were used to."

I thought she might whack him again. Instead, she laughed. I don't think I've ever seen a couple more light-hearted with each other or in love—an uncomplicated love. They have what everyone dreams of.

While Will disappears down the hallway to the bathroom, Sandy directs me to a seat in the living room, a leather recliner with cup holders. Carter would never have gone for this, but she might have grown into an altogether different adult if I hadn't hooked up with her on the street corner that night, if the fire hadn't happened, and if she had never left these mountains. The fake glamour of Hollywood changes a person.

Will enters the room and sits in the chair opposite me. "So, how do you like the mountains?"

"I have to say it's a refreshing change from LA."

Sandy brings a tray with three wine glasses holding what appears to be vodka, with toothpicks holding olives running across them.

"Martinis," she says.

"Yes, I recognize the drink." I say nothing about the glasses, but I immediately want to tell Carter or Kimi this when I return. Then I think how arrogant of me. This woman, naïve about the upper echelons of society, possesses what most of us long for.

"This looks great, honey," Will says. "Did you find this online?"

"No, actually, I just called Dina, who works in one of Harrahs's lounges, and asked her what I couldn't get wrong, and she tells me martinis—only three ingredients: vodka, olives, and brine from the olives."

"Should we drink to something?" Will asks, standing.

I rise from my chair. "I would say to your marriage, but that already looks perfect. Prosperity? You have that going for you, too, in more ways than money."

"Let's drink to you and Carter finding the same," Sandy says.

"Sandy!"

"I'm sorry, Mr. Burke, Arthur, but things are pretty messed up, aren't they? Isn't that why you're here?"

"Honey," Will pleads. "I'm afraid my wife has a way of cutting to the chase."

"No, it's okay. She's right. That is why I'm here. You have something important to tell me, or you wouldn't have called. I hope something that will help both Carter and me."

"It was me who insisted he call," Sandy says. "From what

I've read and pieced together, she's deceiving both you and herself."

Nineteen

KIMI—MONDAY NIGHT

It's seven p.m. I'm in my pajamas, on the couch. I've pulled out the CD, *The Muted Girl,* which I packed in the suitcase with my books, and have placed it in the player. I'm rewatching it for probably the hundredth time. A knock on the door startles me. I push my uneaten dinner aside on the coffee table. I run to the door, thinking it's Arthur. He's returned from his trip and has come straight here from the airport to surprise me.

Even though Arthur is used to my scars, out of habit, I retrieve my veil from the table, placing it loosely over my head. I open the door, ready to fall into Arthur's arms. It's Mrs. Bell.

"May I come in?" she says all bright and cheery.

I want to say no, but maybe she bears news from Arthur, although I don't know why he wouldn't be calling me himself. Then I think it might be bad news. I do my best to hide both my anxiety and disappointment.

"Of course," I say. She stands rather awkwardly, so I offer her a seat.

"I love that movie," she says.

If she had bad news to report, she wouldn't be so casual,

commenting about the movie. I grab the oversized remote and mute the volume.

"Is there some reason for this visit, Mrs. Bell?"

"No, I check on all our residents."

Why do I think she checks on me more than others? But I don't voice this thought.

"I'm doing fine. No need to worry."

I think this statement will end the visit, but she remains seated. A secret part of me is glad. I'm lonely. I hear all the activity in the hallway, the laughter, and sometimes arguments below my balcony, and I wonder why I punish myself like this. What is the point? How will it change anything? I'm like one of those monks who practice self-flagellation.

"Connor Scott, one of my mother's favorites," she says.

"My mother loved him too," I say.

"So good-looking, even in his later years."

She looks at me as if probing, trying to glean some information. I remain silent.

"Do you know the actress Carter Hudson?" she asks.

"No, why would you think I know her?"

"I don't know. Perhaps because you seem so close to Mr. Burke."

"He's my attorney," I say.

"He's also her husband."

"They're divorced, you know."

"Yes, I'm sorry. I didn't mean to pry. I just thought..." She looks down at her lap.

We both sit quietly for a while. I unmute the DVD player, and we watch the scene where the father, played by Connor Scott, and the daughter, played by Carter Hudson, argue—him, in an angry voice, her in inaudible sounds, using sign language.

I want to tell Mrs. Bell how hard that part was. I coached Carter every step of the way except while on set. I could hardly be seen there. Pulling off this strange role took much more talent than a mere observer could ever realize. Learning sign language was the most difficult. Of course, Connor had to learn it, too. I want to tell her who I really am, but I keep my reserve. If I were to divulge I'm Carter Hudson's sister, the one she kept secret for all these years, I'm not sure what her reaction would be. Possibly, she already knows. I don't know what Arthur has told her.

"Do you like old movies?" she asks.

"Old? I guess this movie is old."

"It came out in the eighties, didn't it? Wouldn't you consider it an old movie? Well, certainly not as old as movies like *Casablanca* or *The Wizard of Oz*. Those were the classics. I think this one will be a classic, too, don't you think?"

I realize I'm probably ten years older than Mrs. Bell. Possibly, it's the lighting, but she looks younger than I first estimated. I remember Connor explaining the miracle of good lighting on a movie set.

I nod. "Yes, this movie will stand the test of time."

I wonder why she is here so late. Doesn't she have a family to go home to? But I say nothing. If she were to open up about her life, it might tempt me to do the same.

I stay on the subject of Connor Scott. "When I was young, still a teenager, and even into my early twenties, I used to go on the Hollywood bus tours. I saw his house once."

"So then, you weren't always like this?"

"Like this?" I remember my disfigurement and put my hand up to my veil.

She changes the subject from my face. "I've lived here all my life and have never been on one."

I remain silent, my eyes on the television screen. I sense her eyes are on me.

"Stars are just humans like us. He's no different. We all have our flaws and inner demons," she says, rising from the chair. "Don't get up. Finish your movie. I just came to check on you."

I watch as the door closes behind her. I wonder what made her say what she did.

I can't help but think back to the first day Carter related seeing Connor on the set of *The Muted Girl*. He had his back to her. The director was talking with him as if he were an old buddy.

When he saw me walk in, he directed Connor to turn around. "Connor, I want you to meet the leading lady, Carter Hudson."

She was so nervous that her legs felt like jello.

"Kimi, he took my hand and looked directly into my eyes. A Hollywood icon, the man on the covers of the magazines our mother used to bring home, the man she swooned over."

"It's so nice to meet you, Miss Hudson," he said.

Carter and Arthur were engaged at the time but not married. Connor, who was playing her father, was forty-seven, twenty-three years her senior. The hairstylist had taken careful pains to get the gray just right in his hair to make the role more convincing. Part of Connor Scott's attraction was his youthful look.

"Kimi, he stared at me differently than most men. He never once came on to me the way other men did, regardless of their age. There was this connection between us that I can't explain. He watched out for me."

I eject the DVD and turn off the television. I look at my phone. I am tempted to try Arthur, but the last few tries have said either the call can't be completed or I get his voicemail. I put my uneaten food down the garbage disposal, rinse my dirty plate and glass, leave them in the sink, take a sleeping pill, and head to my bedroom to stare at the blank walls before drifting off.

Twenty

ARTHUR—MONDAY NIGHT

Will's cell phone goes off. "Sorry, I thought I turned the damned thing off." Nevertheless, he looks at it, tilts his head, rolls his eyes in annoyance, and says, "I guess I better take this. Excuse me."

He heads off down the hallway, leaving Sandy and me alone. I'm eager to know what she meant by this deception, but I think I should wait, at least until the three of us are in the room together again.

"It's a council call. Will's on the tribal council. There are only twelve members. It's a great honor for him. He takes his job seriously."

I lift my head in a nod. "Yes, he seems to be influential here."

"Among our tribal community, he is."

"What does a tribal council do? I'm afraid I'm ignorant about such matters."

"Yes, I guess, being a lawyer, this would interest you. Basically, they oversee anything that has to do with the members of our tribe, like planning, business, lands, community services, manpower, investment, education, and housing.

The members are elected and serve for two years. They have the power to legislate laws and solve disputes among our people."

Typically, I would excuse myself from dinner, seeing something important has come up, but I can't leave being so close to the truth. Sandy wants to clue me in on something, possibly one of the missing puzzle pieces to Carter. I fear there is more than one puzzle piece missing.

Will winds down his conversation. I hear him say, "Okay, first thing tomorrow morning." A pause. "Yeah, I'll meet you there at eight sharp."

He looks at me while reentering the room. "Sorry about that," he says, slipping his phone into his back pocket.

"A council call?" Sandy asks.

"What else?"

"Is it about that kid who robbed the convenience store?"

"Who else?" he says.

"I hope it's nothing urgent," I say.

"No, this kid has been an ongoing problem. His father is the chief."

"Oh, I wasn't aware—"

"We still had chiefs?"

"Well, yes."

He laughs. "We do our best to maintain our customs while fitting into the white man's world."

How often have I heard Carter referring to my world as the white man's world?

The subject changes quickly as Will directs me to a seat while Sandy saunters to the kitchen.

"Casino dollars have changed everything for our tribe, even the area. Still, we work hard to maintain the old ways."

Sandy calls out from the kitchen, asking if iced tea is okay to drink. She brings two drinks out, garnished with spearmint.

"I bet you grew this in your garden."

She smiles. "We grow all our herbs, well, mostly what's native to our area. Mint grows like a weed."

She retreats into the kitchen to finish the food preparation.

"We exist on tourism, and lucky for us, beautifully maintained business landscapes appeal to tourists. But since I was growing up, tourism has been the driving force here. You may have noticed all the restaurants and souvenir shops driving into Cherokee," Will says.

"Yeah, they crowded both sides of the road."

"I worked in one of them after graduating high school. I saved enough money to take horticultural classes, my chief love. It's how we met."

"Yes, Arthur," she says, setting a plate of fish on the table. She slides the flower arrangement to the side so as not to block our view from each other. She angles knives on two of the corners where it had been sitting.

"Some Cherokee custom?" I ask.

"No, it's just that this is Allison's masterpiece, and every time she comes over, she checks to ensure I haven't damaged it."

"Yeah, wonder where she inherited those scrutinizing eyeballs of hers?" Will says.

"So, you weren't high school sweethearts. I mean, after Carter left here?"

"No, we didn't even go to the same school. Sandy moved here from Oklahoma."

I try to hide disappointment, thinking Sandy would be the one to spill everything she might have known about Carter.

"Sandy was taking the horticultural class as an elective. Her emphasis was on business."

"Good thing, too," Sandy says as she goes to the kitchen and returns with a flat cornbread and a salad, both new to me. "Will, here, is logical and creative, with ten green fingers, not just a green thumb, but when it comes to business, well, that's where I come in."

"I think you are a perfect pair," I say.

"Please, help yourself, Arthur." She passes me the plate of fish. "Trout. Will caught it this weekend."

"You have time to fish with your business, gardening, and council work?"

"Oh, I make time to fish. Also, it's the time I spend with my son. I should have introduced you today. He was planting trees right alongside me today."

"That's great. I wanted children, but then Carter kept putting it off. Before you knew it, we missed our chance."

I hope this mention of Carter changes the direction of the conversation, but it doesn't. Any other time, this would have greatly interested me—I find myself strangely drawn into their culture, perhaps because it was hers too—but I fear getting caught up in a political conversation. I cringe at the thought of politics taking up the remainder of my dinner with them because politics is never clear-cut, and solutions are never reached. And it's not what I came here to talk about.

"Back in the day, people came here to have their picture taken with the world's most photographed Indian, Chief Henry. He would stand on corners, greeting tourists in a full headdress. Cherokees in this area have never worn headdresses. But it's what people expected. It's what they saw on westerns. It was the Plains Indians who wore them, not us. As you can see, chiefs hardly have the status of American presidents."

"Yeah, tourists would pay to have their picture with him. He also sold magnetic jewelry, which had a healing effect on the body, but it didn't heal his lung cancer. He died a few years ago," Sandy says.

"I'm sorry." I take a bite of the green salad on my plate. "This is interesting and good," I say. "What is it?"

"It's poke salad. Carter never made it for you? It's a weed.

Grows all over the place here. I've heard they're serving it in fine restaurants in New York now," Sandy says.

"Yeah, mostly, Cherokee has stayed afloat over the years with crafts and reenactments to satiate tourists. I remember Carter's mom, Kaya, made all kinds of crafts. Her baskets were fabulous, and she sewed."

Kaya. I don't admit that I didn't remember Carter's mother's name or that Carter never told me.

"Honey, didn't you tell me she also worked in a beauty shop?"

"Yeah, I think part-time. I don't know. It was so long ago."

"And didn't her dad work at Frontier Land?"

"Part-time." Will looks at me. "Wes wasn't one for work. He drifted from job to job, mostly sales jobs. He tried to farm but wasn't very good at it. He was rather pathetic. He was an alcoholic. A lot of Indians are, but especially back then."

"What's Frontier Land?"

"It used to be where the casino is now. When Frontier Land opened in 1964, kids could get in for a dollar. Wes snuck Kimi and Kachina in all the time, and sometimes me too, when he worked there. Even a dollar was scarce back in the day. It could buy sugar or flour and wasn't to be wasted on frivolities. Frontier Land was something in its day, at least to a kid. It covered 140 acres. You got into the park via a wood-burning steam train or a gondola. You got to explore Indian Territory, with over twenty Native American structures and war dance performances, Fort Cherokee, a huge replica of a frontier stockade, and Deadwood Gulch, a full mock-up of a hardscrabble 1860s Western town. Indians and cowboys. That's what made the town money back in the day. But it was all seasonal. In the off-season, we may have had three store-fronts open." Will laughs. "One of them was Bingo. Like Bingo was important.

"Even the tribal government would shut down in the off-season because they didn't have the money to pay employees.

"Frontier Land closed in '83. A water park took its place. I don't recall how long the water park lasted, but the casino opened in '97. Rosa works there."

"Rosa?"

"Our daughter. She works in one of the control rooms where they observe the gamblers. She has a knack for seeing things others don't see," Sandy says.

"Yeah, Arthur. She was born deaf. Because of this, she relies on her other senses, which she has perfected."

"Oh, I'm sorry."

"Thank you. She's perfectly healthy otherwise. It's her daughter who made the flower arrangement." She looks at Will. "Remind me to put it back after I clear the table later." She looks at me. "Her mom is working the early shift, so she'll come here for breakfast and catch the bus tomorrow morning. The first thing she does is inspect her flower arrangement. I think she is gearing up for Mother's Day.

"It was Rosa who alerted us to something about Carter. We were all watching an award show, and when we saw Carter, I couldn't help but tell her that her father once knew her."

"She couldn't believe it," Will says.

"Carter Hudson? You knew Carter Hudson, Dad?" she exclaimed in her facial expression while signing.

"Yeah, your old man went to school with her. But she was Kimi back then."

"Then why did that man whisper Kachina in her ear while they were walking up the red carpet?"

"Are you sure he didn't say Kimi?" Will asked.

"No, definitely, Kachina. His mouth wasn't fully up to her ear. He definitely said Kachina. Isn't Kachina, Hopi?"

"Yes, one twin had a Hopi name, the other a Cherokee name."

I'm shocked that she saw that. It makes me wonder how many other lip readers noticed it. I'm sure if any did who had been willing to share it, it would have been in the gossip rags. And Carter, who wanted that name secret, would have had a fit. I also wonder what else her daughter might have seen me saying, something she might not have wanted to repeat to her parents. I remember that night, well, barely. We had a few celebratory drinks before the ceremony.

"Why do you keep insisting she's Kimi if your daughter saw me whispering Kachina in her ear? And you said over the phone that only their mother could tell them apart."

"She was wearing a backless gown. Kachina had a big scar running across the right topside of her back and shoulder. I doubt if makeup or plastic surgery could have fully covered it. Growing up, she was always self-conscious about it. She got it falling off a rock cliff. I think we were twelve at the time. We liked to go out into the woods, climbing rocks and the like. Kachina fell off a pretty steep cliff one day. She could have died. Instead, she only got cut up pretty badly on one side. Maybe something could have been done about it today. The casino has helped us bring in a nice hospital, but back then, the only place to go was to Gatlinburg, and Indians weren't given priority. She always covered it up. It mostly ran down her right shoulder, if I remember correctly. It stood out, even at a distance."

"Tell me, if you know all this about her, how many others know Carter was one of the twins?"

"I doubt if anyone does but me. I was close to Kimi. In a way, I was to Kachina. All the guys at our school were, if you get my drift."

"Yes, I get your drift."

"Well, Kimi, as far as I know, left here as a virgin. I don't know; maybe the man who took her away changed all that."

"No, he didn't," I say, feeling a need to protect her.

"How about dessert?" Sandy jumps up from the table.

I'm not sure at this point if I can handle dessert. After hearing this, my stomach is a little unsettled, but I don't want to offend them, and I'm afraid if I refuse, the evening might come to an abrupt halt. There is still so much I want to know.

"It's rhubarb pie. Have you ever had it, Arthur?"

I smile, or instead try to, what they've just told me, stirring my ulcer to life. "No, I haven't."

"Is coffee okay with it?"

"Yes, black, if you don't mind."

She clears our plates and heads back to the kitchen.

"I'm sorry. All of this is a bit disconcerting," I say to Will.

We hear her phone go off while she's in there. She returns. "It's Allison. She has one of her headaches and needs me."

"You go. I'll get the desserts and coffee. I'll even clean up the kitchen."

She looks over at me. "I'm sorry, Arthur. She sometimes gets these, and—"

"No one can take them away like her nana," Will finishes.

I say I understand, even though this kind of family life is foreign to me. I barely knew my grandparents. They died while I was young, plus they lived abroad. I only ever met them twice.

I get up from my seat and thank her for the marvelous dinner.

She grabs her purse and heads out the door. I hear her car pulling out of the driveway. I head to the kitchen with Will. He cuts two pieces of pie, places them on mismatched plates, one with a chip, and pours the coffee into dissimilar mugs. I can see Sandy's disapproval in the form of a whack on the arm or something similar. I smile, thinking of this, and say, "It looks great."

We move back to the dining room table. After we're seated, I ask him if he knew Victor.

"No, he just showed up. We saw him hanging out around the school a few days before he went to their house. Didn't Kimi tell you anything about him?"

"Not much. Only that he deserted her on the outskirts of LA. She's always been reluctant to talk about that night."

"I have, too. It always gave me nightmares. Sandy insisted I tell her what was wrong. She didn't know I knew her until we watched television that night. I didn't like to talk about the fire. I probably would have never said anything, but when Rosa told us that, it slipped out that I knew her. I remember saying, 'Kachina, that's not Kachina. I can't remember the film she was up for."

"She was a presenter that night. The only award she was ever up for was *The Muted Girl.* She was only twenty-four then. Although she acted as if she didn't care, the loss devastated her."

"Anyway, Rosa, sixteen then, was watching with us and was already an expert at reading lips. We didn't have close captioning then."

"Will, you said her mother was still alive."

"Yeah, she survived the fire, just barely."

"Is she here, in Cherokee?"

"No, after she healed somewhat, she went back to Arizona, where she was from. She said she had nothing left here and wanted to return to her people."

"The Hopi."

"Yes, the Hopi."

"Carter told me she died."

"I'm sure she thought she did."

"I don't understand. Why didn't anyone tell her Kaya was alive?"

"Because no one but me knew Kimi survived the fire. At least, as far as I knew, no one else knew."

Connor knew. Somehow, he knew.

Twenty-One

ARTHUR—MONDAY NIGHT

Seeing my frustration, Will suggests we go outside for fresh air and enjoy the garden's aromas. "There's a full moon tonight," he says.

I haven't enjoyed a full moon for a long time, although I sense enjoyment is not necessarily the purpose. I get the impression that, based on what he's about to tell me, he needs to be outside howling at the moon as much as I do.

We sit on a bench in his garden. He pulls a beat-up pack of Camel cigarettes and a lighter from beneath a rock in the asparagus plot and offers me one. "Sandy hates asparagus."

"I quit smoking years ago," I say. Still, I take one.

"Yeah, me too, but sometimes I cave. Tonight is one of those nights. I wish I had more than a cigarette," Will says.

If I hadn't had to go through a TSA line, I might have been able to oblige him.

He takes a long drag on his cigarette and says, "Sandy would kill me if she knew I was smoking."

"Obviously, since you are hiding them under a rock in your garden."

He laughs and stretches one of his legs as if repositioning

his body will make it easier for him to tell me whatever he needs to say. I think he probably wishes he never made that phone call, but then, upon finding out it was Sandy who urged him to make the call, I'm sure she would have nagged him until he did.

"It was the night of their party, doubling as a Halloween and sweet sixteenth birthday party. I never even got to give her my gift. I spent a week making her a dream catcher. It's still in a box in my closet.

"I walked most of the way to their house. Some guys I had been with earlier dropped me off partway. I intended to get there early to help finish the decorations, but the guys I was with had something else in mind. If I hadn't been with them, I think I could have changed some things. Maybe Kachina might still be alive.

"A storm came up suddenly. It wasn't in the forecast. There were multiple lightning strikes and thunder loud enough to shake the ground. One of the lightning strikes hit the barn, but not right away.

"Kimi told me a day earlier about Victor, that he wanted to take her and Kachina to California. I asked her what she was going to do. She told me she was thinking about it, but Kachina planned to leave with him. She had a bag packed and hidden under her bed. Kimi swore me to secrecy. She made me promise, Arthur. I regret I kept that promise. I regret a lot of things about that night.

"Kimi was still fuming because the drama teacher had given Kachina the part of Frankenstein's monster. She could have a temper sometimes."

"Tell me about it. Did Kimi and Kachina not get along?"

"Oh, no. They were best friends. Except for the scars on Kachina's back, they were perfectly identical in looks. In personality, they were as different as night and day. Kimi was the smart one. Everyone expected her to leave the reservation one day to make something of herself. Who would have thought she would have gone so far?"

I wanted to say it wasn't without costs, but I didn't want to interrupt.

"Kachina had trouble in school. I know Kimi did a lot of her homework. In retrospect, I think she resented Kachina for a lot of reasons. Kaya held Kimi up to higher standards than she did Kachina. With Kachina, she let everything slide.

"I've built up a good life. I love my wife, my kids, and my grandchild. I might have been able to put that night behind me if she hadn't become so famous. You go into the drugstore, and every other magazine has her on the cover. They provide a constant reminder.

"Kimi worked hard on that costume. The only aspiration she ever had was to be an actress. If there was anyone who could leave the reservation and make that fairytale come true, it was Kimi. When we were growing up, it was rough living here. Life has been a lot better since gambling became legal. People have jobs. Oh, there's still unemployment and now drugs, but that's true all over.

"It was a dry storm—no rain. Only horrendous thunder and lightning that lit up the sky like it was daylight. I started running toward the barn, thinking a downpour might let loose any moment, but it never did. I was maybe one hundred yards away when I saw Kimi. She was wearing the monster costume and carrying a lantern. From that distance, I wouldn't have been able to tell it was her, especially in the costume, but she told me she planned on wearing it that night. She told me she planned on giving the performance of her life."

"She caught the barn on fire, didn't she?"

"Initially. At least that's my conclusion since I saw flames coming from the barn when she reappeared outside, no longer carrying the lantern."

"Are you saying that lightning never struck the barn?"

"No, it did, but the flames were well underway before the lightning hit the barn. All I know is that she was walking toward the barn, carrying a lantern. Moments later, I see a flame. It came from the barn's entrance, where Kimi was standing. She comes running out of the barn screaming, beating sparks from her frayed pant leg, no longer carrying the lantern."

"Do you think she caught the barn on fire on purpose?"

"You don't know how often I've struggled with that question. I only know how mad she was that her sister got the part. I want to think it was an accident. A horrible accident. Anger can cause us to lose all sensibility. It's like the story of the two wolves."

"Two wolves?"

"Yes. It's a Cherokee legend—at least, it's attributed to our people. A boy came to his grandfather because another boy had done him an injustice, and he was angry. The grandfather explained to his grandson that two wolves were fighting within him. One is good, and one is bad. The good one lives in harmony with nature and those around him. He lets things slide off his back and only fights when necessary. The bad wolf is always angry, seeing everything as an insult, and always prepared to fight. The grandson took a moment to reflect on this. At last, he looked up at his grandfather and asked, "Which wolf will win?" The old Cherokee gave a simple reply. "The one you feed."

"Carter has been feeding the wrong wolf ever since I've known her, not because of anger but because of guilt. The night of her forty-ninth birthday party, I think she was trying to release that guilt. I should have been there for her, but she had said something to me, something I took the wrong way, and the angry wolf in me took possession. I stormed from the house. Do you know she had the house decorated like a barn?"

"Yes, Sandy brought home a newspaper with the article on the front page. CARTER HUDSON THROWS PARTY ENDING IN DISASTER. I read it, went into the bathroom, and threw up. That night, I told Sandy the whole story."

"Tell me, Will. What do you think she was trying to do this past Halloween? Do you think she intended to set herself on fire?"

Will shakes his head and pulls back his extended leg. "I don't know, but it's what I suspected."

"She could have killed everyone there," I say.

"Yeah, that crossed my mind—many times."

"I'm afraid everyone else did as well." I finish my smoke, stomping my butt into the ground, and carefully place it under the rock. Will's somber countenance lights up briefly into a smile. "You know, there was all kinds of speculation why she chose that theme. I knew about the fire and thought she was acting that night out, but to what end, I didn't know. She wouldn't talk about it to me. I seriously doubt she confided anything to her therapist. As far as what happened thirty-three years ago, to my knowledge, only one person and I knew some of what happened, if you don't count Victor. Reporters hounded me. I had no answers for them when I couldn't avoid them. Other than Carter, you're the only eyewitness."

Will does the same with his cigarette, placing the dwindled butt under the rock, stretches out his other leg, and continues, "A few seconds later, another flash of lightning lit up the sky. I heard a loud crash. I knew it hit the barn on the other side. When I got closer, I saw that the whole side of the barn had collapsed. Both entrances were blocked. I was shouting Kimi's name, but with the thunder and the roar of the fire, she couldn't hear me, or maybe she was in too much shock to hear me. She runs to the back of the barn. I figured she was going to climb the ladder back up to the loft. Other than part of the front, it's the only part of the structure that still hadn't caught fire. I think she thought she might be able to save her family from up there.

"There's another crash. This time, it's the front, the part I was running toward. I see Kimi running back around. She's standing there, her mask now off. Her face registers utter horror, and I'm sure mine does too. I'm trying to get to her. I'm still about fifty feet away. Blazing chunks of timber, most of which are already rotten, are falling from all sides. The heat is overwhelming. I had never seen a fire catch so fast, but that old barn was on its last legs. Wes was about as good at carpentry as he was at gardening. He always used discarded wood to repair, but then, he couldn't afford to buy new lumber.

"A car speeds past me, throwing a cloud of dust into the already overwhelming heat and smoke. I see it's the Victor guy. He doesn't see me, but he sees Kimi, who is now standing at the edge of the barn, screaming and waving for him to stop. I see Kaya trying to crawl through part of the collapsed barn. I know Kimi sees neither her mother nor me. Kaya appears to be stuck. So, I run toward her instead. I'm pulling her through, dragging her body over the charred wood."

Will lifts one of his arms toward me. "Burns from that night. I always told Sandy it was cigarette burns that happened during a drunken spree. I came clean the night I confided about the fire. It's nothing serious. I didn't go to a doctor. I just used some herbs my grandmother gave me. The scars serve as a constant reminder of that night, not that I need a reminder. Anyway, Kaya's on her stomach and coughing really bad. I turn her over and see half of her face looks as if it's melted. On top of everything else, I'm trying not to puke. I pull her away from the fire, which is spreading like crazy. Sparks are shooting out, and I think the entire field will catch. I'm coughing from all the smoke myself. At the same time, I'm trying to comfort Kaya. I look up and see Victor's car leaving with Kimi in the backseat.

"By now, other cars were pulling up, some coming to the party, others who saw the blaze and smoke and came to see what was happening. It was the end of October—off-season. There were no tribal police or firefighters. I couldn't have even called anyone. The Ahokas didn't have a phone. Not too many people on the reservation did then. It was 1977. Someone in town must have called the police and fire department in the next town. Smoke filled the air. An ambulance followed not too far behind them.

"Kaya was listed as the only survivor. The ambulance drove off with her."

Will kicked his foot against the dirt.

"I should have spoken up about seeing Kimi leave. I don't know why I didn't. I thought it would break Kaya's heart if she knew Kimi was the one who had caused the fire and that she had left, abandoning her family. I was a scared seventeen-year-old kid, much like Kimi. I'm a parent now. I know it wouldn't have mattered. A parent only wants their child alive.

"I thought about going to the hospital later and telling her. I heard she was in there for months because the burns were so bad. Then I went away to school and met Sandy. I wanted to forget the whole thing. I didn't even know what happened to Kimi. It wasn't until I was married that I saw her in that movie, *The Muted Girl.*

"I asked around town about Kaya. She was in an Asheville hospital for a long time. Someone told me that after she was released, she left for Arizona to be with her people, the Hopi. I married Sandy not too long after that—six weeks after meeting. I thought marrying and starting a family would put the fire in the past, and for a while, it did. Almost immediately, Sandy became pregnant with Rosa. We had our hands full with her being born deaf. Within another year, Sandy was pregnant with our son.

"I wanted to do the right thing but had a family to worry about. Time passed. When Sandy read about the episode this past Halloween—about the party Carter gave—I told her what happened that night—what I just told you. She insisted I contact you."

We sit in silence. I'm in shock, and Will has tears running down his cheeks. I want to cry, but I'm numb. A part of me wants to go somewhere other than LA and live out the rest of my life in seclusion, but then I think about all the times I've disappointed my father. I had run away from every difficult situation in my life until Carter.

"What will you do now, Arthur?"

"I guess I will try to find her mother if she's still alive. The only thing I know for sure is that I won't desert Carter, or Kimi, or Kachina, whoever this woman is that I've loved since the day I met her."

I stand. "Tell Sandy how great the meal was. I thank you both for everything. For this." I hug Will and head back to the hotel. I hope I can sleep. I'll figure out my next step in the morning.

Twenty-Two

KIMI—TUESDAY MORNING

I'm back on the farm where I grew up, and Arthur is with me. It's strange seeing him here, but I feel comforted he is. He holds my hand as we walk through the house. It's so tiny. I see cracks in the floor, exposing the dirt beneath. How could the four of us have possibly lived here?

I call out, "Mama, Papa, Kachina." No one answers. We are in the kitchen. There are plates on the table but no food. "Arthur, there are only four plates. They didn't know you were coming." I rub my finger over the dish on the table where my mother used to sit. I look to see it covered in dust. The dust turns to soot. It is the same for my father's plate and Kachina's. But my plate is clean.

We walk outside, dodging a mean rooster. The barn still stands. We walk inside. My parents and Kachina, all sitting on hay bales, look in our direction. In unison, they say, "We've been waiting for you."

I look at Arthur, who dissolves before my eyes into nothingness. I look back in my family's direction and see they have done the same. I run back into the house to see Victor sitting in my chair. He laughs and laughs. I run back outside to see the barn's smoldering remains. I'm all alone.

I wake, drenched in sweat. My first impulse is to push one of the buttons or pull one of the strings for help. Perhaps if I do, Luke will come. I'm being foolish. It was only a dream— one of many over the years I thought I had left behind by coming here.

Rupert, the rooster's name, pops into my head. I remember my father telling me he named him after a mean white man he knew. One day, the rooster attacked Kachina. Our father picked him up, broke his neck, and we had him for dinner.

I reach for my phone on the nightstand. Eight a.m. No messages or calls from Arthur. I won't call again. If this is what he wants, so be it. I rise, shower, and think I might go downstairs again, but I remember reading in the manual that breakfast is buffet-style. So, I call and see about having something sent up to my room.

By the time I've showered and dressed, Luke arrives with croissants, coffee, and orange juice. He places everything on the kitchen island. I hope the visit is only social, but his nurse bag hangs over his shoulder.

"I thought we might check your blood pressure while I'm here.

"If that's what it takes to get you to stay," I say.

He smiles. Dimples melt into the stubbles on his face. I know this is the style for a lot of men today. Luke epitomizes its appeal. His face could be on a billboard.

He pulls out a blood pressure cuff. "If you don't mind rolling up your sleeve?"

"Does it matter which arm?"

"Which do you prefer?"

I roll up my left sleeve, not wanting to reveal the scars on my right side. As I do, my veil slips slightly, and I jerk.

"It's okay," he says. He stares as if he recognizes me.

I pull the veil over the right side of my face more securely.

"Hey, listen, you don't need to wear that around me. Your secret is safe."

"I don't know what you're talking about," I respond.

He is pumping the cuff tighter. He releases it. "It's 140 over 80."

"What should it be?"

"The top number is a little high, but it's understandable. I'm afraid I agitated you a little. We'll retake it after breakfast."

"You mean you're staying."

"Of course."

I take a sip of coffee and a bite of croissant. I see he's brought two. I hand one in his direction.

"No thanks. I've already eaten. I won't tell you what you missed out on at the breakfast bar."

"Luke, I've been thinking. I used to paint. I need something more to occupy my time. If I write out a list of supplies, can someone bring them to me? I'm so used to having Arthur take care of all of this for me, but I haven't..." I hesitate, not wanting to know the man who brought me here dropped me off like an orphan child. "Well, he's out of town on business, and it's taking longer than expected."

"Sure, get me a list. I'll give it to Mrs. Bell."

I finish one croissant. "I'll leave the other for later."

"Did you hear about Frank Bellamy?"

"Frank Bellamy?"

"I guess you haven't had a chance to meet many of the residents yet."

"There was a Frank in the dining room at lunch the other day. He was worried about his grandson, who was in rehab."

"Yeah, that's the one. I'm afraid he had a heart attack last night."

"Was it serious?"

"Sadly, he died."

"Oh, that's too bad. I guess that happens a lot here."

"Actually, not as often as you would think, considering the age of most of the residents."

"You take good care of them," I say.

"I try to." His dimples are more pronounced with this smile.

"Tell me about yourself."

"I guess the biggest thing in my life is that recently, I got engaged," he says.

"Oh, who's the lucky girl?"

He laughs. "You mean lucky man. His name is Clark." He pulls out his phone and shows me a picture they posted on Instagram.

I try to act casually upon hearing he is gay, but then it figures. He is so easy to talk to. Carter was always telling me who was and who wasn't. "People used to keep it a secret for fear it would ruin their career. No more," she said.

"He's a good-looking man," I say.

He sees the time on his phone and frowns slightly. "I have to be upstairs in thirty minutes. He can be a bear if you're late."

"You know him?"

"Not really. He's a hard man to get to know." Luke laughs. "The staff, including Mrs. Bell, refer to him as the man in the high castle."

"I don't understand," I say.

"You know, the Philip K. Dick book?"

"I haven't read it."

"It's a sci-fi classic."

"I've never really been into sci-fi. That's what you like to read?"

"Yes, I'm a big Philip K. Dick and Issac Asimov fan."

He pulls his blood pressure cuff back out and places it

around my arm. While he's pumping it up, I say, "Can you tell me his name?"

The pressure releases. He looks. "The top number went down a bit. It was my fault. I got you all excited."

"I think you probably excite a lot of women *and men*, but I think you're changing the subject, Luke."

"You know it's against the rules, Miss Stone."

"Kimi, remember."

"Okay, Kimi. You know it's against the rules." He puts the blood pressure cuff back into his bag, stands, and hangs it over his shoulder, ready to depart. "He'll ask if I've seen you this morning," he says before turning to leave.

"And will you tell him speaking about the residents is against the rules?"

With his back to me, he says, "Rules don't apply to him," and walks out.

Why would he want to know if Luke has seen me?

Twenty-Three

LUKE—TUESDAY MORNING

I could kick myself for saying what I did before leaving. I
didn't even turn around to see her reaction. Something
about this whole situation doesn't sit right with me. If she
should repeat this to someone else, especially Mrs. Bell, I could
lose my job. But I don't think she will. I think I can read
people fairly well.

I'm sure I look mopey, perhaps hostile, when I run into
Mrs. Bell in the hallway.

"Aren't you supposed to be on the third floor now?" she
asks. She doesn't say it in a reprimanding way. I think Mrs.
Bell is a good person. She's here to serve everyone, but more so
him than anyone.

"That's where I'm headed," I say.

"Is everything okay, Luke?" We both stand in front of the
elevator. She waits for me to press the button because we are
going in opposite directions. She's eager for me to get up there
to him. He puts everyone around him on edge, especially his
assistant. Kyle needs to find an outlet, a way to chill. I hear
Kyle's been by his side forever.

From what I've read about Scott, he's an okay guy, but his

cocktail of medication has side effects. Some aren't pretty. Getting off even some meds won't be easy. That is supposed to be what I'm here to help him do. I had put on my resume that besides my nursing degree and a minor in psychology, I had a background in naturopathy. That was my initial instructions, but somehow, things have subtly changed. He's used to having everything right now. He has little patience. This restlessness he's exhibited since she moved in only exacerbates the situation. It has something to do with her. Yet, she doesn't seem to have a clue as to his identity.

Although I see other residents briefly, my main focus is to be on him and her.

I lie to Mrs. Bell. "Everything is fine. I'll take the stairs. I could use the exercise."

"I should take the stairs myself." I watch as she presses the elevator button and says, "Maybe tomorrow."

Trying to convince Mrs. Bell that I love what I do and don't question the changes in my job description, and I suspect nothing strange is going on, I practically sprint down the hallway to the stairwell. Still, when the door closes behind me, I stop, pressing my back against the metal. I take in a deep breath and let it out. I know who she is. Most of the staff know, yet all the files say she is Kimi Stone. Why is she using the name Kimi Stone, and why does she cover half her face and head with scarves and veils? She's only forty-nine. It's rare for anyone under seventy to be here. It has something to do with her breakdown that was spread across all the tabloids. Perhaps I could do my job better if I were privy to more information.

It's odd to see her without makeup, although I prefer it. In her movies and photos, it's thickly applied. Possibly, she thinks its absence adds to her disguise. She's beautiful without it.

And why is he so interested in her? And why am I suddenly her babysitter? I'm trained in geriatric nursing. Possibly, it's because I have a minor in psychology. More than likely, it's because she has taken a liking to me. Perhaps she has requested me. Possibly, they are both in on this together, but I don't think so. Like most people around here, she seems sincerely curious about the man upstairs. Even though I know his name and have seen some of his movies, I'm just as curious. What's the connection? What's his interest in her?

I'm just a naive gay guy from Idaho who doesn't have a clue. I met Clark, a struggling actor, online, fell in love, and now, I guess I'm here to stay.

I bang the back of my head against the door, take another heavy breath, and head up the stairs to his suite. I hope he's in a good mood.

Twenty-Four

ARTHUR—TUESDAY AFTERNOON

I hear banging. I realize someone is knocking on the door. Momentarily, I forget where I am. I yell, "What is it?" I feel drool coming from my mouth, running onto the pillow as I do.

"Maid service."

I open my eyes fully and see I'm in a hotel. The intricate designs on the burnt orange carpet become more in focus the longer I stare. It's slowly coming back to me, the trip, this whole last six months. I remember I'm in rural North Carolina, grasping for facts about an event that happened over thirty-three years ago. I've concluded the only one who can answer my questions is back in LA, where I left her. Her words, "The truth shall set you free?" keep playing over in my mind. I think it comes from the Bible. I didn't come from a family of churchgoers, nor did Carter, to my knowledge.

I yell, "Not now. Come back."

Last night, the bar was too tempting. On the drive back from Will and Sandy's, I replayed everything Will told me. Could Carter have set a fire intentionally? Would she even tell me the truth if I asked her? Not only has she harnessed the art of acting as a career, but she has it embedded in every fiber of her being.

I have to believe it was accidental—an accident that has messed her up more than I ever imagined—an incident so tragic that an adult couldn't overcome it with years of therapy, let alone a sixteen-year-old girl. Kachina, Kimi. She hid them under the guise of Carter Hudson as if a name change could erase the past.

Why had he never suggested hiring a therapist? There were tutors for her schooling, diction, and acting coaches when what she needed the most was a psychiatrist.

I grab my head. It's pounding. How I even made it to my room last night, I don't know. I suddenly remember a woman. She had long, dark hair like Carter's. Her face is fuzzy. I kept buying her drinks. "Oh, shit!" I rise suddenly and yank the sheets back. I sigh in relief to find I'm the only one in the bed. One more complication is all I need.

Oh, my God, I hope I didn't talk about Carter to her. I squint at the clock to see it's almost noon. I've slept most of the day away. I had planned on trying to catch an early flight out of here. To where, I don't know. Either somewhere in Arizona or back to LA. That's what I was trying to decide at the bar.

The phone light is flickering away. Has Carter located me? Or worse, has he?

I hit the message button.

"Hi, Arthur, this is Will. I never got your cell number, so I called the hotel, and they directed my phone call to your room. I know it's late. They didn't say you had checked out.

"The thing is, Sandy came home and saw how upset I was. We talked until two in the morning. She said I need to go back to the scene of the fire. I've avoided that road since it happened. I always go miles out of my way, even if that road is a direct route to a job. I've run out of excuses. My son, who's often in the truck with me, thinks I'm crazy. He knows nothing about what happened.

"I thought you might like to see it, maybe get a sense of where they lived. I've heard the house is abandoned, crumbling to the ground.

"I guess the thing is, I don't want to go alone. Sandy would go with me. But you know Kimi, and Sandy only knows her from me and the movie magazines.

"If you could—"

Beep

Will's all about long messages.

I glance at the clock again and see it's 12:30. My head hasn't let up. I open the refrigerator and pull out a small can of tomato juice. It doesn't matter that it costs seven dollars. I gulp it down. I pull out a second one. I pop four ibuprofen in my mouth with this one.

I don't know why the thought of visiting the scene where all this happened didn't occur to me. Possibly, I'll get some psychic download from it. Carter might say precisely that, but I don't believe in such things.

I grab my wallet from the dresser to pull out Will's card. I remember him saying it has his cell on it. When I do, I see my watch lying beside it. She gave it to me for our first anniversary. She said she could afford to buy me an expensive gift after making *The Muted Girl*. I promised her that this would be the only watch I would ever wear, and I've kept that promise. I knew it wasn't expensive but didn't say anything. She had no idea how much money she made on the movie and thought a five-hundred-dollar watch was extravagant. She hadn't a clue about money. I knew she didn't have it growing up, and I've handled everything since she was sixteen. She almost fainted when I told her how much they paid her for the movie.

"That much, Arthur?"

"Yes." I laughed. "You're rich."

Immediately, she wanted to return the watch for one that cost ten times as much, but I told her no, I made a promise—that night ended in ecstasy.

I punch in Will's number.

"Catawnee Landscaping."

"Will, it's Arthur."

"I thought you didn't want to go, that maybe you might have caught a plane home."

"No, I'm actually just waking up. I stopped at the bar last night and woke up just a few minutes ago with a wicked hangover. I haven't had one of these in a long time."

"The last time I had one was before I met Sandy."

"You're lucky. Do you still want to go? I don't know why I didn't think of asking last night. I can get ready in thirty minutes if you can get off work for a while."

"You forget. I'm the boss."

"Where are you?"

"Outside the casino, planting some bushes. It's close to the same spot I was at yesterday. Wow, a lot has happened in less than twenty-four hours."

"I'll say. I'll be down in a jiffy."

Twenty-Five

LUKE—TUESDAY MORNING

I hold my fist in the air for a second before knocking. My knuckles are against the door when Kyle opens it.

"We've been expecting you," he says.

"How is he?" I ask.

Kyle shakes his head. "I'll sum it up in one word: agitation. But I'll let you see for yourself. He's been eager to see you all morning."

I stand in the doorway of his bedroom. Dr. Ferguson stands at his bedside, his stethoscope out with the diaphragm against Mr. Scott's heart. He removes the earpieces. "Your heart's strong," he says.

"Just not the rest of me, Doc," he says.

"As long as you keep taking your medicine, we can slow the progression of the disease down."

Dr. Ferguson and I are on different paths regarding this. From what I understand, he's been doling out medication to the stars for so long that it's become mechanical for him. He knows no other way.

"I feel my body is eating itself from the inside out. Death

will be a blessing, but there are some things I have to take care of before I die. Things I have to rectify."

He looks over and sees me standing in the doorway.

"Luke, you're here. Good!"

Dr. Ferguson puts his stethoscope back into his bag and closes it up, nodding at me. "I'll check in downstairs and give you my report. Otherwise, I'll return next Tuesday unless you need me before then."

Dr. Ferguson, a squatty little man whose bad posture only emphasizes it, nods again as he walks past me and out the door. I'm reminded of Toulouse-Lautrec carrying paints and brushes in his black bag instead of a blood pressure cuff, stethoscope, and thermometer. Checking downstairs? At first, I think of Mrs. Bell, but then I wonder if he means Kimi. I'm pretty sure Dr. Ferguson saw her when she first arrived.

I walk over and stand by Mr. Scott's bedside. His dog, Bear, which looks the part, lies on his bed on the floor beside him. It would be hard to pin down any particular breed since Bear resembles a mixture of everything imaginable, possibly including bear.

While pets at The Woodlands aren't expressly forbidden, you need special permission to have one. The only other pet I've seen since I've been here is a Bichon Frisé dog that sits on Mrs. Bono's (no relation to Sonny) lap most of the day, watching soap operas with her. "This breed was a favorite of Italian royals," she said. I refrain from commenting on Italian's love of telenovelas.

Mr. Scott once told me Bear was what you call a rez dog.

"Rez dog?"

"It's what they call strays on reservations. Bear is my fourth rez dog."

"It's good you take them in," I said, for lack of anything better to say, not being an animal person.

"Kyle tells me you're agitated."

"I think you would be, too, if you knew you didn't have long but had so much to set right, if that is even possible. Not to mention having to deal with a frail seventy-seven-year-old body."

"Your mind is as sharp as ever," I say.

I wonder why I'm here, considering Dr. Ferguson just checked him over. I think sometimes he's lonely. He sees only a select handful of people, most of whom he's grumpy with. I heard he had a pleasant demeanor before the disease. The medications he's taking have some nasty side effects. I'm sure I'd be disagreeable, too, if I were on all those pills.

"Luke, I'm contemplating making another movie—something cultural, deep, and long-lasting. One that will hold up through the years, possibly taught in schools, like *To Kill a Mockingbird.* My next movie has to have significance and speak to people. What do you think?"

I immediately think of Clark, not that he's not already on my mind more than a dozen times a day. I'm dreaming. This isn't his type of movie. But if the opportunity should arise, I'll mention him to Mr. Scott. Clark couldn't believe it when I told him I attended Connor Scott daily.

"The star maker?" he exclaimed.

"The one and only, but you can't tell anyone."

When I started working here six months ago, Clark was on my mind nonstop. I had more time to think then. My duties changed when Mr. Scott moved in a little over three weeks ago. I told him right up front I was gay.

"Oh, so do you have a boyfriend?" This was right before Clark and I became engaged, both officially and unofficially, since we're still waiting for a law to be passed to marry legally. I was so lovesick at the time I told him Clark was a struggling actor.

"Oh? What has he been in?" he asked.

It surprised me he took an interest.

"At present, only some commercials, and he's done some modeling." I left out his stint in the porn industry, which he can't seem to break away from.

"You could model, you know, Luke."

"I'm only about helping people by being a nurse."

"I know, people like me, a geriatric. A word of advice, Luke. Never get old."

"I went into nursing because of my father."

"Yes, because he was a hospice patient while you were in college. You regretted not being there for him. And you went into psychology because you had a rocky relationship with him."

I must have a look of shock on my face at his bluntness. I wonder how he has this information. I stutter, "How did you—"

"Know?" he finishes. "It's easy to deduce. I didn't have you checked out if that's what you think. Not extensively, anyway. Of course, I read your resume before I had Mrs. Bell send you up to see me. I thought we had something in common, something a lot of men have in common—a need to please an overbearing father. But the first time I met you, I knew I wanted you as my nurse five minutes into the conversation."

He revealed this to me the first week I tended to him.

"Well, sir, I'm not in the movie business, but if you're going to make one, that would be the kind to make."

"Do you think I have the stamina for it? Do you think I have enough time left?"

"Honestly, Mr. Scott, I think it would be good for you."

He smiles.

Where Kyle sees agitation, I see someone getting a new

lease on life. I've been in nursing long enough to know someone driven by a desire to do something significant before they die has shaken off the illness and lived for years longer than expected.

Kyle likes everything as calm as possible. For everything to run smoothly with no disruptions or changes in plans. I've heard he's been with him since he was a kid. I figure he's got to be almost sixty by now, ready for retirement, but I'm sure he'll stay with him until the end.

"Have you seen Kimi today?"

I think he knows this already, but I respond, "Yes."

"And how was she?"

"Her blood pressure was a little up?" I probably shouldn't be giving out her medical information, but I'm sure he knows practically everything that goes on in this place, and saying someone had a high blood pressure reading is vague.

"Oh?"

"After she had breakfast, I retook it, and it had gone down."

"What do you think caused it?"

"I'm fairly confident it has something to do with Mr. Burke."

"Of course. Arthur." He scowls.

I shouldn't have mentioned his name. There is a definite change of mood, and not for the better. I know Arthur also has some connection with him.

I saw Arthur on this floor several times after Connor Scott moved in. I didn't know who he was. I thought he was some man who had business with Mr. Scott. Then I saw him again the day she arrived.

The staff was abuzz with whispers. "That's Carter Hudson's husband," they were all saying.

"Does she eat healthy other than poppyseed bagels or croissants for breakfast?" he asks, changing the subject to food.

I'm wondering how he knows what she has for breakfast.

"I only know she likes croissants. She has a lot of salads, too much tea, and not enough water. Yesterday, she requested a hamburger, fries, and an Orange Crush."

He laughs as if hearing something his grandchild did for the first time. I read his only son died in an auto accident years ago, right after he received the Oscar for *The Muted Girl*. It also won for best script, although the writer wished to remain anonymous. Connor Scott had a penchant for screenplays written by someone who wanted no credit. Most believed the scripts, which were beautifully written, were his own.

After losing his son, he quit acting and became somewhat of a recluse, but he still worked behind the scenes in the movie industry. Even though he refused interviews, that didn't stop tidbits about him showing up in gossip rags and actual news about his projects in more respectable mediums. They called him *The Star Maker*. Until a few years ago, he was still producing movies—the kind that got nominated for Oscars and sometimes won them, the ones coming from an unknown writer who wanted, for some reason, to remain that way.

"Did you see she got it?"

"Althea had the chef make it for her. I was taking a shortcut through the kitchen and overheard Althea telling one of the staff that Miss Stone wanted an Orange Crush. I sprinted down the street to the nearest convenience store and got her one."

"Good man!"

I omit the fact Althea told the chef little Miss Special had to have something that wasn't on the menu. "And to top it off, she wants an Orange Crush with her hamburger and fries," she said in a disgusted tone, like she was the one standing over a hot grill making it.

Chef Henry yells to one of the assistant chefs, "Charlie, see if we have some of that good steak burger on hand."

Charlie, unlike Althea, is all too eager to please, "Yes, sir."

Chef Henry, who doesn't care much for Althea, asks, "Does she want Orange Crush, the drink or the soda?"

"I don't know. I didn't know such a thing as an Orange Crush drink existed."

I pipe in, "I think the soda would pair better with a hamburger."

Henry laughs, his belly bouncing to the binaural beats of the music they pipe through this place to the point of stretching his white apron to its capacity.

His laugh tapers off, and turning back to Althea, he scowls. "Well, go back and see how she wants her hamburger cooked."

Althea snarls when she has her back to him.

I so want that woman fired, but I'm not the one to take her down. She's doing well enough on that front all by herself. Maybe I'll start a betting pool as to the day.

Mr. Scott laughs to the point of coughing. I help him sit up and give him a drink of water. "That's great, Luke. I know she likes you."

I realize Mrs. Bell must have told him she does.

"The feeling is mutual. Oh, she wants some drawing stuff. She said she would make a list. I told her I would get it to Mrs. Bell."

"Give it to Kyle, would you? Mrs. Bell has her hands full with the other residents."

"Sure," I say. "Mr. Scott, if there's nothing else, I have some other people I need to check on."

"Yes, yes, of course, but before you go, look in the desk drawer, the top one."

I go over and pull the drawer open.

"There's a script in there."

I see a thick manila envelope closed with a small red string. It appears to be the only thing resembling what might be a script. I hold it up and see a title scribbled across the backside. "*The Water Spider,*" I ask, holding it up.

"Yes. Please take it down to her. You can wait until you've tended to your other patients. Tell her it was left anonymously by her door, something like that. Don't tell her it came from me."

"Sir, she doesn't know who you are."

"And I don't want her to—yet."

"What if she doesn't want to read it?" I've seen Clark laugh at scripts he thought were stupid, toss them in the waste can, and then pull them back out. "Until something better comes along," he would say.

"She won't be able to resist the title."

"If you say so, sir. I'll check on you tomorrow."

As I leave, I hear him instruct Kyle, "Kyle, see to it the dining room adds hamburgers and Orange Crush to the menu. And find Arthur."

I walk down the hall with the script in my hand, wondering why he wants his identity kept secret from her and what connection her former husband has with him.

I look at the name on the manila envelope, *The Water Spider,* and think, what an odd name for a movie. They made a movie together, his last acting role. He's over twenty years her senior, which matters little in this town. Did they have an affair? According to Clark, many actors on movie sets do. He was married then, lost his son a short while later, and he and his wife divorced. A lot of couples do after losing a child. He never married again. Nor could anyone connect him with another woman, also according to Clark.

Twenty-Six

KIMI—TUESDAY AFTERNOON

Once again, I'm wearing the carpet thin. Luke can't just walk out on me like that, saying what he did. How often have I mentioned the man upstairs to him, or rather what he calls him, the man in the high castle? He usually only smiles as if his white teeth and sexy dimples get him out of any unpleasant conversation, and I surmise my questions about this man are unwelcome.

And sometimes, I think I hear a dog. I haven't seen one dog since I've been here. Maybe he's watching Lassie reruns. Arthur said people here were stuck in the black-and-white era.

I wonder what other people around here know. I also wonder why I'm so interested. If Arthur would only call, my mind wouldn't dwell on this mysterious man. He's a diversion, something to occupy my mind—something other than Arthur's absence.

I walk over and open the balcony doors. Instead of bothering with a veil, I stand with half my body behind the curtain. There is a table below on the poolside filled with people having lunch. One woman raises a glass that looks like iced tea, possibly Long Island tea, and says, "To Frank."

Everyone follows suit, toasting the man. Suddenly, I feel like walking around the pool for some fresh air.

Mrs. Bell looks at me strangely as I walk down the hall in shorts, flip-flops, and a hoodie. I keep pulling the hood to my nose to hide the damaged part of my face.

"Miss Stone?" Her mouth gapes open in surprise.

I say, "I'm going out to the pool," while I walk past her. I'm sure she has stopped in her tracks and is staring at my backside as I walk toward the doors leading to the patio.

I find a lounge chair not too far from the table roasting Frank. I want to listen in on their conversation. I'm still pulling the hood half-way across my face. I sense the occupants, four women and one man, staring at me. I don't know for sure, but their conversation has grown quiet. Possibly, they are whispering things. I look in their direction. They continue to stare, with no remorse at being found out. I guess honesty is one perk or curse of old age.

"What is that drink you're having?" I ask the woman who first raised her glass to toast Frank.

"It's Long Island Tea," she replies.

"I thought as much. How do I get one of those?"

The man at the table struggles to rise from his chair. The lady next to him grabs his arm and pulls him back down. He's barely made it two inches off his seat. She yells, "Derrick, we need another drink over here!"

Behind me, a young man in the same green polo shirt bearing The Woodlands logo and khaki pants appears. "Another tea, Mrs. Marcum?"

"Not for me. For her." She points to me.

"Right away," he says, trotting away.

"I'm Nancy Marcum," she says.

The other ladies introduce themselves, and the man says, "I'm Ralph Bellamy."

"Bellamy? Didn't..."

"Frank was my brother," he says.

"I'm sorry. I heard about his death."

"Thank you," he says. "He was my younger brother."

The woman, whose name I remember being Gloria, nudges him.

"Only thirty minutes younger. We're twins."

"I'm Kimi Stone," I say.

The women look sideways at each other like they don't believe me. I say, "Did you know that one in forty-two children are born a twin?"

Ralph says, "That many. Seems a lot."

"I know. I rarely ever meet twins," I say.

I remember reading that. Yet, growing up, Kachina and I were the only twins in school, and there were way over forty-two students.

"We weren't identical," he says.

"Those are even rarer. The odds of identical twins are one in 250."

"You're a fount of wisdom," Nancy says.

"I read a lot of books."

Derrick brings out my drink, pulls a table to the side of my lounge, and sets it on a napkin. I smile, thank him, and tell him I may need another one after finishing this one. I bring the straw to my mouth, holding the glass with one hand and my hood with my other.

They strike up a conversation with me, my first real one at The Woodlands, if you don't count Luke or Mrs. Bell.

One woman says, "Frank's wife was here with him, but she died a while back."

"Frank took it hard. They were together for forty-two years," Ralph says.

"Not quite forty-two," the woman says. "Candice died two days before their anniversary. Suddenly. Heart attack. Just like Frank. We were planning a big party for them, too. Such a shame she couldn't have lasted two more days."

Ralph rolls his eyes. "Are you still angry about not having the party?"

"I went to a lot of trouble to arrange it," she snaps.

"The staff went to the trouble, not you."

She looks my way. "You have to forgive Ralph. He's angry because his brother died."

"I'm not angry. I'm sad, Martha. There's a difference."

"Are you married, Ralph?" I ask.

"Not presently," he answers.

The same woman, who seems to be Ralph's nemesis, says, "Ralph, here, holds the record for the most marriages. Five."

Hmm, beat Carter by two.

"All exes. All still alive, too."

"Because they're all younger," Martha says. "Quite a bit younger," she adds with a roll of the eyes.

Ralph let it roll off like an old joke he'd heard too many times, something not worth attention. "None of them ever came to see me. When my doctor told me I could no longer live alone, I let Frank talk me into moving in here with him after Candice died. Now, I'm all alone again."

"You're not alone," Martha says, putting her hand over Ralph's arm and looking up at him with woeful eyes.

"Aren't you hot in that?" the woman dressed in all pink says, changing the subject. I've already forgotten her name, but I don't want to ask. Maybe I should bring up name tags to Mrs. Bell.

"No."

I take another sip with my head turned away from them. Another woman, I think Gloria, starts talking about her days as a concert pianist.

At three o'clock and four drinks later, I'm still sitting beside the pool. Derrick went off duty after two drinks; otherwise, he would have cut me off. The congregation at the table all left, one by one, talking about dinner as they moved like stalled traffic past my lounge chair. They only just finished lunch. Is that the life here?

The last two to leave are Ralph and Nancy; Ralph complains to Nancy about how Gloria brings up her days as a concert pianist in every conversation.

My legs look red. The thought of sunscreen never occurred to me. I realize I've been sitting in direct sunlight. How long has it been? I look at the empty glass beside me— the liquor. The drinks have numbed me to the sun shining directly on my legs.

I look over to see John, who replaced Derrick, taking away the plates Ralph and the others left behind.

I rise to my feet too quickly. I stumble. The next thing I know, I'm choking in four feet of water. As I'm coming up for air, I hear plates crashing on the Saltillo tiled patio. While drowning in embarrassingly shallow water, I'm hoping the tile didn't chip because, having it near the pool at home, I know how fragile it is.

I don't see lights, and I don't go through a tunnel. I see the double doors leading back into the building, and I'm being carried through them.

"Arthur?"

He doesn't answer. I open my eyes and see it is John who brought me my last two drinks. In a panic, I reach for my hood, which is nowhere to be found, at least not near my face, but I keep raising my hands for it to no avail. Then, my hands, my arms, and my whole body go limp, and everything goes black.

I wake up in my bed—not the one I've grown accustomed to over the years, but the one at The Woodlands, the one a maid comes in every morning to make up for me—the one Arthur doesn't share with me. I try to sit up, but strong arms push me back down.

"Easy now." I recognize Luke's voice.

"My head is splitting."

"I guess it would be after four Long Islands."

"I'm dry. I have a robe on." I look at him in surprise.

"You were soaking wet."

"But—"

"I'm a nurse, remember? Plus, I'm gay."

"I feel so—"

"Embarrassed," he finishes.

"Yes."

He laughs, and I do, too.

He hands me a manilla folder.

"What's this?"

"A script."

"Something your fiancé is looking at?"

"No."

"Why give it to me? I know nothing about scripts."

"Kimi, I think we know better." He sits on the edge of the bed beside me. "Please read it. For me."

I look at the title while he holds it up in front of me—*The Water Spider*.

"Who would give me this? Do you know what it means?"

"No, I don't."

"It's Cherokee. It's a story about the first fire."

"Interesting."

"Did Arthur leave this for me? Was he here while I—?"

"Passed out?" He shakes his head. "No, it wasn't Arthur."

"Please, Kimi, just read it." He lays it on my nightstand.

I guess I have nothing better to do.

Luke tucks me in and says good night. "Croissants or poppyseed bagels in the morning?"

"How—"

"Shh," he puts his fingers to his lips.

"Surprise me," I say.

"I expect you to tell me what this script is about in the morning," he says. "Promise?"

"Yes, I promise."

Twenty-Seven

ARTHUR—TUESDAY AFTERNOON

I sit in the passenger seat of Will's pickup truck as we drive past houses and mobile homes sparsely spread between fields of brittle grass shaking off the morning frost, each blade vying for the sun's warmth. Lines of trees sit back in the distance. Rusted vehicles, some with flattened tires and others on cinder blocks, line the roadway like scattered graves. I might comment if we weren't on a mission of self-reflection. I look over at Will, who sits with his back rigid against his leather seat, his knuckles turning white from his tight clasp on the steering wheel.

He slows. His fingers curl tighter around the steering wheel.

"It's right around this corner," he says.

I look up ahead. To the left, I see a pile of weathered boards rotting into the ground. The chaotic arrangement is about fifty yards back off the road, peeking through patches of taller grass than the rest of the field. Will pulls off the road, parks his truck a few feet into the open field, opens his cab door, and gets out. I follow suit.

We walk on hard ground and sweaty grass through the field.

"It seems so small," he comments.

"What's left of it, you mean?" I say.

"I suppose people have carried away the best boards, and someone has turned in the roof for money at a metal recycling place."

What he's talking about is out of my expertise.

"It's been thirty-three years," I say.

"It's honestly surprising to see this much left, considering how quickly nature reclaims dominance."

I remain silent as he walks around the residue of a haunted past. Charred pieces of wood, no bigger than my fist, and a few blackened rotted boards are all that remain. If I hadn't known otherwise, I would have guessed someone had built a huge bonfire here once.

He travels around in a wide rectangle, pacing off what he remembers as the outline of where the barn once stood.

"The barn had two wide openings, one on each side." He detours to the middle of his imaginary rectangle, pointing. "Over here was the side Kimi disappeared behind, the side I saw Victor follow her to. There was a ladder on the outside going up to the loft." Will walks to the other end. "Here is where Kaya escaped. There used to be a hole at the bottom at this end where water seepage from a broken gutter rotted the bottom boards. Wes always said he was going to fix the gutter and the hole."

"Lucky for Kaya, he didn't," I say.

"I guess his ineptitude paid off. Or not. Some people say it would have been better if she had died in the fire that night along with the rest of her family. What did she have to live for with her family gone, barely alive herself, mostly burned beyond recognition? Before the fire, she was as beautiful as her girls."

Will studies the minuscule pile of rubble that has all but become a part of the earth over the decades. Just a few rotted pieces of wood marking the spot of a tragedy thirty-three years ago. A chilly gust of air beats against our bodies as a couple of vehicles whip by us.

He nods his head upward toward the road. "Just beyond the hill lies a recently developed residential area. I have a client there."

"I see no signs of a house," I say.

We walk across the road and onto what once might have been a driveway. One deep rut makes the ground uneven. Another rut, higher up, runs parallel, indicating what once used to be a driveway. A clump of trees and brambles hide the remains of what had once been a clapboard house. One large oak tree and a smaller one have burst from acorns, overpowering and subduing the flimsy man-made structure.

An arm of a white plastic chair, now yellowed, sticks through the dirt and some tree roots. Half-rotted shingles, broken-up cinder blocks, and thin clapboard strips with flakes of dirty white paint crumble into the mixture of other house remains. An enamel kitchen sink, faded wallpaper glued to pieces of oak board, and piles of unrecognizable possessions mesh together in clumps. It reminds me of a tangled mess of Christmas tree lights that no longer work.

I fight off tears. I wonder how anyone could have lived in what I perceived the house might have originally looked like. But then, while traveling through Appalachia, I've seen similar dwellings.

"Do you think they were happy?" I ask.

"As happy as any family around here struggling to make ends meet. The four of them were together. That was a lot."

"You talked about Wes's drinking."

"Yeah, a lot of men drank. He was an okay guy, a good

husband, and a good father to the girls when he wasn't. That was about half the time. He wasn't a mean drunk."

"This is certainly different from how she lived as Carter Hudson."

"It looks like nothing now. But standing out in that field, for a moment, I could see it like it was yesterday. I could still hear the screams. They haunt me. It haunts me I ran. I didn't tell you that part. I denied being there, even though I knew some people saw me. I was always in trouble back then. Kimi wanted to date me because I had the reputation of being a bad boy. Kimi tried to emulate Kachina, who was popular with the boys. But she couldn't quite pull it off. I had been with Kachina. Most of the boys around here had. I never touched Kimi, well, in that way. Anyone who knew her could see the drive in her, the purity of her soul. I think she mostly lived in a fantasy world, though. She cut pictures of female actresses from her mother's movie magazines and taped them all over her side of the bedroom wall.

"Kimi was the most like her mother. A dreamer. But she had ambition. I think her mother convinced her she could be anything she wanted. Both girls were on their own a lot. Kaya was always working. Had to keep the family afloat. Wes wasn't much for work, but Kaya worked at a beauty shop, took on sewing jobs, and made baskets to sell in the craft shops. Her baskets were top-notch. It was a shame they all got destroyed in the fire. She used one stall of the barn as her workshop.

"She depended a lot on Kimi to keep tabs on Kachina. That girl could give promiscuity a good name. She bragged she couldn't get pregnant. It had something to do with her falling off the cliff that day. She had scars on the inside as well as on her back and shoulder.

"Sandy told me about *The Muted Girl* and insisted we see it. We were newly married, and I had just started the business. A movie wasn't in our budget, but she said we needed a night out. She told me the girl on the poster was beautiful and wanted to see it. Sandy was eight months pregnant with Rosa at the time.

"When I saw the poster for that movie, I couldn't believe it. I knew it was her right away. She was older, more developed, and wearing makeup with her hair all different, but I'd spent too much time with her. It was her, all right. I don't think anyone would know she was part Cherokee or part Hopi. Her look defied definition. Maybe exotic. That's the best word I can think of."

"Carter worked hard on that look. She stayed out of the sun, even though she loved to swim. She did all her swims at night. She said it relaxed her. When she swam and at night were about the only times I ever saw her without makeup. I always thought she was more beautiful without it. Even now. She wasn't wearing it when I first met her, but she was careful never to be seen without it after she started acting. 'All illusion, Arthur,' she used to say. Makeup turned her into someone she was not. Kimi never wears makeup."

"Sandy and I went to see the movie. I couldn't even tell you today what it was about. All I could see was Kimi. I watched every gesture, every muscle twitch. I closed my eyes sometimes to concentrate on her voice, or rather her grunts and strange pronunciations of words. I could relate to the overbearing father. I saw my father in him."

"I think a lot of us see that."

"I didn't tell you my father was once a tribe chief, did I?"

"No, you didn't."

"It was strange; the subject was about a deaf girl. Rosa wasn't born yet. When our child was born deaf, I thought it might be retribution or karma. Not so much from the running away part, but I might have somehow prevented the fire. I was supposed to have been there earlier to help with decorations."

"But wasn't part of it lightning? You couldn't have prevented that."

"No, but the lightning didn't strike the barn until after the fire from the lantern was well underway. I had gotten sidetracked. On the way there, I ran into a gang I sometimes ran with. We robbed a gas station that night. Like I said, I didn't have a good reputation.

"Kaya hated Kimi was seeing me. Even though she was in shock, she knew it was me who dragged her the rest of the way out of the barn. She looked up at me, one side of her face hideous. I don't even think she felt the pain. I can relate to how that might be now, being a parent. It's adrenalin. She said her daughters' names, then her eyes caught mine, and she whispered my name. Then she passed out.

"Not long after the fire started, it was a circus. Townspeople were coming to see where the flames and smoke were coming from. The police from the next town over were the first official ones to arrive. They were from the same town where the gas station was located. Another reason I hightailed it out of there. I feared they would think I might have had something to do with the fire or that they knew I was one of the boys who had robbed a gas station hours earlier. I ran into the darkness of the field and hid on the edge of the tree line. I watched the commotion. Finally, the paramedics arrived and were running toward her."

"How do you know she's still alive after all this time? She'd be in her late sixties, not that that's old, but considering all her injuries?"

"As of the Christmas before last, she was still alive. She sends me a Christmas card every year. Well, up until last year. I guess, in gratitude. She said she would keep my secret if I would keep hers. I suppose, in a way, they are one and the same."

"You have an address for her?"

"Not an exact one. Only a post office box number. It's postmarked from a tribal village in Arizona. Also, as of the Christmas before last, her mother was still alive—ninety-eight."

"Do you mean Carter's grandmother?"

"Yeah. From what Kaya wrote on the last card, she's one fierce woman. She's called Honovi. It means strong deer in Hopi."

The mountain wind blows through Will's hair, which he wears long today, while we stand by the house's ruins. A few of my speckled-gray strands whip across my forehead. I suddenly remember having an appointment at a lush spa in Beverly Hills for a trim and to have my nails done, which seems so mundane and superficial compared to this.

Every few minutes, a car or truck flies past us. My pants ruffle like a flag in the wind when they soar by. None of it is helping me digest what he is telling me. I can feel my ulcer. "Do you think we could sit in your pickup's cab?" I ask.

We walk back over, get in, and shut the doors we both left open.

"So, you are saying that you not only saved her mother's life but have also been in touch with her all these years."

"Yes."

"She knows her daughter, one of them, is alive?"

"I don't know, but I've always suspected she did."

"I don't understand."

"She never mentions either of them in the cards she sends. It's always a sentence or two, some generality about her life there, something about how different the weather is in Arizona, how, if truth be told, she preferred the mountain air. Sometimes, she would write Hopi verses; at other times, she would write Cherokee ones. Never once did she mention Kimi or Kachina, or even Wes."

"But when you wrote back to her, didn't you ask about Kimi?"

"No, I didn't know what to say, so I avoided it. I would tell her about my family, something always simple. I didn't know what had happened to Kimi after that night. For all I knew, that man Victor could have murdered her and buried her body somewhere in the desert, and no one would have been the wiser. I thought possibly one day, if she was still alive, she might return here, but then why would she? It would be nothing but pain for her. I didn't have a clue what had happened to her until I saw her picture on that poster with Connor Scott."

"Connor," I say with a dry mouth.

"You know him? I guess you do, considering your wife made a movie with him."

"I know him because I'm his lawyer." I don't see any reason for keeping this from Will since he is baring his soul to me. "So, does this make us blood brothers, Will?"

He smiles. "I think it does, Arthur, but there's something else I have to confess if we are to seal the deal."

During a meditative facial pose, waiting for the words, his eyes come back alive, and he points. "Do you see it?"

I see a black female bear running with two cubs close to the tree line. "My first black bear sighting," I say. I remember all of Connor's dogs. I think there have been six of them, one right after the other, all mutts, all named Bear.

For the brief time we watch the bears, the complexity of our lives with Carter leaves us. We watch until they disappear into the woods.

"What I told you about working at one of the craft shops to earn enough money to go to school wasn't exactly true. I had some money saved, but not nearly enough. Then, one day, about a year after I graduated high school, out of the blue, I received a registered piece of mail. The return address was a Hopi charity foundation in Los Angeles, with only a post office box. I pulled out a note with a cashier's check made out to me. It was more than enough to enable me to get a four-year degree with all my other expenses paid. The note was hand-written on plain paper without official letterhead or contact information. Nor was it signed. I tried to find the organization, but there were no listings. I called the bank, who wouldn't tell me anything, and I called the offices over the Hopi Tribe. They had never heard of it."

"You received an anonymous donation to put you through school. Do you think it was from her?"

"The one time I answered one of her cards myself was to ask her about this. She said, 'No, it wasn't me.' If she knew who it was, she had no intention of telling me. When I saw how big Kimi had made it, I thought it might have been her."

"No, it wasn't Kimi. I handle all of Kimi's financial affairs. Besides, Kimi had hardly any money of her own at the time you would have received that check. Her first break was that movie." I say nothing because I could be totally off the mark, but I have an idea, although I don't know how he would have known anything about Will. Unless...

We sit for a moment, staring at the tree line. We hope to see the bear family again, but we don't.

"What will you do now, Will?"

"What that bear family told me to do."

He recognizes the puzzlement on my face.

"There is a Cherokee legend that says you never actually kill a black bear. It simply returns to its life in the forest. I will do the same. How about you?"

"I'm unsure if I have a life to return to."

We drive in silence back to the hotel. When he stops in front of the entrance, he reaches into the back seat and hands me a bag. I glimpse inside to see something wrapped in foil with a beautiful red bow.

"Sandy wrapped it. Please give it to Kimi when you see her again. Tell her who it's from and that I wish her Nvwadohiyadv."

I repeat the word back to him slowly.

"That's correct. It's Cherokee for peace. May you have it too, Arthur."

He reaches into the glove compartment and pulls out a business card that has been separated from the pack. "The name and location of Kaya's village are on the back."

I shake his hand, gripping it with the force of a blood brother, and thank him for everything.

Twenty-Eight

KIMI—TUESDAY NIGHT/WEDNESDAY MORNING

While sitting in bed, I pick up the script Luke left on my nightstand. How many times did our father sit Kachina and me on his lap, one of us on each knee, and tell us about the creation of fire? Our mom had told us plenty of Hopi stories. Papa said he had to have equal time. It's funny how both stories were about spiders.

The Water Spider is a story about the first fire in Cherokee tradition. Arthur wouldn't know this story—at least, I don't think so—but he's the only person who would have sent it to me. Obtaining this script must have been his urgent business. Is he back? Luke said it wasn't him, but he said it was also anonymous. It had to have been Arthur.

He's never accepted Carter's death. He thinks I'm her. Does he believe, in my condition, I can act?

I stay up most of Tuesday night reading the script. The leading part is for an older woman damaged in a fire years earlier. Like the spider, the woman created an air pocket around herself, and an unknown boy pulled her to safety.

It's clearly about Kachina, but the character's name has been changed in the script. Or, I think it is about Kachina. The character is alive, living on a Hopi reservation. I read every line over and over. It's also about me. There is a mixture of us both. How can someone know my story? Our story? There are no names on the script to show who wrote it.

I only know this role was specifically written for me and that whoever wrote it wants me to play it. But that's Carter's job, not mine. I'm Kimi.

A banging on the door wakes me. I look at the clock and see it is almost noon, and the script is half-opened on the other side of my bed. I yell from the bedroom, "Who is it?"

"It's Luke."

I tell him to come on in. I know he has a key card, and I'm not even worried about him seeing me like this. He already has.

He comes through to my bedroom. "I checked on you earlier. I knocked, but you didn't answer, so I let myself in. You were sound asleep. I knew you needed rest. I'm afraid I ate both the bagels."

He laughs.

"I saw the script on your bed and figured you had read it. I'm curious."

"You don't know what it's about?"

"I know nothing."

"It's based on a Cherokee myth about fire."

"Oh?"

"Did you know I'm Cherokee?"

"No, but now that you tell me, I can see it in your complexion and possibly your features."

I automatically cover the side of my face with my hand.

I've been playing this role for six months. Living it night and day. Luke removes my hand.

"Kimi, you don't need to do that."

"Maybe you're right, Luke. I don't know why I needed to do any of it. I only know I was doing it for her—for Kachina and my mother."

"Kachina?"

"My sister."

"I didn't know you had a sister."

I pick up the script. "If I take this part, the entire world will know."

Twenty-Nine

ARTHUR—WEDNESDAY MORNING

I'm at the Asheville airport, headed to Arizona, thinking about how much has happened in such a short time. It has only been three days since I was supposed to meet Kimi for lunch at The Woodlands.

There have been numerous calls and messages from her, as well as from Connor. It crosses my mind that she might harm herself if she doesn't hear from me soon. So, I send a brief text:

ARTHUR BURKE

> I'm fine, but I'm still busy with urgent business. I will contact you as soon as I can.

I can't bring myself to add any emojis. I've never been particularly keen on them. Carter used them to excess. To my surprise, she doesn't text back right away. I expect her to be livid, demanding to know where I am. Nothing.

I call Mrs. Bell, who tells me that, other than falling into the pool after four Long Island teas, she's fine.

"And, Mr. Burke, I'm afraid your secret is out. Too many of the staff and residents recognize her."

I'm shocked that she has even left the room, but Mrs. Bell tells me she has been eating in the dining room—all thanks to Luke.

"Luke?"

"He's a nurse on staff. Mr. Scott has taken a liking to him and has asked him to take good care of Ms. Hudson."

Of course, Connor would see to her every need. I don't know why I worried.

I asked Mrs. Bell if the word had gotten out that she was there. I bypassed the newsstand. Carter could have been plastered all over every magazine and newspaper there.

"So far, the news has been contained to The Woodlands. I cautioned the staff about privacy issues and the potential loss of jobs if anything leaked out. The only person I worry about is Althea."

"Althea?"

"A lady we fired yesterday. She said what she thought more times than not, and her thoughts weren't pleasant. She left, disgruntled. I can't say what she might divulge. I went directly to Mr. Scott, who said he would take care of it."

"Will you please not tell Carter or Mr. Scott about this call? I'm on business and hope to return in a couple more days. Don't worry, I'll settle everything with Mr. Scott."

"If that's what you want, Mr. Burke."

I end the call, hoping she will be true to her word even though Connor is her boss. I'm tempted to text him. I know I should since he's my employer. I put my fingers over the letters and begin typing but keep backspacing. I have too many questions. They are calling for me to board. I slip my phone back into my jacket pocket and get in line.

It's 9 p.m. when I arrive at the motel near the Hopi Cultural Center in Second Mesa. I drive my rental SUV into the potholed parking lot of a hotel that looks like the one used in *Psycho*, but I don't care. The lady at the desk, who appears to be Hopi, hands me a key card and tells me not to worry about my vehicle. The police patrol the area carefully. I only look at her and turn.

I'm whipped and beaten down by all this. I drive the rental around to the other side of the motel, but instead of parking in front of my room, which is on the first floor, I park directly under the pole light on the other side next to a beat-up Chevy that probably belongs to the woman working the desk. No need to wake up to a stolen vehicle on top of everything else.

I toss my carry-on onto one of the two double beds with thin white bedspreads. The room is cheap but clean. I check my phone. Still no return text. She's pouting. I've come to expect this reaction over the years. It's what she does when she's mad. Or she is so taken with Luke that she has forgotten about me. Our history has been interlaced with brief affairs on both our parts. They've never amounted to anything. We've played these games with each other for as long as I can remember. I want to hear her voice but can't bring myself to call. I know she would answer, only to act like she doesn't care. Even if I knew what to say, and I don't, I'm too dead tired. I feel as if I could sleep for a solid twenty-four hours.

I shower and go straight to bed, hoping I can have a blackout sleep, dreamless unless it's something pleasant with no one I know in it. As for finding Kaya, I'll figure it out in the morning.

The second person I asked told me right where to find her. "Everyone in the village calls her the fire woman," he said.

"You mean she's still living?" I asked, relieved.

"Well, she was earlier this morning when I saw her at the post office," the man said, removing his hat and rubbing his fingers through his long hair.

The post office was the first place I went looking. I could have walked right past her, but I guess not, not from Will's descriptions of her burns. I couldn't have missed her.

I thank the man and head for my vehicle.

It's easy to find the house. It's modest but nice. A plump, fifty-ish woman answers the door. I tell her I'm Arthur Burke and am here to see Kaya Ahoka. I half expect her to shut the door in my face, but she opens it wider and beckons me in.

"She's been expecting you." She leads me into a modern kitchen and asks if I want a cup of tea or coffee.

I tell her I stopped at a convenience store and picked up something along the way.

"Expecting me?"

"I'll let her tell you."

A slender, petite woman walks in with a cane. Half of her face is scarred beyond recognition, but she doesn't hide it.

The woman who answered the door says, "If you don't need me, Kaya, I'm going to have my coffee out on the back porch and finish the book I started."

When the woman disappears, I say, "I have so many questions; I don't know where to start."

"I'm sure you do, Mr. Burke, or should I call you Arthur? After all, you've been my son-in-law three times. Not currently, but you're still together."

She sees my surprised look and says, "Oh, I keep up. Are you sure you don't want something?"

I tell her, "No, I'm fine."

"Your preference," she says. "Well, it's a long story. Let me start at the beginning." She props her cane against a chair and sits at the table, where a cup of coffee awaits. My appearance must have interrupted their morning ritual. She motions me to take the seat across from her.

She takes a sip of coffee from the side of her mouth. I can tell she has mastered this.

"They said I had been in a coma for two weeks. It was probably for the best. When I think back on it, it was my body's way of healing as much as possible. When I awoke, the pain was unbearable. They quickly gave me morphine, something they had not done while I was in a coma.

"Things were foggy at first. I only knew I wasn't home. They told me my name was Kaya Ahoka. I remember saying, 'I don't know.' I would drift in and out of sleep. I dreamed. Sleep and dreams were all I had. I couldn't remember who I was or if I had a family.

"The doctor said that, in addition to everything else, I was in shock, that the amnesia was only temporary. Trying to remember only gave me a headache on top of the already excruciating pain. But when I slept, I remembered. My family returned to me, and my physical pain went away. I clung to the memories of the dreams while lying in bed in the morning, but within minutes to an hour, the recollection vanished. On some days, there were faint memories—flickers here and there. You know how dreams are, Arthur.

"I tried so hard to remember the dreams because they were of happy times. I worked on recalling by writing them down every morning before the nurse came in to check on me or give me my breakfast. In my dreams, I lived on Hopi land with my husband and twin daughters. I was so in love. My mother didn't even mind that he was a white man. I met him when he was backpacking through Hopi land. Even my mother, who wasn't too keen on me marrying a white man, said he was the most handsome white man she had ever seen.

"Eventually, the memories of this reality, not my dream one, returned to me. I wasn't on my native land. I hadn't married the backpacker, but I did have beautiful identical twin daughters. I saw my husband's face. I remembered the good times and the bad."

She smiles. Or one side of her mouth does.

"There were more good than bad. I saw him die. Lightning struck. It was as if the entire planet had lit up at that moment. There was this horrendous cry of the thunder god. It was loud. It was so loud I didn't even hear the crash of the beam as it struck, crushing his skull. I still have nightmares. The blessing is he died instantly. I screamed and screamed.

"We hadn't had rain in weeks. Not only was the barn old with aged wood, but because of the party, we borrowed extra bales of hay from a neighbor for the party. Plus, we strung crepe paper streamers across the barn like spider webs, a torch waiting to be lit.

"Amid my screams, my thoughts turn to Kimi and Kachina. I didn't know where they were. The last time I saw them, they were in the house. They said they would come out to the barn in a bit to finish the decorations. I prayed they were still safe inside the house, but I remembered seeing a light approaching the barn. Maybe a flashlight. One figure. I didn't know if it was one of the girls.

"All these thoughts going through my head happened in a matter of seconds. I was suddenly aware of my situation and that I was blocked. Then I remembered the boards missing at the bottom of the side of the barn I was in. Everything was lit up enough, but the smoke made it impossible to see. But I knew I could feel my way if I could manage to crawl a few yards. The hole would be wide enough for me to crawl through. I only knew I had to find my girls.

"I didn't even realize I was burned. All I could think about was getting to them. The next thing I remember was waking up in a burn unit in Kentucky. I wasn't even in North Carolina anymore. I asked, 'How long…' The nurse said two months.

"I lost all track of time, and no one could tell me about my girls. In my heart, I feared they were afraid to tell me. Why hadn't they been here to see me? But Kentucky? How would they get here? Did anyone even know where I was?

"Then, one day, a tribal member came to visit. He told me I was the only one who made it out alive from the fire. I felt the bed with me on it was plummeting into the deepest pit of hell.

"People were saying Will Catawnee saved my life. There were a few who saw him kneeling over my body after pulling me to safety. Slowly, I remembered. I never liked Kimi dating him. He hung out with a bad lot. He denied saving me, saying people were mistaken—it was dark, and the air was so full of smoke that they weren't seeing correctly. But it was him.

"Over twenty-five percent of my body suffered burns. They told me I was doing well. Perhaps if the burn was on a part of my body that wasn't visible, I might have agreed, but the right side of my face was hideous, more than it is now. Or perhaps I've grown accustomed to looking at myself over the years. The burned area runs from my head down the right side of my torso, stopping at my waist. The hair on that side of my head will never grow back. I had such beautiful hair."

Kaya strokes one side of her head, still covered with hair, not gray but white.

"Valorie, my burn technician, was always encouraging me. She reminded me of my mother, not in looks, but in her manner. Valorie was a plump redhead with freckles. I guessed her to be only a few years older than my daughters. She told me I was her very first patient and that she had just graduated nursing school. She changed my bandages, gave me my treatments, and evaluated my progress each day. I was still on an IV. After they removed it, all I could eat was soft foods such as ice cream or yogurt. I drank ice water through a straw, holding the straw to the left side of my mouth. I couldn't tolerate anything hot. I couldn't eat during the treatments, but I could watch television. I hadn't been into soap operas before the accident, but I got involved in them. Television programs, movies, and books kept my mind off things. It's funny how other people's tragedies, even imaginary ones, can take your mind off your own.

"Valorie was kind, but I rarely talked. I'm sure she was used to it. Depression is a side effect of being burned to the point of disfigurement. And then there is losing your whole family along with it. My mental anguish was almost as great as the physical pain. Well, it's gotten better—the physical pain, that is. Most of the pain I have these days is from old age.

"Back in the burn unit, while Valerie changes my bandages, I watch my favorite soap opera. She apologizes for interrupting it because she knows I look forward to it. A young girl, a new actor, comes into the scene. She is the daughter of a regular cast member looking for her biological mother. Chills go from head to toe through my body, and I let out a small scream. Not much of one. I had suffered smoke inhalation and had first-degree burns to my lungs, esophagus, and tongue. I couldn't speak for a long time. The tears running down my face bring comfort to my skin.

"Are you okay? Did I do something that hurt?" Valerie asks.

"No," I say, sitting up straighter in bed. For a moment, I've forgotten about my situation. I try to speak but can't. I motion for my pen and pad and write, 'The actress,' I point to the screen, 'is my daughter.'

"She looks at the screen attached to the wall. She thinks I'm hallucinating. If only she could see the resemblance. But how could anyone? I know, Mr. Burke, I'm a hideous monster. Why I came back to my people. They don't see me that way.

"She only had a walk-on part. I watched that soap opera religiously, hoping she would be on again.

"After two more months, I'm ready to leave the hospital. I think, how am I going to pay for this? I've been here forever, but I'm told it's all been taken care of and that I'll have a private nurse for as long as I need one. There is nothing left for me in Cherokee. Intuitively, I know it is him. Somehow, he learned about the fire, about the girls. It's through Connor I find out Kimi survived. I want to go to her, but what would she think of seeing me like this? Connor assures me he is taking care of her and that she'll have everything she needs— proper schooling and possibly a movie career if it is still what she wants. He tells me about you. At the time, I needed constant care, and he was married with a son. Considering our situations and the fact that I didn't want to complicate either of their lives, we agreed to rely on you. I longed to see my mama again. Her wisdom, which I didn't appreciate growing up, was what I needed.

"Valerie said she always wanted to travel out west."

"Yes, and I've been with Kaya ever since," Valerie says as she walks back into the kitchen for a second cup of coffee. "Are you sure you don't want one, Mr. Burke?"

"I think I will," I say.

"Sugar? Cream?" she asks.

"Black."

She places a cup in front of me just as a cell phone rings on the kitchen island's edge. Valerie picks it up and looks at the screen. "It's Connor." For a moment, I think she means me, but it's her cell, not mine. "Do you want to take it?" she asks Kaya.

"No, you answer. Tell him I'm talking to Arthur, and I'll call him back."

Thirty

KIMI—WEDNESDAY AFTERNOON

Wearing a sleeveless top and shorts with nothing covering my face, I walk down the hall with Luke. I've put on light makeup. I haven't worn makeup since the night of the party. I wore a different makeup that night—stage makeup, which one uses for special effects and disfigurement.

Since coming here, I've taken baby steps to emerge from the hermit lifestyle I've condemned myself to for the last six months. I feel I'm ready to begin anew as my true self. It was a good decision to come here.

There is no one in the hallway other than Luke and me, but I can hear the commotion of the dining room, the drone of voices intermingled with the clanging of glasses and silverware as we draw nearer. The room grows quiet in waves as we enter through the double doors. Stares and whispers permeate the room. I'm light-headed. I see all the tables occupied except for the one I've sat at the few times I've eaten in the dining room. Luke takes hold of my arm to offer support.

"I think I must still be suffering a bit of a hangover," I whisper.

"Steady. You've got this," he says.

I see Ralph Bellamy sitting with the same four women I saw him with yesterday. One of them, I think Gloria, nudges him and says loudly enough for me to hear, "I told you it was her."

Luke and I are sitting at the far corner, the table that would be the least desirable in a fine restaurant, but it's where I feel the most comfortable. I also think it has become known as my table. A girl in The Woodlands' uniform places a glass of water with a lemon on the table, not taking her eyes off me. She almost spills it.

"Sorry."

I see her hand trembling. The name tag reads Jennifer.

"It's okay, Jennifer," I say.

"So what will it be?" Luke asks. "Hamburger and fries?"

Jennifer is standing, ready to write.

"I think a salad and some fruit."

"So, you are going to take the role?" Luke says as Jennifer walks away.

"Why do you say that?"

"You're watching your figure. I've heard the camera adds twenty pounds. I hear it enough from Clark."

"Ah, your fiancé."

People have gone back to their eating, but most look my way every so often.

"Oh, your art supplies should be here by tomorrow."

"Great, you got them."

"Well, not me."

Jennifer returned with a cup of fruit, one lone pear she thought I might like, and a colorful salad with oil and vinegar on the side.

"Aren't you going to have anything?" I ask Luke.

He looks up at Jennifer. "I hear you have hamburgers on the menu now."

"Yes, sir."

"Medium rare, with fries and a Coke."

"Yes, sir."

"I can remember the last time I had a hamburger before the other day. We had a hamburger and hotdog joint in the town where I grew up. Whenever we could scrape together the money, a few of us kids would go there."

"And where was that? No one seems to know anything about your history. You just showed up one day on the big screen and have been famous ever since."

"It didn't quite happen that way. I did all kinds of bit parts, mostly commercials or walk-on roles, one-liners if I said anything. That went on for eight years."

"That's been going on for ten years for Clark."

"I hope he makes it."

"Yeah, me, too." I take a bite of salad. "So, if I tell you about my past, is there a nurse/patient confidentiality clause written somewhere? Is there such a thing?"

"If there's not, we'll make it a thing. A pact between you and me."

"I had a steady boyfriend, Will Catawnee."

"Sounds Native American."

"It's Cherokee."

"Oh, like the script?"

"Yes, like the script."

"You haven't told me about that yet."

"I grew up on a Cherokee reservation, technically not a reservation, but a nation was the name given to it. My family lived on a small farm on the outskirts of town, although calling it a farm was a joke. My dad had a black thumb but knew how to entertain my sister and me, while our mother worked several jobs. He would sit us on his lap and tell us stories. He called them the stories of our people. Cherokee legend states that a long time ago, half the world was covered in darkness and half in light. Animals inhabited the Earth then. They prayed to Unetlanvhi, the Creator, asking Him to send something to the dark side of the world to keep them warm. He sent Thunders, a clan of powerful storm spirits who live in the sky and can command thunder and lightning. Some tribes say the Thunder spirits are birds, but the Cherokee say they are humans and sons of the corn mother.

"They sent a bolt of lightning to a sycamore tree. It glowed with yellow and orange light, the first fire ever seen on Earth. The tree was on an island.

"The animals on the dark side of the world held a meeting looking for the bravest animal who could get that fire for them. At first, a raven went. The bird was strong with a large wingspread, but a gust of wind sent embers to his wing, burning him. He returned without the fire. Next, an owl went. He was also strong, with a large wingspread, but a gust of wind blew embers again. They landed on his eyes, turning them red and the area around them white. The council of animals met once again. They sent animals of every variety out —one by one. They all failed to bring back the fire. They were at their wit's end.

"A small voice said, 'I can go get the fire.' All the animals looked to see where the voice was coming from. They saw a tiny female spider on the ground. They had sent their bravest, and this minuscule creature wanted to go. They laughed and laughed.

"The spider paid them no heed. She was determined. She spun a web, making a pouch. She put it on her back and carefully glided across the water. When she reached the island, she climbed the sycamore tree and placed an ember in her pouch. She swam back, at first slowly, but she could feel the heat of the ember burning her back, so she swam faster. She made it back to the animals, delivering the ember, but had burned a small red spot that remains on her back to this day. But she had succeeded in bringing fire to the animals and all humankind."

"This is what this script is about? Are you playing a spider?"

"No. The story is a myth with a moral."

"Which is?"

"The spider was small, not big and strong like the other animals, yet she saved the world."

"Or that a woman might save the world?" Luke says.

"Exactly."

"Right on, Sister!" a woman in the room yells.

We hadn't noticed the room had gone quiet, the residents hanging on my every word. Luke's hamburger arrives, and I finish my lunch. He gulps it down quickly and says, "I have some patients to check on. Do you want me to take you back to your room?"

"No, I think I'll stay."

He smiles.

While Jennifer is clearing our plates, one lady at the table beside Ralph asks what made me want to become an actress. I'm amazed by such a banal question, yet I'm relieved she didn't ask about the night of the party. Since Luke has already left, I ask Jennifer if she might find someone to move the plant that partially blocks my table from the others. An all-too-familiar face appears. I recognize John, the guy who saved me from drowning.

"I never thanked you," I say.

He seems embarrassed but says, "I'm glad you didn't drown."

I turn toward the lady. "What's your name?"

"Alice, and this is...," she announces the name of each person in the room. There is no way I will remember everyone, but a few names stick with me.

"Well, Alice. I think the desire came from my mother. We

were poor. Dirt poor. Besides working in a white woman's beauty shop, my mother made baskets to sell at one of the craft shops in town."

Someone calls out, "You were Cherokee?"

"Part. My mother was Hopi, my father was Cherokee."

"Oh." She draws it out as if I'm revealing some big secret, which I am.

"I'm Jewish," one lady says.

"I'm Greek," another one says.

I think they are reminding me that America is one big melting pot. However, I see no other Native Americans here, nor any African Americans, other than some of the wait staff. I smile and nod, knowing she didn't intend to be patronizing.

"My mother's name was Kaya. She was the best mom in the world. I had a twin sister, but she, along with my parents, died in a fire. I was only sixteen."

I stop to acknowledge the sympathetic words and gestures circulating through the room. I can see from some of their faces that they are connecting the dots—my family being killed in a fire and the fire the night of the party that was in all of the papers. I'm not ready to answer those questions. I start talking right away, not giving anyone the opportunity.

"We didn't have a television at home, but the lady who owned the beauty shop had one in her store. While my mom fixed women's hair, she watched old movies and brought old movie magazines home from the shop. They were usually way out of date, but I didn't mind, nor did my mother. She would tell me about the stars in those magazines. The stories were so real that I thought she knew them personally. I wanted to be one of those women more than anything. Not that I wanted to be a star, but I wanted to act. Most mothers would discourage their children from going into show business, but my mother told me I would be a great actress one day. Possibly, it was only dreaming—a tribal mother living in a fantasy world, instilling unrealistic hope into a child reared in poverty. The thing is, the way my mother described this world seemed real, and at a young age, I only knew I wanted it. My father, even though he failed miserably at most things, told me even though I was small, he knew I would do great things one day. Like the water spider, I believed I could do anything if I set my mind to it."

Applause fills the room. I get up, take a bow, and say, "I think I need some rest after almost drowning yesterday." I wink at John, who stands off in the corner.

I see Luke has returned and is standing in the doorway. He walks over to my table, and we walk out together. We pass a staff member taking down an egg tree left over from Easter last Sunday. I whisper, "Tsuwetsi."

"What?" asks Luke.

"It's Cherokee for eggs." I get a chill remembering my father bringing in an egg from a chicken he threatened to butcher if she didn't start laying.

Luke hands me a pear. "You didn't eat this at lunch."

Again, I'm reminded of my father. I've felt his presence all morning. He would bring us pears from a neighbor's pear tree who lived down the road. I seriously doubt if the neighbor knew about it.

We get on the elevator. Luke presses both the second— and third-floor buttons. I don't ask about the man upstairs because I know it will do me no good and partly because I'm still reeling from what happened in the dining room. As we ascend, he asks me how I feel about what happened. I'm smiling from ear to ear. "Maybe I've made some progress. What do you think?"

"I think you have."

The elevator door opens.

"Do you need me to walk you down the hallway to your apartment?"

"No. I think I can manage," I say.

I step out of the elevator. He's holding the door open. "Do you have your keycard?"

I reach into my pocket and pull it out, holding it up for him to see.

"Then I shall see you later," he says as the door closes.

The hallway looks vacant, but as I approach my apartment, a voice from behind shouts Carter Hudson. I turn to see someone in a Frankenstein monster suit, a poorly designed one, but that doesn't occur to me until later when Mrs. Bell and a security guard who works on the premises question me. At the time, I was too busy screaming and trying to shield myself from the cell phone pointed in my face set in the burst picture-taking mode. The figure turns and runs toward the emergency exit. I drop the pear to the floor, and with a shaky hand, I reach for the cell in my pocket and call Luke.

Luke is massaging my shoulders while I sit on the floral couch, drinking a cup of chamomile tea. I'm shaking, not because a paparazzi member managed to get into The Woodlands and snap photos of me, but because of the costume.

"Our entire security team has been called in. No vehicles have been reported leaving the premises, and we are currently checking the license plates. We protect our residents," Mrs. Bell assures me. The smile is forced, manufactured to reassure me, just like her handshake when I first arrived.

Her cell rings. Somehow, I know it's the man upstairs. I wonder if he is calling because he feels his security has been breached. Mrs. Bell walks out to the balcony, but not before I hear her saying, "I knew it was a mistake to let her come here."

Before I finish my tea, there is a knock at the door. The security guard answers and greets a male staff member. At the moment, I suspect everyone. "Since they were wearing the costume, couldn't it have been someone who works here?" I say.

Mrs. Bell is off the phone now. She returns from the balcony and whispers with the staff member she addresses as Matt. She turns in my direction and says, "We've apprehended her."

"Her?"

"Althea Rubins. We fired her a few days ago. When we let her go, she turned in a fake pass key. Her original pass key only worked in certain downstairs areas because she was kitchen staff, but it was enough to get her in the building. She intended to sell the pictures to the highest bidder."

"I remember her. She is the one who brought me the hamburger and fries the other day."

Mrs. Bell's smile turns almost genuine. "I assure you, Miss Stone, if that is what we are to keep calling you, this matter will be handled as delicately as possible."

"I would like to ask that you don't press charges."

She looks surprised and relieved. "I'm glad you feel that way, Miss Stone, because we don't want this kind of publicity for The Woodlands. Charlie, our senior security guard, who has worked here for twelve years and has the trust of our senior staff, will be posted outside your apartment. Someone else will be sitting by the pool outside your balcony. We want no more intrusions for you or any of our residents. Her eyes drift upward. I feel she is covertly trying to tell me something, or maybe she is expressing exasperation at the added responsibilities of having Carter Hudson as a resident.

Everyone but Luke leaves. He sits at my bedside, waiting for the sedative to take effect. At first, I tell him I don't want anything, but he insists it's mild and probably won't even put me to sleep. I'm relieved because I want to pray to the Great

Spirit or my mother, whoever will listen and ask for forgiveness.

I tell Luke to leave. "I will be all right," I say. It's what I want to believe. He shuts the bedroom door behind him, telling me to call him if I should need him.

Any other time, I would pick up my cell and call Arthur, but a numbness invades my body and mind. Perhaps it's the sedative that Luke gave me. When I hear the outer door shut, I pray aloud, "Mama, Papa, if you can hear me…"

Thirty-One

ARTHUR—WEDNESDAY AFTERNOON

At noon, the three of us, Kaya, Valerie, and I, are sitting at the kitchen table having Hopi corn stew.

When I told her how Carter had made it for me once, a smile spread across her face, and she said, "Then, I must also make it for you."

She tells me her mother died several months ago, and I tell her I'm sorry.

"It was a peaceful death. She died in her sleep. She could no longer get around like she used to, but her mind was sharp until the end. After a while, she accepted Kimi had gone the way of the white man. She watched all her movies. Valerie would make us popcorn, and we would sit and say the lines along with her. We had them all memorized."

Valerie rises, gathers our dishes, and puts them in the sink.

"I'll take care of them later," Kaya tells Valerie.

"Thanks, Kaya. I need to be off. Check on my husband and grandbaby."

"Oh... I assumed."

"That she has been only my private nurse all these years?"

"I guess."

"Valerie married a Hopi man shortly after coming here. Over the years, she has taken care of me and many others in the village, as well as my mother to the end."

Valerie bends down and kisses Kaya on the cheek. "Do you have everything you need?"

"Yes."

Valerie hugs Kaya long and hard. "Then I guess…"

"I'll let you know."

Valerie turns to me and says, "It was nice to meet you finally, Arthur."

I rise and bid Valerie goodbye.

After the door shuts behind her, I say, "Kaya, what I don't understand—"

"Why did I never come forward? Why did I let Kimi believe I had died?"

"Yes."

"In the beginning, I was in terrible shape, in a coma part of the time, and when I came out of it, I didn't remember. And when I did finally, I didn't want to be a burden. When I was ready to leave the hospital and found out someone had paid my bill, and I would be cared and provided for—for the rest of my life—"

"You knew it was him."

"Yes."

"He was the backpacker."

"Yes."

"And he's Kimi and Kachina's biological father."

Kaya nods.

"But still."

"I think Kimi told you about Victor?"

"Yes."

"Did Connor know? Well, what am I saying? Of course, he knows. Behind the scenes, he groomed her for stardom while he groomed me to be her husband."

"Arthur, it's not exactly like that. Nothing is ever that black and white. Do you think I planned to get pregnant? No, but this handsome young man, who I didn't know was famous at the time, shows up in our village. I had never even seen a movie. All I knew about them was what I saw on the covers of magazines in grocery stores.

"He was backpacking alone. He said he had to get out of the city and escape the pressure of his father's rule. I remember thinking he could be on the cover of one of those magazines. Little did I know he was.

"Well, I caught his eye. I was only fifteen but looked older. He was twenty-four. I told him I was eighteen. We fell in love. He liked I hadn't recognized him. He confided things in me he had never told anyone—mainly about his relationship with his father. We went to the nearest town, and he gave me money to go to a drugstore and look for a particular magazine. There he was, his picture and a story about how he was taking a break from movies and was believed to be somewhere in France.

"I show him the magazine and say, 'But you're not in France.' 'No, I'm here with you. My agent planted that story.'"

"He stuck around for three months—long enough for him to fall in love with me and a mutt that hung around us. He called him Bear because that's what he looked like. He asked me to marry him and return to LA with him, but I knew his father wouldn't accept me based on what Connor had confided in me. I insisted he return without me and get his father's approval first.

"He agreed after a week. Instead of taking me with him, he took the dog. Said Bear would have to do until I could join him.

"He sent me letters and postcards of every place he visited on his way back, along with pictures of him and Bear. He told me he would show me the world one day.

"When he arrived home and told his father about meeting me and our plans to marry, his father exploded. 'She's Indian!' There was still a lot of prejudice then. Besides being an Indian, I was primitive and uneducated. That wasn't precisely how Connor said his dad put it, but it was the essence of the conversation. His father threatened to cut him off. He was already furious about the cross-country disappearance trip. I almost think Connor might have defied him, but his father sent a private investigator to our village who discovered my age."

"Then?"

"Connor was heartbroken that I had lied to him, and his father won. You must know, Arthur, about overbearing fathers and sons who, no matter how successful they become, their approval is all that matters?"

I hold my head down.

"Connor collects the type—men like you who have this need. I couldn't tell you why. Only a psychologist could do that. Possibly, he finds them eager to please and easier to control, or maybe he sees himself in them, rooting for them and wanting them to break free. Even after his father died, Connor still wasn't free. He exerted the same control over his son, although he didn't see it until it was too late."

"His son died in an auto accident. It almost seems the gods wrote it in the stars, doesn't it, Arthur?

"Losing his son devastated him. It was right after making *The Muted Girl.* Before that, he wanted to announce to the world that Kimi was his daughter, but I asked him not to. I wanted her to think she had made it on her own, that she wasn't being helped the whole time. In retrospect, I was probably wrong. I don't know. We all have our dark sides, Arthur. Mostly, we're shades of gray. There are a few moments when we are as close to pure light as we can get when we're still on

Earth. Those are the moments of pure, unadulterated love, the kind you have for a child.

"I couldn't tell you if it was my dark side or my light side that kept me from telling Kimi I was still alive or that Connor was her real father. Maybe the decision lay somewhere in the gray. I want to think I was doing it for her good. All any parent wants is what's best for their child. I also felt I was being disrespectful to Wes's memory. He showed up at just the right time."

"You were pregnant, and you hadn't told Connor."

"Exactly. By the time I found out, he had already told his father about us. At that point, I didn't think it would make a difference. Still, I would go to a newsstand every chance I got. Two months after he left, one month after the private investigator came, I saw a magazine with him and his fiancee on the cover."

"And Wes came along."

"That very night. I was already two months pregnant. Since twins usually come early, he never suspected. He was great with the girls when he wasn't drunk. He was the one who raised them.

"Wes never knew the girls weren't his until much later. Not until right before the fire. It was as if every bit of karma came due at once. Wes and I had a big fight a few days before the girls' sixteenth birthday. We were having such a hard time of it. I thought if Connor knew, he might step in, see to it they got a break in life, and see to it they could attend college. I drove to the nearest phone booth. I still had the agent's number. I hoped it was still good. I left a message for him to give to Connor and told him I would wait by the phone for an hour, and if I didn't hear from him, I would know he didn't want any part of the girls' lives. A man was waiting to use the phone. Although he pretended he wasn't listening, he must have been."

"And that man was Victor Wildman."

"Yes, an opportunist. Either Connor Scott would reward him for bringing his girls to him or would pay him to keep the secret."

"But Victor was a wild card."

"Yes. You know the story from there."

"So, the agent gave Connor your message. But how did he know about Victor?"

"Victor also got a message to Connor's agent that he was on his way with one girl, Kachina. He never showed. Connor had someone find him. All he said was that she was too much for him, stark raving mad—how could she not be after what happened—and she got away from him somewhere outside of LA. I thought to myself that sounds more like Kimi than Kachina. That's when Connor called your father's private residence to use whatever legal means were necessary to locate her, but you answered the phone."

"And Connor relayed what I told him about Carter to you."

"Yes."

"But you still could have told her."

"Look at me, Arthur. Kimi was doing great. She was achieving what she always wanted. I would only be in the way."

"Tell me. How did you know it was Kimi and not Kachina?"

"Don't you think a mother knows her daughter?"

I rise. Kaya reaches for her cane and rises slowly.

"No, please, don't get up. I don't know what else I can ask. I'm glad I met you. It will be hard not to tell Carter."

"You won't have to tell her. I will. I'm going with you. I'll call Connor, who will arrange a private plane for us. The only other time I was on a private plane, any plane, was when I was coming here to live, but I was sedated at the time. This time,

I'll be able to see our people's land from the air. I already have my suitcases packed."

"You were telling Valerie goodbye earlier."

She nods.

"I'll go in the back and make that phone call to Connor, now, Arthur."

I watch as she walks slowly down the hallway with the aid of her cane. My eyes catch a computer on a desk in the room's corner. The screen is lit up. I walk over and see what appears to be a movie screenplay—*The Water Spider*.

Some things suddenly become clear—where Connor got his anonymous scripts. She returns as I'm standing by her computer.

"We're all set. Connor says the plane will be at the airport first thing in the morning."

"You wrote *The Muted Girl*, didn't you?"

"It was about Kachina, indirectly. She no longer had a voice. I would write little plays for the girls when they were young. Kimi was a natural at it. She taped pictures of movie stars all over her side of the bedroom. Kachina could never remember her lines. Kimi always had to help her. Kachina loved big houses and mansions, in particular, the Versailles Palace. Those were the pictures she put on *her* wall."

"This one, on the screen, *The Water Spider*...?"

"This one I wrote for Kimi."

"Do you think she will ever act again?"

"Oh, yes. I know she will. And this one will win her that Oscar."

"Pick me up at six sharp in the morning, Arthur."

Thirty-Two

KIMI—THURSDAY AFTERNOON

Noisy chatter, clanging silverware, and smells of rosemary and garlic flood the hallway as I near the dining area. The rich aroma does nothing to entice my appetite. I'm wearing one of my prettiest dresses, or Carter's, as I'm now ready to embrace her fully, not as Kachina but as Kimi.

At first, there is a nudge from Mr. Brockman to Al Goodman when he spots me. Last night, Luke went over all the residents with me, bringing a folder from the office with their pictures, telling me their names and a bit about each one. He thought it would take my mind off yesterday's misfortune, and to some extent, it did. He quizzed me, and I surprised myself by remembering everyone. It was like going over lines with my mother when I was young. I always remembered them then, too.

You could hear a pin drop in the dining room as I walked in. Like Pompeii, the entire crowd is frozen in place, not ashen gray but in the mismatched bright colors of senior citizens long past any regard for fashion sense. The last sound uttered is that of Mrs. Whisman, who looks up from her plate through her Coke bottle glasses and says, "Is it her? Has she finally decided to grace us with her presence?"

Yesterday, I was a hero to them, but they've had time to talk, speculate on my situation, and reiterate my flaws to each other. The Althea incident has spread like an LA fire. Fire. It has always been my nemesis. Today, they theorize what went haywire and why I went crazy a little over six months ago—how I ended up here while still in my prime. One thing I've learned in this business is that yesterday's golden child is tomorrow's villain.

As I look over the room. I see only the residents and staff, no strange faces, or rather, the familiar faces of the paparazzi. Luke told me after yesterday that The Woodlands hired extra security.

I ignore Mrs. Whizman. Audrey, sitting next to her, says, "Shh," possibly worrying that I'm offended and might not continue what I started yesterday. I know Mrs. Whisman speaks to everyone like this—one of those little tidbits Luke filled me in on. I think she might even be rude to Jesus if he were to appear.

I feel as if I'm walking on stage for the first time. I'm Kimi, and all eyes are on me. It's how I envisioned it to be if I had won the Academy Award that night instead of Mitsy. I half expect applause, but there is none. After all, this is the dining room of The Woodlands, not the Kodak Theatre.

"Tell us, however did you pull this off?" Gary asks as soon as I'm seated in my usual spot. They have moved the enormous fern out of the way and to the room's far corner. One server stops pushing his food cart and stands temporarily frozen when I enter. Coming out of his daze, he resumes rolling it in my direction. He stops at my table, removes the stainless-steel lid from a platter, revealing a delicious-looking plate of lamb, scalloped potatoes, and asparagus, and begins to set it in front of me, but I motion for him to put it back under the warmer and tell him, perhaps I'll have it later in my room. Neither my nerves nor my stomach can handle food at this moment.

My audience awaits, and I'm playing to a packed house. I see Mrs. Bell standing by the column with some of her staff. Some still call me Miss Stone, even though they know who I am by now. I think most suspected from the beginning. Some obviously haven't yet gotten the memo that they can drop the ruse and call me Ms. Hudson.

"Who did you use to decorate?" Mr. Martin asks.

"Decorate? Is that important?" Audrey, who sits clear across the room, shouts.

"She used Carl and Meg. Who else?" Opal says as if they are the only choice in town. "I use them for all of my parties. Well, did."

It is so typical for this crowd to get off track.

"Let her tell the story," Morris says, waving his hands.

Morris Goldman, who I've noticed always loosens his belt during dinner, puts his fork down, and pushes his half-eaten German Chocolate cake aside, is the conclusive proof I have a captive audience. I wonder if today's dessert selection might offend Harvey Goldstein, who sits in the back of the room with his arms crossed, waiting for me to begin the story I started yesterday. It was only natural to think that German Chocolate Cake came from Germany. I read it was named for Samuel German, who developed a type of dark baking chocolate in 1852, and he was American.

"Yes, I used Carl and Meg," I say, winking at Opal. The wink is a reaction for me, like an uncontrollable twitch. It's one of my trademarks. The room grows silent again as if I've used a Jedi mind trick on them. I pause before continuing.

"When I told Carl and Meg I wanted the room filled with hay bales, you should have seen the look on their faces. They thought I had gone mad."

"You did go mad, didn't you?" Gloria, two tables away from me, says. "You were trying to kill yourself, weren't you? Go up in flames like the rest of your family."

The Carl and Meg thing was merely a ruse, something to address the elephant in the room, a way to lead up to the night of the party.

I look at her, suddenly realizing something profound. "Yes, you're right—well, partially right. I knew that was a possibility, and I was prepared. I never intended to hurt anyone. I thought, somehow, I could take Kachina's place. At the same time, I think I was finally ready to come out of my madness—a madness I suffered for years—but I'll let you judge."

I feel two hands on my shoulders. No one has to tell me that Arthur is behind me.

"Bales of hay? I thought you wanted something resembling Dracula's castle," Carl complained more than asked.

"Dracula's castle was my idea," Arthur says.

I reach my right hand over his and squeeze it.

"A last-minute change of plan. Can you make this room look like the inside of a barn?" I asked Carl and Meg.

"If I can find a farmer in LA," Carl said while Meg looked around the room, already calculating how it could be done.

"I denoted sarcasm in his voice. I expected it. I tell him to add it to the bill, even though I know it will be cheaper to scatter hay and some rustic boards about."

"As long as it doesn't involve animals. I'm sure the city has regulations regarding animals," Meg chimes in.

"It's just a barn, minus the animals. If I decide to throw a Noah's Ark-themed party, we'll look into the city's ordinances." I laugh, but the two of them stand there like I've lost my mind.

"Oh, no!" Mrs. Bono exclaims. Her Bichon Frisé dog whimpers. She looks down at the dog dressed in pink frill and says, "Shh, it will be all right, Isabelle, you're safe from the flames."

I tell them, "I realize this is short notice, and you've already gone to the trouble of decorating the outside like Dracula's castle. That can stay, but I want this room to resemble a barn. The furniture will have to be moved out, of course. I will gladly pay extra for all this."

"That won't be a problem. Just show us where to put it," Meg says. I can tell she is warming up to this change with the expectation of a blank check.

"We'll get on it," Carl says. He's smiling now.

"And some pumpkins and orange and black crepe paper decorations. You know, the kind we used for Halloween parties in elementary school," I shout as they go out the door.

"They both look back at me as if I'm crazy. I've turned their elegant decorating scheme into a gaudy affair, but they give me a thumbs up before the door shuts behind them because, well, you know how it is in the town…"

"It's all about the money," says a man I can't see clearly because Mrs. Morton's outrageous hairdo blocks my line of vision.

"But why?" Alice, sitting at the table next to mine, asks.

"Why turn part of my house into a barn? And then set it on fire, with guests fleeing for their lives, although they were never in any danger. I used fire retardants in such abundance that I'm sure I was breaking environmental laws. You know how California is in such matters. There was only one place I didn't use it—"

"On your costume!" one of the staff shouts.

"Correct. It all has to do with an event that happened one Halloween thirty-three years ago. The Eve of All Saint's Day has been my curse. It also happened on my birthday, but I was determined not to let the event ruin my birthday. I also vowed never to try to look younger unnaturally." I see Olivia Roberts glaring at me with eyebrows pinched to her hairline. "My family never got to grow old. They all died in a tragic fire that night, all of them but me—my mother, my father, and my twin sister, Kachina.

"I dread Halloween and all it represents to me. Over the years, I tried certain rituals to rid myself of it, but nothing worked. Once a year, on Halloween night, I would disguise myself and go out, first in the neighborhood and later into other city areas."

Agnes raises her hand, and I point to her.

"Why *did* you dress as the monster on the night of your party?"

"The monster destroys himself with fire," Adam answers.

"That is not how Mary Shelly wrote it. You are referring to the movie version, Adam. Have you even read her book?" Audrey scoffs.

I interrupt their bickering. "My sister played the part of the monster in a school play. I'll admit I was jealous." Arthur's hand is more firmly on my shoulder.

"I wanted the role. I decided to perform some of the monster's role at my sixteenth birthday party. I wanted to outdo her. While everyone was in the barn, finishing the decorations, I was in the house, putting on the costume. An awful storm was brewing."

"Just like the night of your party six months ago," Ralph Bellamy says.

"Yes. Lightning struck the barn, and it caught on fire as I headed toward it. A beam collapsed. It fell on my father, killing him instantly. I could see his face through the flames. I heard the screams of my mother, but the smoke was so thick I couldn't see her, nor could I get to her. The hay was so dry it crinkled. As a kid, I thought nothing of it, but I remember my parents complaining about our fall crops and the lack of rain. I only knew it hadn't rained in weeks.

"My mind goes from my mother when I hear Kachina calling for help, but I can't get to her. I go to the back of the barn, where I know there is a ladder and that I can climb up in the loft. That part of the barn hadn't caught fire yet. I see Kachina down below. I'm reaching for her, begging her to climb. She tries, but she slips. The fire is getting closer, and she's screaming."

I realize I have my eyes closed and my hands over my ears, and I'm shouting and screaming myself when Arthur pulls my hands down and whispers in my ear, "It's all right. I'm here."

I take in a deep breath. I see their statuesque poses with open mouths, the forks of those eating hanging in midair.

"I watch as the fire takes my sister. I see her beautiful face, my face melting into the flames. We were identical. I tell her we will trade places."

"And so you did. But you can be you now," Arthur whispers in my ear.

I'm crying after relating part of my story. I feel like collapsing in his arms as he takes my hand and leads me from the dining area.

I wait until we get in the elevator by ourselves to speak. "Arthur, I have to tell you something. I didn't tell the entire story. I left out parts."

"Yes, I know."

"You do?"

The elevator door opens because neither of us has pushed the button yet. It's Mr. Brockman with his walker. Arthur asks if he would please take the next one. He nods. The door closes, and Arthur presses floor two but stops me from getting out when the elevator door opens. He lets the door close again, and we hang between floors.

"There is so much I need to tell you, Kimi. Is Kimi what I should call you now?"

"Yes, I think that would be good," I say.

"Well then, Kimi, what you said about my relationship with my father the day before the party—my being a disappointment to both you and him..."

"Yes, I know, Arthur, and I'm sorry. I was stressed. I didn't mean it."

"I know you didn't, but It's okay. You were right. I *was* a disappointment to my father and sometimes to you too."

"It's okay, Arthur. Really."

"No, you said, 'The truth shall set you free,' and it's been playing over in my mind ever since. I never told you I had a gambling problem when we met. My father was always bailing me out, holding it over me, and telling me what a disappointment I was."

"But Arthur, I've never known you to gamble."

"No, it stopped when I met you, or maybe it was upon hearing about my father's death. You see, I was hired—"

"Hired?"

"Yes, hired to find you."

"I don't understand."

"You will soon. My father was abroad on business a few months before I found you on the street corner. And he died shortly after that. You went to his funeral."

"Yes, of course."

"In early November, I went to his house while he was away to get a few things. While I was there, the phone in his study rang, and I picked it up. One of his clients, an influential and important one, wanted him to find you."

"Me?"

"Yes, and that will be explained. The thing is, I did find you two months later when my father was away on business again. We still hadn't spoken since our last argument. He knew nothing about you or that I was trying to locate you. I wanted to prove myself in his eyes by doing something right. He had a heart attack while in New York. I never got the chance to apologize. That, plus finding you, changed my life. I think I was gambling only to defy him. I certainly didn't need the money. I went to Cherokee."

"What?"

"You see, I got a phone call. I had every intention of coming last Sunday, but someone named Will left a message about you."

"Will Catawnee?"

"Yes."

"It's funny. I haven't thought about him in years, but suddenly I was, even talking to Luke about him in the dining room yesterday."

"I stayed at Harrah's. There was something in the deepest recesses of my mind that I might start gambling again. I walked into the casino, but it sickened me."

Arthur hands me a paper bag that, in all the excitement, I had neglected to notice. "For you."

I pull something round wrapped in tissue paper and a bow out. I unwrap it to discover a dreamcatcher.

"It's from him. He made it for you and intended to give it to you at your sixteenth birthday party."

A flood of tears overwhelms me, and the elevator door opens. It's a staff member. Arthur asks if he can catch the other elevator or take the stairs.

"There's a lot we have to discuss, but Kimi, I love you and will be by your side as long as you want me there."

I'm too choked up to speak. The wetness running down my cheeks saturates his shirt as we embrace.

Arthur presses three, and we begin to ascend.

"Did you forget? I'm on two?" I say, wiping away the remaining tears.

"I know, but I have a surprise for you."

Arthur and I stand in front of one of the doors on the third floor. I'm about to meet the mysterious man.

"I know this man, don't I, Arthur?"

He smiles and gives me a reassuring look. His hand rises, ready to knock. As it does, it brushes against my arm. He brings his hand back down, pulling something from my sleeve. He examines it.

"What is it?"

"A fruit sticker."

I remember the pear. "I hope I'm not conventional."

"Carter, I mean, Kimi, you are anything but conventional, and that's a good thing. He holds the sticker, which is still on the tip of his finger, up to the light and declares, "Organic."

He removes the sticker with his other hand and slides it into his pocket before gently knocking on the door, as if someone on the other side is waiting, eager to open it for us.

Thirty-Three

KIMI

Although it's been years, I recognize him immediately. He appears frail and weathered, wrinkled, but not exceptionally so. Despite the progression of years robbing him of the youthfulness exhibited on magazine covers, Connor oozes charm, the legendary kind of old Hollywood. Dressed immaculately, he stands before me, clean-shaven, sporting a thick mop of hair, once an umber brown, now cloudy gray. He's not the same Howard-Hughes-looking recluse I saw gazing out the window that day. My skin flushes in embarrassment, and my heart swells in joy, presuming the change in appearance is for me.

He flashes an electrifying smile. My lips spread wide in imitation. I reach for him, and he embraces me with a force that borders bodily strangulation. I cling to his torso just as vehemently. It's not until after an enveloping momentous reunion pushing the concept of time from the scene that I notice the figure of a woman standing directly behind him, her face hidden by a black-lace veil. I almost shriek at the irony and know there is a purpose to all this, but my mind is still riding the wave of release from my dining-room confession and of being reunited with Connor.

The woman, however, intuits a slight disturbance in my being, albeit small, unbalancing me for the briefest second despite Arthur, Connor, and Luke's comforting presence in the room.

"Don't be afraid," she says.

Her voice has an inappreciable raggedness to it, suggesting age, but I recognize it, but how can it be? Of course, I remember the sound of our mother's voice. It's like the small waterfall behind the house where we grew up—soothing, kind, unconditionally loving, I say silently to Kachina. At this moment, I feel Kachina's presence more than I've ever felt it. I realize there is no simulation, no conjuring her into existence, which I've realized I've been doing all these years since coming to The Woodlands—initially gradually, then in these last few years, obsessively.

Connor steps aside, and the others in the room, Arthur, Dr. Ferguson, Luke, and some older-looking, balding man with wire rims, who I assume works for Connor, fade into the background like extras on a movie set. Even though the curtains are fully drawn, and the room is bathed in sunlight, the woman, dressed in black with the black veil, captures center stage. She demands it. She reaches both arms and grabs my hands with hers, drawing me into the spotlight to share the credit of the final act, although I fully expect an epilogue. I fall into her arms, my face against the lacy material of her veil. Streaming tears, a minute version of a tsunami, bind our cheeks together like cement.

Dr. Ferguson and Luke are here for a reason—I suspect to convince me I haven't had a total collapse or to assure I won't have one—that what I'm experiencing is real.

It's been two months since leaving The Woodlands. We lingered there for another two weeks before I returned to my house, which I swore I'd never return to. It exudes a brighter aura with Arthur here and my mother living in the elusive west wing, the part of the house I once tried to confine my shadow self to, although it eventually grew too strong to cage.

My mother walks freely about, her scars exposed, a constant reminder in the flesh, but one I'm slowly coming to terms with. The other side of her face has the wrinkles of normal aging. I remember her in her thirties. She comforts me by saying the wrinkles and scars have helped her grow in wisdom. Connor is a regular visitor, although officially, he resides at The Woodlands, which I found he hastily bought and moved in, thinking it might be the solution for both him and me after the fiasco of a party. Luke even periodically checks on my mother, me, and Connor, who can be found in the west wing with my mother most of the time. He also talks with Arthur, who is as immersed in all this as the rest of us.

My mom and Connor work on scripts behind the closed door of the west wing. That's what they say, but I've sometimes walked down the hall past the door, and I hear them giggling like kids. I'm glad they've rekindled their once-forbidden love, but I can't help but wish the father I grew up with and Kachina were here.

Bear wanders the house and property freely—as freely as an old, feeble dog can. The dog racks up more vet visits than doctor visits for Connor, my mother, and myself combined. Arthur had a giant doggie door installed for him, but one of us usually needs to help him through it.

Unlike Bear, Connor's demeanor reflects a new spirit and resolve. His last check-up was good. Arthur reminds me of what I had said on the day we left for the Woodlands about the truth setting one free. A part of me still feels the truth hasn't fully revealed itself.

My mother's latest check-up was not so good, but she denies anything is wrong and that the surgeries over the years haven't taken their toll. I fear she won't be here long—that I'll be losing her almost as soon as I find her. I plead with her to take it easy. She insists on cooking most of our meals even though Marie returned to housekeep and cook for us. It turns out that Arthur never took her off the payroll. He said he knew I would one day return to normal if anyone knows what that truly is and would return to the house, that Marie was too much of a gem to lose. He's correct. Marie was always loyal, never uttering a word to anyone about what went on in our household.

She and Mom have become best friends, although they sometimes argue over the correct spices to put in a dish. They trade stories about their backgrounds. Marie grew up as poverty-stricken as us.

Mom won't stop writing, and she and Connor hash out scenes together for the next movie even though we haven't started the production of *The Water Spider* yet. Connor and I insist she is credited for the script, even though she pretends not to hear us.

"This movie will make me a star," I tell her as if I'm still her teenage child, only dreaming of being in the movies one day.

"You're already a star," she replies. "That happened with *The Muted Girl.*"

"No," I say. "That movie made Kachina a star. This one will make me a star. Perhaps I'll even win an Oscar for it, like Kathryn Hepburn."

On the surface, everything seems good, but Arthur and Luke observe something different. Although the house has a new life with a regular influx of people, mostly work-related— some from the movie industry, others repairing and redecorating, there is something ghostly as if Kachina is beckoning me to finish something. I want to talk to Mom about it, but I can't bring myself to broach the subject.

I paint, hoping to find some resolution through art. I'm no longer painting simplistic landscapes but scenes and symbols relating to the Hopi and Cherokee. I look at them, and while stylistically, they are correct, like me, they are missing a component. They are only a facsimile of the heritage I denied for so long. My mother knows this. I see it in her eyes. Still, she brags about them like any mother would boast about her child's creations and insists we infuse them throughout the house to tone down the grandiose decorations resembling the Palace of Versailles. I am reluctant to abandon the style entirely because it was what Kachina liked. Mom says what a sixteen-year-old likes changes with maturity.

Amid the new-found joy, an underlying tension snakes its way through the house, re-making it into a prison—albeit different from the one before, but nevertheless, a prison in which our negative emotions concerning the abrupt changes are pushed aside. Luke says we haven't completely dealt with them or reconciled the past.

The unspoken reality of this slaps us in the face one night in June when, after a fierce heat wave, a thunderstorm breaks loose. At three a.m., my mother and I run down the hall into each other's arms. She never told me she was as fearful of storms as me. Everyone in the house wakes up except for Bear. Connor goes back to the bedroom to check on him and returns shortly with tears in his eyes, carrying Bear's limp body.

Thirty-Four

Forgiveness is a funny thing.

I'm not sure who had more to forgive—me due to the resentment when it dawned on me that my mother had been alive all these years and had not contacted me nor told me Connor was my biological father—or my mother who suffered deformity and the loss of a husband and daughter because of me. Even though my mother expressed forgiveness and was happy we were now together, I felt no exoneration.

With Bear's death, which even brought Arthur, who had grown to love the dog, to tears, we realized what we had been denying—that we had been using our happy reunion to cover the past that still haunted us. When Arthur suggested couple's therapy because he could think of no better term, my mother insisted it be with Grandmother Sarah, the wise woman of the Hopi village.

"She will help us to find a balance. Besides, you need to see the land where you were conceived."

The four of us, now family, traveled there.

Only through Sarah's expertise did my mother even hint at

blaming me for that night. My mother asserted that the censure toward me lasted no longer than the flitter of a butterfly wing. She said that although I may have been the one to bring the lantern into a barn that was nothing more than a giant tinder box, it was Victor who kicked it over and started the fire. In the deepest part of my heart, I knew it wasn't true, but such is a mother's unconditional love, which, not having children of my own, I couldn't relate to. The closest thing I could compare it to was the bond I had once shared with Kachina.

I can't blame my mother for keeping her survival hidden from me for so long. She had her scars to deal with, the least of them being physical. She confessed culpability. What mother in her right mind would allow a party in a rickety old barn, a danger in itself, although not much more than the house they lived in, when they hadn't had rain in a month, where drink and cigarettes were a given?

Grandmother Sarah brought so much out into the open for us. She said, "Having lost so much, we were both fragmented and needed to become whole."

Grandmother Sarah, in addition to being Hopi, had family relations among the Navajo. She suggested a sweat lodge for the four of us, one for my mother and me and another for Arthur and Connor, since the sexes are to be separated in traditional sweat lodges. Both my mother and I are reluctant. She grasps my hand, and we look at each other. We are both thinking of the fire element of a sweat lodge.

"How could this possibly help," I ask.

Grandmother Sarah makes a circle in the soil with her cane. She looks at the ground below, the tip of her cane stopping short from finishing the circle. She closes her eyes as if in prayer. When she reopens them, she says, "You must come full circle." She then moves her cane to close the crude ring of dirt.

Grandmother Sarah says I was trying to relive the experience of thirty-three years ago at my party, hoping for a different outcome. After contemplation, I conceded she was right. I attempted to create some made-up ritual to release me from my guilt.

Grandmother Sarah made a phone call, and the four of us, early the next day, without breakfast because fasting beforehand is required, gathered appropriate clothing and towels, piled into the rental SUV, and traveled North to visit the Navajo rez. The trip would take an hour. My mom and Connor are in the back seat. Arthur is driving. None of us know much of what to expect, and under the advice of Grandma Sarah, we shouldn't speculate or anticipate. Though my mother and I have indigenous roots, neither of us has experienced the sweat lodge. I had never even heard of one taking place during my sixteen years in Cherokee, but then, as a teenager, I was preoccupied with other things. Oh, there were plenty of drumming ceremonies and various reenactments for tourists. Those were hard to miss. I knew sweat lodges were sacred, not meant for tourists. That's what I was taught in school on the rare occasions we studied our own history. I only know the generalities, like they're spiritual, cultural, and practical. I never questioned any further. Nor did any of the other students, according to my recollection. We were too busy with puberty and being blended into the white man's culture.

Later, after achieving stardom, I was invited to participate in several sweat lodges, administered mainly by new-age types who were not privy to the authentic customs of our people. I politely declined, not giving any reasons. In my mind, I looked down on their inaccuracy, while in reality, I was secreting my heritage to make it in the business.

Grandmother Sarah said all we needed to know for now was that the purpose of the sweat lodge was to connect with the Creator and nature, and it would help us restore order and balance in life. The sweat lodge is also a place to connect with Indigenous heritage and culture.

We sit quietly in the SUV. Arthur is driving. I check the mirror and see my mother and Connor holding hands in the back seat. Over the last couple of months, I've noticed that she almost always has her scarred face on the opposite side of him. I'm sure he doesn't see it.

There is some small talk, nothing important. We are driving toward the important stuff. I gaze at the scenery from my window. In my mirror view of the backseat, I see Connor's hand clasped over my mom's. Arthur's eyes are straight ahead on the road. The sky is a brilliant blue, dotted only with occasional puffs of clouds. In contrast, barren red dirt, buttes, plateaus, piñons, and cedars with their roots claw into the arid soil on both sides of the barren road.

In the back compartment of the SUV, we have a variety of canned goods and blankets, which Connor generously purchased before leaving Hopi land to offer as gifts to the Navajo.

Halfway there, a scrawny, half-starved dog darts in front of us. Arthur swerves to miss him. "It looks like a wolf," I say.

"No, a German Shepherd, although possibly part wolf," Connor says. "Pull over to the side of the road," he instructs Arthur.

Arthur does but says, "What are you going to do?"

"Anyone have a knife, or better yet, a can opener," he asks.

"Will this do?" I ask, pulling a toenail clipper with a nail file attached from my purse.

"It will have to," he says.

Meanwhile, the dog waits patiently by the side of the road, either curious or too tired to move on.

"What if he's dangerous?" Arthur says.

"No, I think he's fine," Connor says while departing the vehicle.

He shuts the door and cautiously approaches the dog, who cowers in fright, his tail tucked between his legs. Connor pets him, and within a minute, he is wagging his tail. He goes to the back of the SUV, opens the hatch, and pulls a can of tuna from a sack carrying the canned goods. The dog follows him, still wagging his tail. With the end of the nail file, he punctures the can enough to remove the tuna in small chunks.

We all turn around in our seats, watching. Connor pulls a water bottle from the back and pours it into a pottery bowl I purchased at the trading post. The dog laps it up furiously. My mom leaves the vehicle to assist Connor. It's evident that Connor doesn't want to leave the dog in this predicament, but we are on our way to the sweat lodge, and someone named Running Bear is expecting us. We are already running late.

After my mother and Connor pet the grimy creature one last time, they reluctantly get back into the vehicle, leaving the dog in our wake, hoping he makes it. The three of us turn in our seats, observing the dog until he is out of sight. Even Arthur looks back intermittently through his rear-view mirror.

The lonely road finally ends, and we park in front of a similar-looking trading post where we had purchased the pottery on Hopi land. The pottery bowl now sits some distance back on the side of the road, its intention to hydrate a malnourished mutt.

The four of us exit the SUV and pass an elderly man, his yellowed-gray hair trickling down his bright red shirt in two long braids, almost reaching his belt bearing an enormous silver buckle inlaid with turquoise. His sun-toughened skin glistens in the morning sunlight. It's ten a.m. His face, with its many lines, resembles a computer circuit board. He sits in a rustic twig rocking chair beside the door in front of the display window. His eyes are closed, and we all wonder if he is alive or perhaps a well-crafted wax figure luring tourists into the shop. We walk past him, enter the shop, and ask the woman at the register where we might find Running Bear, the medicine man Grandma Sarah told us to ask for.

"You here for the sweat lodge?"

"Yes," we echo simultaneously. The woman points toward the window to the back of the frizzy-gray-haired man with the almost perfect part running down the middle, who we just passed coming in.

The woman pays no heed to my mother's face, which always happens when any of our friends or acquaintances meet her for the first time after coming to live with us. My mother gives me a look like she knows what I'm thinking. There are times when I feel Kachina's spirit resides within her.

"You see why I preferred to live here," she whispers.

As we leave the building, the tingle of the bell tied to the door wakes the man. He shades his eyes from the sun and squints up at us. "Grandma Sarah?" he questions.

"Yes, that would be us," Connor offers.

The elder pushes himself up from the seat, balances himself, and says, "Follow me."

"Can I leave the vehicle here?" Arthur points to the SUV.

"Fine. Towels? Clothes change?"

"Aoo," my mom says.

"You speak Navajo?" I look at her, surprised.

"Only a few basics. Aoo means yes," she says.

Arthur removes our offering of canned goods and blankets from the vehicle. Running Bear directs him to leave them inside the shop. We get our bags carrying towels and a change of clothes. While in the sweat lodge, we'll be naked— at least, I think that is the case. I confess I Googled it last night before going to bed. The trouble, though, is that one finds conflicting information with anything on the internet. It was the same when I once summoned the courage to

Google my own name or the one I decided to use nearly thirty-three years ago. I cried and cried. Arthur held me, encouraged me, made love to me, and told me never to search for my name on the internet again. "Nine times out of ten, Carter, it's not true. It's all about making a buck, and people are vultures."

I immediately thought that in Cherokee culture, turkey vultures are called the "Peace Eagle" because they refuse to kill in order to live. My father had a different interpretation, though, and said, "Their feet are useless for killing, so they let the other animals do the dirty work." Since Mom has returned, I'm reminded of more things about Dad and Kachina—trivial things but memories that make me smile.

Running Bear, aptly named, gains momentum. I remember my leap up the stairwell on that first day at The Woodlands. Except this man is spry for his advanced age and much lighter on his feet than me. I was in an air-conditioned stairwell. I surmise the difference can be attributed to living in nature rather than the city. He's also used to the oppressive heat. Worried about my mom, I look at her, but she and Connor seem to be doing fine. Of course, this is home to her. And Arthur, well, it's finally sinking in how much this man loves me.

Arthur asks if it's a long walk, but the man doesn't seem to realize Arthur is talking to him. We soon discover what he said a few yards back was what little English he knew, a memorized script to answer the inevitable white men's obsession and question of where to park. He yelled something in the Navajo tongue to a young man across the street, who ran swiftly over.

"You're not tired already, are you, Arthur?"

He winks at me. "No, I felt bad for him. Maybe I should have offered to drive us."

I return with my signature wink, which I've neglected since my mother returned to me. Arthur is laughing, and

Dave's eyes grow big, causing him almost to stumble while walking alongside us.

"You're... You're...?"

"Yes, she is," Arthur says between laughs.

I turn sideways, smile at him, put my fingers to my lips, and shake my head.

"Oh, sure, Mrs. Hudson. No one will ever know."

Oh, I'm a Mrs. now, I wonder to myself. I admit I've been thinking about it again. Arthur has even hinted at it. A fourth marriage proposal with the same bride and groom is only alluded to in almost inaudible whispers. After the history between us, there is no deep-knee bend proposal, especially not at Arthur's age. His only deep-knee bends are picking up his golf tees.

The younger man says, "Hi, I'm Dave. Running Bear speaks very little English. I'm to interpret."

I introduce everyone since Dave already knows who I am. After the introductions, I say, "I was born with the name Kimi Ahoka."

"That's pretty," he says before filling Running Bear in on our names.

As we walk on, the ninety-year-old medicine man speaks in Navajo in a melodic tone.

Shortly, we come to a hogan. An older woman with a round belly in a brown summer dress falling mid-ankle greets Running Bear.

"This is Mona. She will be your sweat lodge guide. She speaks English," Dave says. Mona nods toward each of us as Dave introduces us.

Here, we part ways—my mom and I following Mona and Arthur, Connor and Dave veering off behind Running Bear, trying to match his rapid pace, while Mona walks like a tortoise. I also read in my Google search that you're given a sacred name during the sweat lodge ceremony. I wonder if Mona's is Turtle.

We come to a clump of evergreen trees. Just beyond is one of the smallest structures I've ever seen. It reminds me of a pizza oven. The split cedar frame sinks in two feet of ground and arches four feet high. Red Arizona dirt covers it. I wonder how the four of us can fit.

A log fire, competing with the sun, blazes a few feet away. She directs us behind a small wooden enclosure and asks us to remove our clothes and return wearing our towels. I feel embarrassed, not for me, but for my mom. I've never done a nude scene, but I've gotten as close as one could get in a string bikini on an Italian beach while shooting a movie. Arthur always forbade me to do nude scenes. Now, I know it was Connor. That movie was a fluke. I agreed to it while vacationing in Italy between divorces. Arthur and I weren't speaking to each other during that one separation. I haven't seen my mom naked since my youth. She was beautiful then.

Mom smiles at me as we enter the ramshackle dressing room. "Are you okay?" she asks.

"Yes. Are you?"

"This reminds me of when the three of us went to town after your father had a month of successful sales. We tried on matching dresses in the minuscule closet the shopkeeper called a changing room."

"I remember that," I say.

Mom unbuttons her blouse and takes it off. She's not wearing a bra. Reading my thoughts, she says, "I got used to not wearing one because of the burns. I never could return to them."

"I understand." My eyes are running up and down her side. It's not as bad as I envisioned, but then I imagined something resembling the creature in the movie *Alien*.

"Do you want to touch the scars?"

I gently rub my hand along the length and width of the scarring in a wavy pattern, then kiss my mom's disfigured cheek. We hurriedly remove the rest of our clothes, place them in our bags, and cover ourselves with threadbare beach-sized towels we purchased at the Hopi Trading Post. Outside, we hear Mona stirring the fire.

She looks up as we come out. We see a pile of glowing red rocks in the center through the small lodge doorway. Mona carries another pile on a shovel and places them on top. She beckons us inside. I think it must be two hundred degrees. I'm already sweating from the walk here in ninety-degree heat and the ground scorching my bare feet the few yards from the changing station to the lodge. Stepping out of the bright sunlight, we duck down to enter and sit about six inches apart. Mona drops the wool blanket to cover the doorway and sits on the other side of my mom. It's pitch black. All I see are the dull gleam of rocks.

We sit in silence. My posterior finally cushions itself into the coarse weave of the towel against the rough bark on the floor. My skin is already baked, and rivulets of water trickle down my body. I worry about my mom, but I know this is a sacred time, so refrain from asking. Instead, I listen to her steady breath and convince myself she is alright. I feel her arms loosening the front of her towel, and I do likewise. The sweat dripping from her arms mingles with mine.

Mona begins a chant in her Navajo tongue and then translates it into English. She summons the spirits of Earth, Air, and Water to weave our bodies and souls with the elements. She tells us of a time long ago when her people rose from the Underworld and gathered in a tq'ache, the Navajo word for sweat lodge, to create chants and hymns dedicated to our life changes.

Steam rises when Mona pours a brew of cedar and piñon needle water onto the rocks. The water crackles as it hits the red stones. Steam rises and dissipates just as quickly, leaving a lingering odor of the burned needles.

Mona's voice penetrates the darkness. "Only needles from trees struck by lightning can be used. They cure," she says. "Inhale them, drink their brew. They make you well."

Although I can't see my mother's expression in the darkness, I'm sure she thinks the same thing as I do, but neither of us speaks. I can't help but wonder if Mona somehow knows our story.

After drinking, my mother passes the bowl to me. I press it to my lips, and I sip the organic brew. Mona begins another chant, at first in Navajo and then in English. She calls on the Greater Powers to bring healing and blessings to us and the village's residents. Afterward, Mona explains that the chants were handed down through her tribe only to certain people, including herself and Running Bear, in this generation.

There is an elongated silence. I take it we are to meditate and reflect. Possibly twenty minutes go by. My mother begins singing. I recall it is the Kachina song she used to sing to my sister and me when we were small, the one I so feebly tried to sing before the party. Possibly, it's hearing her sing the song again, or the heat of the fire bringing back that night, or both. A flood of tears streams down my face, intermingling with the wetness of the sweat. I'm openly crying. Loudly. My mother reaches for me and holds me. Our naked bodies cling together. At this moment, I ache to crawl back into her womb and start all over, but I realize Kachina won't be there, and my crying grows even louder.

I know little about the Catholic faith, but suddenly, the sweat lodge seems like the ultimate confessional. I blurt out in a hoarse voice from my wailing that I didn't tell the truth about Victor dropping me off.

"It was only something I told myself. He threatened it plenty of times, and I thought it would serve me right. I should be abandoned." With this, I felt my mother's arms grip me even tighter. In the background, I hear Mona chanting in a low voice in Navajo.

"Victor stopped at a used clothing store outside of Los Angeles. He said he had to make me presentable. For what I didn't know. I still had the costume on the whole way up until that point, and it smelled of soot. Victor was telling the woman he was trying to do a good deed, that he picked me up on the side of the road, a runaway he hoped to return to her family. I knew you were right about Victor, but like me, the lady was eating it up. While he was busy flirting with the lady, I guess the owner, I asked if I could use the restroom and clean up before trying on the clothes. She pointed, and I made my way to the back of the store. I turned to see her and Victor laughing. They were standing in the far corner. While they weren't paying attention, with the clothes in my arms, I detoured, ducking between the clothing racks, and made my way past the cash register and out the entrance. The ding on the door must have alerted them. I was nearly a block away when I heard him cussing and yelling for me to come back. Then I heard the lady yelling even louder, telling him he had to pay for those. I ran through back alleys and side streets for a mile, maybe more, before a stitch in my side brought me to a dead stop. Days later, after living on the street, I once saw Victor drive by slowly, looking in all directions. I turned my back to him and pretended to be in a crowd of people until he passed. I am so sorry. I'm so sorry."

My mother repeats over and over, "It's okay." She continues to hold me and rub my hair backward from my forehead with her fingers, the way she used to with Kachina and me when we were small. Only instead of her fingers, when we were little, she used one of the combs my dad sold so long ago. "Dad said we would never run out of combs." The memory of this somehow signals my tear ducts to halt. A slight smile comes across my lips. I feel my mother's lips against my wet hair.

Mona douses a bowlful of the brew on the hissing rocks, and another burst of steam assaults our nostrils. In the light of the rising flame, I slightly turn and see my mother smiling as well.

With an impassioned and vibrant voice, Mona begins another chant, asking for our travels to be safe. She removes the blanket to reveal the opening and motions us out. With our damp towels wrapped around our bodies, my mother and I crawl through the small doorway, both of us squinting into the bright sunlight.

Mona doesn't follow. She continues to sing. Mom tells me she is chanting a prayer of thanks to the spirits of the sweat lodge. The song also asks forgiveness for errors she might have made in the chants or protocol during the ceremony.

Mona, shielding her eyes from the sun, emerges from the sweat lodge and instructs us to change back into our clothes. She patiently waits for us after we use the extra towels we brought to dry the sweat from our bodies and return wearing our original attire. She takes each of us aside. We are each given a sacred name to be shared only with our husbands. She says this will also be the case in the men's sweat lodge. I think this partly prompted the double wedding ceremony between Arthur and me and Mother and Connor before leaving the Hopi Nation. In my heart, I know this fourth marriage will take. During the feast following the sweat lodge ceremonies, we are told that the number four is sacred to the Navajo.

On our wedding night, the one in which our bond was truly consummated in body and, most importantly, soul, I shared my sacred name with Arthur—Joyful Wolf. When Mona gave it to me, she said, "Now, go. Don't let the bad wolf eat your joy."

My joy swelled when Arthur told me his.

"Running Bear told me he was ignoring precedence in giving me my sacred name." Arthur whispers in my ear, "Orpheus. I didn't know what it meant and didn't know whether I should ask, so I didn't. Do you know what it means?"

"Yes. It means you will travel to the underworld and back for me."

Arthur kisses me and smiles. "Yes, I would."

Epilogue

I didn't win the Oscar for *The Water Spider*. However, my mother did for best screenplay. Elation and joy in her success swelled my heart to such a degree it demolished any disappointment in not winning. Connor's, Arthur's, and my hands were raw from clapping so hard. Connor was given a lifetime achievement award, for which he praised my mother and me in his speech.

From that point onward, I knew we would work as a team to bring Native culture to the forefront through movies and documentaries.

We attended no parties that night as we only longed for each other's company. Arthur, Connor, my mother, and I settled in front of the fireplace, staring into the blaze with its slow, steady crackle, something neither my mother nor I no longer feared. Nor did lightning or storms bother us. Well, not so much as before. I saw my sister's face emerge momentarily within the flames, winking at me. I look over at my mother. I'm sure she doesn't see what I see, but then there are some things that only twins who have inhabited the same womb share.

Two years later, we are in Cherokee, on location, amid another production. I hand over Amara Kachina to Rona, our nanny because the director is ready for me. Rona is neither Cherokee nor Hopi but Lakota. She came highly recommended as a nanny. Arthur and I decided to halt birth control and let the Great Spirit decide our fate concerning children. At nearly fifty-one, she was a miracle. Women over fifty have only a ten percent chance of getting pregnant. Perhaps it was my mother's constant prayers to every Native American spirit in the universe for a grandchild that caused us to conceive. It was only natural to name her after my sister. Since names have meaning, Arthur and I decided on Amara, which means eternal and unfading and embodies the enduring nature of a new beginning and the transformative power of embracing change. If it had been a boy, we would have named him Wesley.

As with our traditional Hopi wedding with lots of corn involved, when Amara Kachina was born, we followed the Hopi birth ritual of secluding her for nineteen days indoors, cared for by the elder woman of the family, my mother. She wrapped her in a blanket alongside an ear of perfectly formed corn.

"To make up for what I should have done for you and Kachina," she said.

The town of Cherokee is different than I remember. The casino has given it new life, and the natural beauty and hiking trails draw a new generation. My mother and Connor sit in a sunny spot next to each other in wheelchairs, blankets over their laps, looking on as I say Kaya's lines. Wolf, the mixed breed with part German Shepherd, we looked long and hard for on the way back from Hopi land, lies lazily between them. My mother's idea was to name him Wolf, departing from the usual name Bear. I wonder if she knows something. Wolf seems at home in Cherokee.

The bright sun catches the right side of my mother's face at an angle that blends the web-like burn marks like nature's perfect makeup. Possibly, I no longer see them. I don't think Connor ever did.

It seems as if most of the town, including tourists, watch while we shoot a scene. I think this film of our life story employs every out-of-work citizen of Cherokee. Occasionally, I look out and see Will's face in the crowd. Sometimes, I glimpse him and Arthur talking like long-lost friends.

I'm playing two roles: my mother and my present self. A young girl, a new actress Connor says has great potential, plays both the younger Kachina and me. A younger woman should play the part of Kaya, but Connor insists I can pull it off. He teases they can do anything with AI and soft lighting these days.

The crowd is silenced. Amara Kachina is asleep in Rona's arms, so I don't worry about her crying. I'm on my mark. The clapper loader shouts, "*The Two Wolves Inside Me*. Take One," and snaps the slate shut with a heavy bang. The director shouts action.

I sometimes feel guilty that I've accepted Connor as my father so readily. I pull up memories of the only man I knew as my father in an effort to keep his memory alive. It's not hard to do standing on the soil I grew up on. Mother assures me telling our story, the one she, Connor, and I wrote together, will make him proud.

We have avoided visiting where our house and barn once stood for weeks. When we finally make the trek, my mother has forgotten the road, but Arthur remembers.

Arthur and I take a shovel and cooler from the vehicle. The cooler holds Amara Kachina's carefully preserved placenta. Since vowing to bring the story of Native Americans to the forefront, I've read about many different traditions and customs. The Navajo's custom is to bury a child's placenta within the sacred Four Corners of the tribe's reservation as a binder to ancestral land and people. In New Zealand, the Maoris have the same tradition of burying the placenta within native soil. In their native language, the word for land and placenta are the same. Arthur and I both agree that Amara's placenta should be buried here.

Afterward, Arthur, Connor, and Wolf return to the SUV at my mother's request to give us a private moment. With one arm, I hold onto her, thinking the stress might be too much and that she might faint. In the other, I hold Amara. I am barely steady myself. The day is bright except for a few clouds.

"They are cloud people now," she says while gazing upward.

I don't have to ask who "they" are. I know she is referring to my father and Kachina.

Will informed us the tribal council had voted to erect a memorial for both of them where the barn once stood—a nice gesture, especially considering the movie we're making will be premiered in Cherokee. We've decided on the off-season to add an extra boon to the town.

"You know, your father always dreamed of being famous one day."

"Really?"

"Oh, not a movie star. He just wanted to know his life

meant something and that he would be remembered. I'm sure he is happy about the memorial."

With my arm wrapped around my mother's tiny waist, I take another look at the sky before heading back to the vehicle. One lone cloud separates into what appears to be figures I could swear are vaporous silhouettes of my father and Kachina before evaporating. I look at my mother and know she has seen it, too.

I look down at my baby, understanding unconditional love. I think not only of my baby but of Arthur, my dad, my mom, Connor, and Kachina. I remember Arthur telling me shortly after our last wedding ceremony how he never wanted the job of caring for me after finding me, but he soon found it was the only job he ever wanted, the one he was destined for.

Acknowledgments

My husband, Chris, offers me tremendous support regarding my writing and most things in life. He is the one who suggested I start writing.

A heartfelt thanks go out to my beta readers: Ann Colbert, a member of my writing group who just published her first book, *Ava Finds Time*; Cynthia Faye Davis, who creates beautiful videos under *Goddess and Heroine Folklore from Around the World*; Charlotte French, author of *Agnes Treading Water*; Giles Kelvage, author of the soon-to-be-published *Prayer to Whooshicree*; Janice J. Richardson, author of *A Reluctant Winner: Lite Women's Fiction with a Twist*; G. S. Tabberner, author of *The Magical Diaries of Charles Lester Seymour*; and Gina Baratono and Daphne Singingtree, both of who helped with all aspects Native American. All gave me helpful, constructive criticism, which strengthened the narrative.

Gina Baratono went above and beyond, gifting me the image of the twin girls and a miniature pair of moccasins, which I will display in my office with my other writing memorabilia.

Finally, to the readers who embark on this adventure with me, thank you for giving these characters a home in your imagination.

J. Schlenker, a late-blooming author, lives with her husband, Chris, out in the splendid center of nowhere in the foothills of Appalachia in Kentucky, where the only thing to disturb her writing is croaking frogs and the occasional sounds of hay being cut in the fields.

https://jschlenker.com/